CREAM PUFF
MURDER

Books by Joanne Fluke

CHOCOLATE CHIP COOKIE MURDER

STRAWBERRY SHORTCAKE MURDER

BLUEBERRY MUFFIN MURDER

LEMON MERINGUE PIE MURDER

FUDGE CUPCAKE MURDER

SUGAR COOKIE MURDER

PEACH COBBLER MURDER

CHERRY CHEESECAKE MURDER

KEY LIME PIE MURDER

CARROT CAKE MURDER

CREAM PUFF MURDER

Published by Kensington Publishing Corporation

A HANNAH SWENSEN MYSTERY
WITH RECIPES

CREAM PUFF
MURDER

JOANNE FLUKE

KENSINGTON BOOKS
http://www.kensingtonbooks.com

KENSINGTON BOOKS are published by

Kensington Publishing Corp.
850 Third Avenue
New York, NY 10022

All Kensington titles, imprints and distributed lines are available at special quantity discounts for bulk purchases for sales promotion, premiums, fund-raising, educational or institutional use.

Special book excerpts or customized printings can also be created to fit specific needs. For details, write or phone the office of the Kensington Special Sales Manager: Attn. Special Sales Department. Kensington Publishing Corp., 850 Third Avenue, New York, NY 10022. Phone: 1-800-221-2647.

Kensington and the K logo Reg. U.S. Pat. & TM Off.

ISBN-13: 978-0-7582-3806-1
ISBN-10: 0-7582-3806-1

First trade paperback printing: March 2009

10 9 8 7 6 5 4 3 2 1

Printed in the United States of America

This book is for Cody and Jacob.

In loving memory of Gladys Gladke Oven, my second grade teacher, and Hannah, who passed her love for my Hannah on to her daughter.

Acknowledgments:

A big hug and kiss to Ruel, my inspiration and in-house story editor. And hugs all around to the kids and the grandkids.

Thank you to Mel & Kurt, Lyn & Bill, Gina, Adrienne, Jay, Bob, Amanda, John B., Judy, Dr. Bob & Sue, Laura & Mark, Richard & Krista, Mark B., and my hometown friends in Swanville, Minnesota.

Thank you to my kind and talented Editor-in-Chief, John Scognamiglio, for saving my bacon more times than I can count.

The same goes for Walter, Steve, Laurie, Doug, David, Maureen, Meryl, Colleen, Michaela, Kate, Adam, Jessica, Peter, Robin, Lori, Mike, Tami, Susie, and Barbara.

Thank you to Hiro Kimura for the luscious Cream Puff on the cover. And thanks to Lou Malcangi for designing such a delectable dust jacket.

Thanks also to all the other talented folks at Kensington who keep Hannah sleuthing and baking up a storm.

Thank you to Trudi Nash, a wonderful traveling companion! And thanks to David for getting along without her.

Thank you to Dr. Rahhal, Dr. and Mrs. Line, and
Dr. Wallen.

Thanks to Joel at L'Affair Café for his expert advice
on cutlery.

Thank you to John at Placed4Success for Hannah's movie
and TV spots. Thanks to Ken Wilson—Let's have lunch.
And a big hug for Lois Brown, food stylist extraordinaire.

Thank you to Connie Martinson for the kind words and
encouragement.

Thanks to the Books-A-Million managers who invited me to
Birmingham. Great folks, great city, great time!

Thanks to Jill Saxton for catching my Minnesota goofs.
Hugs to Lois Hirt for dental advice—Norman,
thank you, too.

Many thanks to Terry Sommers for her incredible Carrot
Cake Cookies, and to Paul for tasting, critiquing, and
carrying.

Thank you to Sally Hayes for sharing the virtual baking.

Thank you to Jamie Wallace for keeping my Web site,
MurderSheBaked.com up to date and looking great.

Hugs to everyone who sent favorite family recipes for
Hannah to try so she'll never run out of yummy sweets to
bake. And thanks so much for all the friendly e-mails and
snail-mails that send me off to write about Lake Eden
with a smile on my face.

Chapter One

There was a loud crash as someone dropped a platter. A split second later, Hannah Swensen reached up to pick a piece of pepperoni out of her curly red hair. She examined it, identified it for what it was, and just barely managed to resist the urge to pop it into her mouth. Although one bite of the traditional pizza topping might not exceed her calorie count for lunch, it could pave the way to a self-indulgent feast from the menu at Bertanelli's Pizza, a popular eatery in Lake Eden, Minnesota.

One glance down at the salad she'd ordered and Hannah almost gave way to temptation. It was a perfectly good salad, crispy lettuce in three varieties, several slices of tomato, strips of yellow and red bell pepper for color, and a dressing of balsamic vinegar and olive oil on the side. Salads were good. Salads were healthful. Salads were much better than pizza when you had to lose at least ten pounds because everything you owned was too tight around the middle, including your very favorite pair of jeans.

"What's that?" her sister Andrea asked, watching Hannah wrap the meaty missile in a napkin and set it aside.

"Pepperoni. I heard a crash right before it hit. One of Ellie's new waitresses must have dropped a pizza platter."

Without another word, both sisters picked up their winter

parkas and slid over to the edge of the booth so they could peer out at the other diners. It was Saturday, and Bertanelli's was packed with customers. It was also November in Minnesota, and that meant the coatrack by the door was also packed, and they'd had to stash their bulky outerwear in their booth. Andrea was sharing her side with her husband, Bill Todd, the Winnetka County sheriff. Hannah's lunch date was her sometimes boyfriend, Bill's chief detective, Mike Kingston. This was obviously a working lunch because the men hadn't even noticed the porcine projectile that had landed on Hannah's head. They were too busy discussing a bungled bank robbery that had taken place in a neighboring town that morning.

The interior at Bertanelli's was comfort itself, with carved wooden booths and tables, plastered walls with fake brick peeking through, and Italian scenes painted by the Jordan High senior art class. The candles on the tables were stuck in wine bottles that had been dripped with various candle colors, a tribute to the crafts movement of the fifties. All in all, it was a nice, relaxing place to have lunch, but not today.

"Uh-oh," Andrea said, beginning to frown.

"You said it," Hannah added, spotting Bridget Murphy, who had just righted herself after running smack-dab into the waitress who'd been carrying the pizza that had provided Hannah's unexpected slice of sausage.

Both women watched as Bridget, who was known for her fiery Irish temper, veered off toward the big round booth in the corner where Ronni Ward was holding court. Ronni was flanked by four of Lake Eden's most successful males. Mayor Bascomb and bank president Doug Greerson were seated on her left. Al Percy of Lake Eden Realty, and Bert Kuehn, co-owner of Bertanelli's, were seated on her right.

Everyone had thought that Ronni was gone for good last winter when she got engaged and moved in with her fiancé to help him run his fitness center in Elk River. But Ronni and the man she'd promised to marry had broken it off, and, as

Hannah and Andrea's grandmother had been fond of saying, the *bad penny* had turned up in Lake Eden again. Bill, who was a soft touch for a sob story, had rehired Ronni as the fitness instructor at the sheriff's department, and the word on the Lake Eden gossip hotline was that Ronni was flirting heavily, or perhaps even more, with the deputies at the sheriff's station, regardless of their marital status.

Unable to live on the small salary the sheriff's department paid her, Ronni had found a part-time job at Heavenly Bodies, the new fitness spa at the Tri-County Mall. Her track record there appeared to be more of the same. She'd sold more memberships than anyone else on the staff, but the members she'd signed were almost all male. Several local wives weren't happy about their husbands' resolve to get into shape by joining one of Ronni's exercise classes or hiring her as their personal fitness coach after hours.

"Here comes Cyril," Hannah said as Bridget's husband attempted and failed to intercept his wife before she reached Ronni's table.

The two sisters watched for a moment. At first only words were exchanged, but with each salvo, Bridget's frown grew fiercer and Ronni's scowl etched deeper.

"What's happening?" Bill asked, tapping his wife on the shoulder.

"Ronni Ward's arguing with Bridget Murphy, but Cyril's there and he's trying to break it up."

Almost simultaneously, Bill and Mike reached for another piece of pizza. Hannah thought she knew what was running through their minds. Bertanelli's had the best pizza in Minnesota. If Bill and Mike had to leave to break up a catfight between Ronni Ward and Bridget Murphy, they wanted to finish their lunch first.

"Bridget doesn't look happy," Andrea went on with her running commentary.

Hannah watched Bridget's husband put himself in what might be harm's way to block Bridget's access to Ronni.

The women's voices became louder, and Bill reached for a final piece of pizza. "What's happening now?"

"I think it's almost over," Andrea told him. "Cyril's got Bridget in one of those holds you see on the wrestling channel, and he's hauling her away. I wonder what set her off?"

Ronni did, Hannah thought, but she didn't say it. *She's enough to set any woman off.* "I wonder if Ellie knows where Bert is," Hannah speculated.

"She knows. She's over there at the kitchen door, just staring at Bert. If looks could kill, Bert would be a statistic. One of these days Ronni is going to get hers, and it won't be pretty."

"Right," Hannah said, and then she leaned across the table and lowered her voice. "I just hope I'm there to see it."

"Me too! Maybe someone ought to call Stephanie Bascomb, and Sally Percy, and Amalia Greerson, and invite them to come out here for lunch."

"You wouldn't!" Hannah said, giving her sister a long hard look.

"Probably not, but it's fun to think about what would happen if somebody . . . uh-oh! Bridget got loose!"

Both sisters watched anxiously as Bridget raced back toward Ronni's table. Cyril looked dazed, and Hannah had a sneaking suspicion that Bridget had bitten him on the shoulder since he was rubbing it through his shirt. It took him a moment to recover, and that gave Bridget time to reach her goal. Once she arrived, red-faced and panting, she hurtled herself at Ronni and grabbed her by the hair.

"Have you no shame?" Bridget's voice took on the thick Irish brogue of her ancestors. "He's got a wife and baby, and another one on the way. You leave my boy alone or you'll answer to me!"

"You tell her, Bridget!" someone shouted, and it sounded like Ellie to Hannah.

"Knock it off, will you? We're trying to enjoy our lunch here!" a diner shouted, and Hannah recognized the voice. It was her downstairs neighbor, Phil Plotnik, and he was sitting with a whole table of DelRay workers.

"Be quiet! Both of you!" a woman called out from a booth across the room. "And if you can't, do us a favor and take it outside!"

Several other shouts for Ronni and Bridget to cease and desist came from various sections of the dining room. Almost everyone wanted the altercation to end, but it was pretty clear that there was even more trouble brewing when a half-dozen Jordan High students at a table in the center began to clap and whistle.

"Food fight!" one of the boys yelled, and all six of them started to hurl garlic bread and meatballs.

Pandemonium ensued in very short order. Waitresses squealed and ran for the safety of the kitchen, several metal pizza pans hit the floor with a clatter, and a plastic Coke glass sailed across the room, barely missing the tall, straw-cradled bottle of Chianti that Ellie had placed next to the cash register.

"Time to go to work," Bill said, sliding over in tandem with Mike. "Let us out, will you? We've got to break this up before those Jordan High students do some damage."

"And before Bridget and Ronni really hurt each other," Mike added, and then he turned to Bill. "It's your call. You outrank me."

Bill didn't hesitate. "I'll take the Jordan High kids. You take the women."

"I knew you'd say that," Mike said with a grin. "Okay . . . let's roll."

Once they'd let Bill and Mike out of the booth, Hannah and Andrea sat back down to watch the men in action. For several moments it was a free-for-all as Cyril tried to pull Bridget away. Invectives from the women and the patrons alike rebounded. At the same time, Italian sausage, breadsticks, antipasto, and spaghetti vied for air supremacy. Andrea and Hannah leaned out to catch the action, ducking back when any edible ammunition came within their range. It took several minutes, and Andrea wound up with a splatter of marinara sauce on her arm, but it was clear the tide had turned and the long arm of the law was winning.

"Wow!" Hannah gasped as Mike dashed nimbly over fallen platters, food, and drink glasses to lift Ronni out of the booth. He grabbed her by the waist like a father dealing with a recalcitrant child, and carried her out the door.

"Wow is right." Andrea motioned toward the table of students. Bill had just arrived at the table and as they watched, he disarmed them neatly by grabbing the edge of their red-and-white checkered tablecloth and removing their weaponry in one massive jerk.

"Good thing he doesn't know how to do Herb's trick with the tablecloth," Hannah said, chuckling as she remembered her mother's shock when Herb Beeseman, Hannah's partner's new husband and an amateur magician, had grabbed the edge of the tablecloth at the last dinner party they'd attended and whisked it away, leaving everything on the table intact.

Their lunch dates were nothing if not efficient, and in remarkably short order peace was restored. A squad of Bertanelli's waitstaff hurried out to make the mess disappear, and within a matter of a minute or two, patrons were once more able to enjoy their lunch and hear Tuscan melodies over the sound system.

"That was fast!" Hannah commented. "Bill calmed those students down in nothing flat. Your guy's good at this."

"So's yours," Andrea responded, snagging one of the remaining pieces of pizza.

"He's not mine. I'm not even sure he's *partially* mine, not when Ronni's living in the apartment right across the hall from him."

Andrea picked up a slice of mushroom that had fallen to the platter and popped it into her mouth. "I don't think Ronni will be around for much longer, at least not at the sheriff's department. Bill called her in last week and told her that if he heard one more word of gossip about her and any of the married deputies, he'd fire her."

"Can't be too soon to suit me," Hannah muttered, frowning deeply.

Andrea reached out to pat her sister's hand, a more personal touch than what was the norm for the Swensen clan. Whether it was due to the Scandinavian influence or some other innate cold-climate reticence, warm hugs and embraces were more generally attributed to Mediterranean climates and did not come easily to Minnesotans. "Let me pay, and let's get out of here. And then we'll . . ." Andrea stopped, drew in her breath sharply, and then continued, "I can't believe I forgot!"

"Forgot what?"

"The dresses Mother ordered came in at Claire's dress shop. We have to go try them on now. She called me this morning."

"Claire?"

"No, Mother. She wants us to go for a fitting this afternoon in case there are minor alterations."

"You're talking about the Regency dresses for the launch party?" Hannah guessed. Their mother had written a Regency Romance novel, and the launch party was set for the weekend before Thanksgiving. Delores had asked that her daughters wear Regency-style ball gowns to serve the refreshments, and they'd all agreed.

"That's right," Andrea confirmed it.

"Okay. We're on the same page. But how did Claire know what size to order for me?"

"Mother told her to order the same size as the dress she bought you for Christmas last year."

"*Last* year?" Hannah groaned loudly. "I gained some weight since last year. I can't get into the dress Mother gave me anymore. It's way too tight across the . . . well, you know."

"Backside?"

"Yes, and other places, too."

Andrea looked thoughtful as she signed the check and added a tip. She led the way to the door and as she pushed it open, she said, "We'll have Claire let it out as much as she can and go from there."

Not even the soothing décor of Claire's nicest dressing room could turn Hannah's ordeal at Beau Monde Fashions into a pleasure. Wallpaper the color of green tea with a lovely rose border could not erase the fact that her dress wouldn't button.

"I've been meaning to tell you," Claire said, her voice floating in through the louvers of the dressing room door. "Bob and I are really grateful to you as an enabler."

"Huh?" Hannah was thoroughly puzzled.

"The way you helped us tell the congregation that we wanted to get married."

"Thanks." Hannah remembered the morning in church when she'd made the announcement that Reverend Robert Knudson and Claire were planning to be married. She'd certainly overstepped the bounds of friendship by forcing the issue in such a public way, but everything had turned out all right. She was just patting herself on the back, mentally, for a job well done, when she realized that Claire had used the word *enabler*. "You're seeing a marriage counselor?" she guessed.

"A pre-marriage counselor, someone from the synod. It's recommended when a minister gets married. Anyway . . . I don't have any family and . . . will you be our maid of honor for the wedding?"

Hannah took a moment to think that over. The old saying, *Three times a bridesmaid, never a bride*, didn't apply in her case since she'd walked down the aisle as a bridesmaid five times in the past. "I'd love to, Claire. Thanks for asking me. But you'd better order a larger size dress."

"There's a problem?" Claire glanced in as Hannah opened

the door, and not even the soft pink bulb in the overhead lamp could hide her dismay. "Oh, dear!!"

"What's wrong?" Andrea asked, coming up behind Claire. Hannah glanced at her sister. Of course Andrea's dress fit perfectly. She hadn't gained an ounce since high school.

"Hannah's dress is too tight," Claire murmured, stating the obvious.

"And how!" Andrea shook her head. "Is there anything you can do?"

Claire gave a little shrug. "I can let it out, but not that much. They clipped the seams."

Even though she wasn't a seamstress, Hannah knew that meant she was in trouble. "Can you order a larger size?"

"There's no time. It takes at least two months for a special order, and your mother's party is only two weeks away." Claire thought for a moment and then she turned to Hannah with a hopeful look. "You said you were serving the refreshments. What kind of apron will you be wearing?"

"See-through lace. Mother ordered them from a catalogue."

"Then we've had it. Unless . . ."

"Unless what?" Hannah asked, hoping that Claire had come up with a miracle.

"Unless I put in inserts."

"Can you do that?" Hannah asked her.

Claire picked up the hem of Hannah's dress and looked at it. "There's not much material, and it's a large print. I'm not sure I can match it."

"What does that mean?" Andrea asked, every bit as clueless as Hannah was.

"It means that I'm a good tailor, but it's still going to look like we had to enlarge it because it was too small."

"Okay," Andrea said, turning to Hannah. "Hurry up and change back into your regular clothes. I've got a plan."

Hannah wasted no time in peeling herself out of the dress

and handing it out the door to Claire. In less time than it would take her to beat a meringue by hand, not that she ever would, she emerged from the pretty little dressing room, zipping up her parka.

"I'll call you later, Claire," Andrea said, hustling Hannah out the door.

"What plan?" Hannah asked, turning up her collar as she headed across the parking lot for the back door of her bakery and coffee shop, The Cookie Jar.

"You're already on a diet. You told me that, and it's all to the good. That means we've got two whole weeks to firm you up."

"Firm me up?!" Hannah uttered the words in the same shocked tone she would have used if her cat, Moishe, had barked to greet her when she opened the door. "Does *firming up* mean what I think it means?"

"It does." Andrea braced herself against the wind that almost claimed the little fur hat she was wearing. "I bought a year's membership at Heavenly Bodies, and it comes with a guest pass. I'll get you enrolled in my Classic Contours class. That's a program to discover your ideal shape."

Hannah was about to object when she reconsidered. Classic Contours didn't sound bad, especially if the classic part had something to do with classic art. The women Reubens painted certainly weren't featherweights. Then there were the Gibson Girls, and no one could describe them as sylphlike, and . . .

"Once you discover your perfect shape, you use individual body sculpting to achieve and maintain it. Each one of us has a series of personalized exercises we do."

She'd known it was too good to be true. Hannah gave a deep sigh and put away thoughts of well-proportioned, plus-size ladies.

"Anyway," Andrea went on. "I'll call out there and sign you up, and my personal fitness coach will design an exercise program for you."

"Uh-oh," Hannah breathed, giving a little shudder. The phrase *fitness coach* was not in her vocabulary. Even worse, the phrase *exercise program* brought back painful memories of mandatory calisthenics in elementary school gym class.

"Don't worry. It won't cost you anything," Andrea reassured her, completely misinterpreting Hannah's near-panicked expression. "Roger, my fitness coach, owes me one. I'm advertising his classes on my real estate flyers."

"It's not the money. It's just that I'm not cut out for an exercise regime. It's never worked for me before, and . . ." Hannah stopped and sighed again. She really wanted to tell her sister to forget it, but she knew how disappointed Delores would be if all three of her daughters weren't wearing the dresses she'd bought for her launch party. Were two weeks of her life too much to give for her mother's happiness?

Andrea sensed Hannah's ambivalence, and she gave her closing argument. "If you exercise every day, use the right machines, and stick to your diet, you'll be able to fit into your dress before Mother's party."

"You really think so?"

"I do. Just say yes, and we'll get started bright and early Monday morning."

Tomorrow was Sunday. At least she had one day to enjoy before Andrea cracked down the hammer. Hannah had made a solemn promise four years ago, right after she'd embarked upon a jogging regime that had lasted less than a week. She'd vowed to never again throw herself into an activity she knew she wouldn't complete. It was a waste of time, an assignment in futility, an endeavor that was fated to end in defeat.

"I love you just the way you are, Hannah." Andrea reached out to give her a little hug. "But just think of how proud Mother will be when she sees all three of us in the lovely dresses she chose for us."

Guilt reared its ugly head, and Hannah groaned. Andrea was pulling out all the stops to close the deal, a tactic she must have learned in real estate school.

"Yes?" Andrea prodded.

Hannah felt as if her life was about to pass in front of her eyes, but there was no help for it. She had to make their mother proud. "If you're sure it'll work, I'll do it."

"I'm sure."

"I just wish I'd known all this before we left Bertanelli's," she muttered, opening the back door and ushering Andrea in.

"So you could have ordered your salad without dressing?"

"Not exactly."

"Why then?" Andrea hung her coat on one of the hooks by the door and settled herself on a stool at the stainless steel work island.

"So I could have ordered a jumbo pizza for my last meal."

Chapter Two

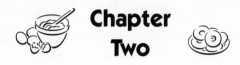

It was early Monday morning, and there was only one light in her bedroom. That was the way Hannah wanted it. She was dreading the event that was about to take place, and shedding light on it would only make it worse. She'd promised herself she'd never do this, but circumstances had changed.

Hannah sat down at the dressing table and addressed the large orange-and-white cat reclining at the foot of her bed. "I'm warning you, Moishe. If you say anything at all, you're history!"

Total silence greeted her, and Hannah was reassured. Perhaps this wouldn't be so bad after all. Other people did it, and they seemed to enjoy it. She'd even heard several say that it gave them a lift, made them more aware and alert, more equipped to handle the stresses of the day.

She didn't believe it for a second. No good would come of what she was about to do. She'd much rather sit here all day debating the pros and cons of her decision, but she had to get going or she'd be late.

"Okay," she said, standing up and addressing Moishe again. "I'm as ready as I'll ever be, so here goes nothing." And then she shrugged out of the robe she was wearing and turned to face the mirror.

There was dead silence in the room. It was the same silence

that followed a terrible disaster, the same eerie stillness that motorists talked about after a multicar pileup on the interstate. It was the total absence of sound that occurred after every catastrophe, and it was even more of a catastrophe than Hannah had thought it would be.

A generous sprinkling of silvering in the center of her reflection could have spared her this moment. Spidery cracks splitting the glass into irregular shapes and turning her image into a Dali painting would have done the trick as well. Even better, the entire mirror could have fallen forward onto the floor, leaving nothing but an ornamental frame around the paper Delores had chosen for the walls of her eldest daughter's boudoir.

"Good grief!" Hannah moaned, echoing Charlie Brown's famous utterance. She'd known it would be bad, but not *this* bad. The screaming yellow accents on her black exercise outfit called blaring attention to the extra padding around her middle. Her legs, encased in black tights, looked like stout tree trunks, fully capable of supporting the oh-so-much larger torso than she'd realized she had. She'd chosen to wear black because it was slimming, but there was no escaping the truth. She was stout, like her Grandma Swensen. And although she'd loved her grandmother with every fiber of her being, she'd never aspired to actually *look* like her.

"At least no one will see me except a bunch of other women trying to lose weight," Hannah told the cat, who was bristling slightly as he regarded her with round, unblinking eyes. "I know I don't look good, but I wish you wouldn't bristle that way."

Moishe made no sound, but Hannah thought the hair on his back smoothed out a bit. It was time for a fish-flavored reward, and then she had to leave. She'd promised to meet Andrea at the Tri-County Mall to go over her exercise routine before class started. Hannah's plan was to learn the exercises, attend the thirty-minute class, and then drive to The Cookie Jar to help her partner finish the baking for the day.

It took only a few moments to get ready to go. Hannah turned on the television for Moishe, made sure his food bowl was full to the brim, and checked to make sure he had plenty of water. Then she slipped into her longest jacket, one her grandmother would have called a car coat, grabbed her purse and her car keys, tossed several treats to the cat who was waiting patiently on the back of the couch, and hurried out the door.

A chill wind whipped her red curls into an even more un-ruly state than usual. This second week in November was cold, and it smelled like snow was on the way. But something was wrong, and Hannah stopped midway down the outside stairs from her second floor condo to figure out what it was.

There were no strange noises coming from any of the con-dos, and the smooth expanse of snow that had fallen during the night was unbroken by human footprints. All the doors and windows in her line of sight were intact, and she didn't see any evidence of burglary or vandalism. Everything seemed to be perfectly normal, but she couldn't shake the feeling that something was wrong.

There was a faint cyan cast to the landscape, and the wood siding on the condos stood out in sharp relief. The scene re-minded Hannah of an old sepia photograph she'd seen of her grandparents' farm. The color was different. The shadows in the photograph were brown, but the shadows she saw now were bluish-black. They were different than anything she'd ever seen before.

Blue light. She thought about that for a moment. Was this some kind of natural phenomenon like a meteor shower, or a blue moon? Hannah hurried down the covered staircase and looked up at the sky. She didn't see anything unusual in the heavens. The only difference between this morning and any other morning was the light. The sky was brighter in the east than it had ever been before.

A delighted laugh escaped Hannah's lips. Her mirth took a visible form in the icy air, and the little cloud of vapor that formed reminded Hannah of the balloon above a cartoon character's head. To carry the analogy even further, the balloon should be filled with a lightbulb to show that she'd figured out what was amiss. Of course things looked different this morning. She was accustomed to leaving her condo at five AM when it was pitch black. On this particular morning she was a full hour later than usual.

Hannah stepped carefully on the sidewalk between the buildings and took the stairs down to the garage. It was underground, stretching the length of her four-condo building and extending across to serve the four units in the building next door. Hannah hurried down the steps. She had to rush to meet Andrea on time, and as she reached the bottom step, she came very close to running into her downstairs neighbor, Phil Plotnik, who worked nights at DelRay Manufacturing.

"Whoa!" Phil said, reaching out to grab her arms. "What are you doing here this time of morning? Did you sleep late?"

"Not really. Lisa's handling the baking this morning, and I'm meeting Andrea at the mall."

"I thought the mall didn't open until ten."

"It doesn't, but Andrea's a member at Heavenly Bodies and she's got a key to their outside door. We're going to work out before anyone else gets there."

Phil looked surprised, but he didn't say anything and Hannah gave him credit for that. Silence was definitely golden when it came to the topics of losing weight and exercising. In lieu of asking questions or offering his opinion, Phil simply walked her to her cookie truck and opened the driver's door for her. "Will you be at The Cookie Jar later?"

"I should be there by the time we open at nine," Hannah told him, and that was when she noticed that he looked worried. "Is something wrong?"

"Sue's been really depressed lately, and I thought I'd stop by this afternoon and get something nice for her."

"That's sweet of you, Phil. But why is she depressed?"

"I think it's because she's dreading the winter cooped up in our condo with Kevin."

Hannah tried to remember how old Kevin was. He had been born at the beginning of the winter, and she was almost sure it was two years ago. This meant that Sue and Phil's son was in his terrible twos. "Kevin just turned two, didn't he?"

"Yes, on November third. It wasn't so hard on Sue when he was little. He slept a lot then, but now he's really active and Sue has to watch him all the time."

Hannah did her best to imagine raising a toddler. It must be difficult to be closeted with the responsibility of a child for twenty-four hours a day. "I'll bet Sue doesn't get much free time."

"You said it! The only time she has is when Kevin's napping, and he never naps for long. She gets time for a shower and maybe a quick flip through the paper before he wakes up, but that's about it."

"How about at night when he goes to bed?"

"We get an hour alone, just the two of us, and then I have to get ready for work. I'm on the swing shift now. After I leave at nine thirty, Sue's usually so exhausted she goes straight to bed."

Hannah was silent. That didn't sound like much of a life at all. "She worked at DelRay before Kevin was born, didn't she?"

"Yes, in the office."

"Did she like it?"

Phil shrugged. "It was okay and the money was good, but what she really wanted to do was teach. As soon as Kevin's old enough for school, she's going to go back to college and get her degree. She's only got a couple of courses to go."

A dim light began to flicker in the back of Hannah's mind, and in less time than it took her to realize that she had to hurry or she'd be late meeting Andrea at the mall, she had an idea. She wouldn't mention it now. She didn't want to raise hopes and then dash them.

"You can relax, Phil," she told him. "I've got something that'll perk Sue right up. What's your schedule like today?"

"It's like every other workday. I play with Kevin for a while so Sue can get some work done, and then I sleep from about eight to three."

"Can you drop by the coffee shop when you wake up?"

"Sure. Are you going to make something special for Sue?"

"You bet. It's impossible to worry about anything when you're eating chocolate, and I'm going to come up with a cookie for Sue that'll cheer her up for the whole week."

It was almost bright enough to drive without headlights when Hannah pulled into the parking lot at the Tri-County Mall. She passed Bergstrom's Department Store, locked up tight until it opened at ten, and headed to the north end of the shopping center where the street door for Heavenly Bodies was located. The parking lot was completely deserted, and Hannah pulled into the space at the right of the door. Andrea wasn't here yet, which didn't surprise Hannah. It had taken a blaring alarm clock, several none-too-gentle shakes on the shoulder, and threats of dire bodily harm to get Andrea out of bed when they were in high school.

The inside of her windshield was beginning to fog up, and Hannah opened her window a crack. There was a delightful scent in the air, a sugary, chocolaty scent with undertones of cinnamon and maple that set her mouth watering and her mind flipping through the sweet possibilities. She knew this scent. She'd smelled it before. But where?

When speculation didn't lead to an answer, Hannah zipped her knee-length jacket and stepped out of her truck. She started to the right, but the scent faded. It was something to her left, and she was going to find it!

When she walked around the corner of the building, she encountered the back doors of several closed shops. There was no way Bianco's could be the origin of this delightful scent. It was an Italian shoe store, and it smelled of leather and packing material. The next store was an upscale kitchen boutique. Unless they were doing a cooking demonstration, which was unlikely since there were no other cars in the parking lot, it couldn't be coming from there either.

Hannah walked on until she came to a likely prospect. It was a small space that had previously belonged to a flower shop. It had changed hands and the new name was stenciled on the door. It read, DORO'S DOUGHNUTS, in thick gold script, and Hannah had all she could do not to knock on the door and demand entrance.

"Hannah?" A voice called her name, and Hannah turned to see Andrea. "You're not going in there, are you?"

Hannah stepped away from the door. "Of course not. I just smelled the doughnuts and wondered where they were."

"Good thing I got here when I did," Andrea said. "How did you do on your diet yesterday?"

"I had a small glass of orange juice, two scrambled eggs, and a piece of whole wheat toast for breakfast."

"That sounds good. Did you scramble the eggs in butter?"

"No, I used a nonstick cooking spray. They couldn't have had many calories. They were perfectly tasteless."

"Excellent." Andrea favored her with a smile. "How about the toast? Did you butter it?"

"Absolutely not," Hannah said, grateful that Andrea hadn't asked about the jar of apricot jam on the top shelf of her refrigerator.

"How about lunch?"

"I'd love to, thanks," Hannah quipped, but she sobered when Andrea frowned at her. "I had a green salad with two tablespoons of diet dressing on it. I did have a cookie for dessert, though. Lisa wanted me to try a new recipe, and I baked a quarter batch at home. Her cousin Tiffany sent it to her."

"What kind of cookie was it?"

"They're called Pistachio Winks, and they're really good.

We're going to bake them today and try them out on our customers."

"I'll have to try one when I come in later. I just love pistachios. But I'm getting sidetracked here. You only had one cookie for lunch, right?"

"That's right." Hannah decided not to mention the fact that she'd eaten several more cookies for an afternoon snack, along with a bowl of vanilla ice cream, just to see if the combination would work.

"How about dinner?"

"Sausage," Hannah said, leaving it at that. She'd been thinking about her missed opportunity at Bertanelli's and how she deserved a last meal before starting her new exercise regime. She'd sworn Ellie to secrecy over the phone, and she'd picked up a double order of garlic bread and a supreme pizza with everything on it to take back to her condo for dinner.

"Did you have any potatoes or rice with the sausage?"

"Of course not. I know better than that."

"And you know that a dieter's biggest downfall is late night snacking?"

Hannah could testify to that. She'd eaten every one of the candy bars she'd been saving to make Brownies Plus.

"Well," Andrea turned to smile at her, "you didn't do badly except for the cookie. I really think diet and exercise is going to work for you, as long as you stick to it."

"Me, too," Hannah said, hoping she *could* stick to it.

"Let's go and I'll show you your exercise routine." Andrea pulled Hannah across the parking lot toward the back door of Heavenly Bodies. "Roger and I worked it out for you. We worked out one for Bill, too. He promised me he's going to go in early and work out in the sheriff's department gym every morning."

Hannah nodded, but she had her doubts. Bill had once confessed to her that he liked to exercise about as much as Hannah did. Both of them had agreed that rowing on a river or riding on a bike path might be enjoyable, but performing the same activity on a stationary machine while staring at a cinderblock wall was about as boring as it got.

"Here we go," Andrea said, marching up to the door. She punched in some numbers on the keypad, inserted her key card in the slot, and opened the door to what Hannah had always thought of as a torture chamber.

"You have to do the keypad *and* the key card?" Hannah asked, stepping into the hallway that led to another door.

"Yes. That way if someone steals your key card, they can't use it unless they know your personal code."

"It's just like a bank machine. You need your P.I.N. and your card to make it work. Does it keep track of when people come and go?"

"It's not *that* sophisticated," Andrea told her. "Bill says that kind of setup would cost a lot more. The owner probably thought he didn't need it since he's got mall security and cameras on the entrances and exits."

The first thing Hannah noticed when she stepped inside the inner door was the scent of oranges. The fragrance had the distinctive artificiality of room freshener, and Hannah suspected plug-in dispensers at strategic points throughout the spa. There was another scent under the citrus bouquet, a combination of damp towels, sweat, and chlorinated water. "There must be a pool," she commented.

"Two. There's a lap pool that runs the length of one wall. That's for the serious swimmers. And there's another pool for hydrotherapy and aquatic gymnastics. There's a sauna, too. It's coed so you have to wear a suit." Andrea stopped and the corners of her mouth turned up. "Unless, of course, you come in at three in the morning with your husband, and there's no one else here."

Hannah's mouth dropped open. She couldn't help it. "You didn't!"

"Not me. You know Bill. He's not that daring, especially now that he's sheriff. Just think of the headlines in the *Lake Eden Journal!*"

"THE NAKED TRUTH ABOUT COUNTY LAW ENFORCEMENT," Hannah said with a grin. "SHERIFF TODD EXPOSES THE BARE FACTS."

Andrea laughed as she flicked on the lights. "Bill would never even consider doing anything like that, but I can't say the same about the rest of the members. I've heard some pretty racy rumors about a couple of them."

"Ronni Ward?"

"Her name was mentioned. And that's one of the reasons Bill is going to phase out her job at the sheriff's department. But she's not the only one."

"Who else?" Hannah asked, following Andrea to a dressing room with the word WOMEN painted on the door. The door across the hall from it read MEN, and Hannah was slightly disappointed. She'd expected some designation to go with the name Heavenly Bodies, a pairing like STARLETS and COMETS, or perhaps even VENUS and MARS.

"Nobody's really naming names, at least not to me," Andrea went on with her explanation. "I think that's because I'm the sheriff's wife."

Andrea sounded a bit disappointed, and Hannah grinned. "Bill's job is a real handicap?"

"When it comes to gossip, it is. Nobody tells me anything anymore." Andrea walked over to a bank of forest-green lockers with bright pink trim. "Put your things in my locker, and let's get going."

Once her purse and jacket were stashed away, Hannah glanced around the dressing room. It was a very attractive place. Hanging plants decorated one mirrored wall, and they were reflected in the mirrors on the opposite wall. Pink-and-white flowers were in abundance, and Hannah turned to her sister. "What are those flowers?" she asked.

"Begonias. The owner told me they're perfect for the moisture level in here. See those lights above you?" Andrea pointed up to the bank of fluorescent lights. "There's another bank that comes on after hours. They're grow lights, and begonias just love them."

"Very pretty," Hannah said, following Andrea out of the dressing room.

"Good morning, ladies," a male voice greeted them, and Hannah had all she could do not to turn around and rush back into the dressing room. Andrea had assured her they'd be alone, and some guy was standing there smiling at them.

"Hi, Tad. Meet my sister, Hannah." Andrea turned to Hannah. "This is Tad Newberg. He's one of the night security guards."

Hannah shook hands with the short, chubby security guard. Tad had what she'd always thought of as a baby face, with round cheeks and freckles. He looked as if he belonged in junior high, but his sandy hair was thinning just a bit on top. He wasn't as young as he looked, and Hannah was willing to bet he was about her age.

"Glad to meet you, Hannah," Tad said.

"Same here," Hannah replied.

"I'll leave you two to your workouts, then." Tad turned on his heel and headed for the door. "If you have any problems, just holler," he called out over his shoulder.

"Tad's a nice guy," Andrea said, unlocking a door with her key. Hannah followed her into a room with stark black machines that looked highly threatening.

"We'll start here." Andrea led the way to something that looked like a bicycle that was fashioned out of the wrong parts. "Just watch me for a while and then you can try it."

Oh, goodie! I can hardly wait! Hannah felt like saying sarcastically, but of course she didn't. Andrea was trying to help her, and she should be more grateful.

"You put your hands here." Andrea grasped the handlebars and placed her feet on the pedals. "And your feet here. And then you push back with your feet and pull forward with your arms."

"Right," Hannah said.

"It's just like a rocking chair, except that you have to work at it."

"Right," Hannah said again, watching her sister push and pull to glide back and forth. It reminded her a bit of an animal in a zoo, mindlessly repeating the same behavior over and over again, hoping for some reward. Wasn't there some way to tone up and lose twenty pounds without sacrificing her dignity in the process?

Andrea hopped off the machine and Hannah noticed that her sister wasn't even breathing hard. "You try it now. It's a great way to tone up, and it really stretches your muscles."

Hannah had all she could do not to groan as she got into the proper position. The seat was too small, and it didn't seem to conform to human anatomy. The handlebars were up too high, and she wasn't sure she could pull herself forward on them. The pedals were set at an awkward height, and she knew her legs would cramp if she spent more than a few minutes riding the infernal contraption.

"All set?" Andrea asked her.

Hannah struggled to duplicate her sister's actions. It had looked easy when Andrea had done it, but her sister's seemingly effortless glide back and forth took real muscle to accomplish. She told herself that it would get easier once she got used to it, but she didn't hold out any real hope that would be the case.

"That's it. You've got it now."

Hannah might have replied, but she was panting too hard from her efforts. Not only that, she didn't trust herself to speak. She'd just glanced at her reflection in the mirrored wall and remembered the time their father had taken the whole family to the circus. They'd all laughed when the baby elephant had ridden a child-size tricycle around the ring, but it didn't seem that funny at all in retrospect!

PISTACHIO WINKS

Preheat oven to 350 degrees F., rack
in the middle position.

1 cup butter *(2 sticks, ½ pound)*
3 cups white *(granulated)* sugar
4 eggs, beaten *(just whip them up in a glass with a
   fork)*
⅛ cup *(2 Tablespoons)* molasses
1 teaspoon salt
1 teaspoon baking soda
3 teaspoons vanilla
2 cups finely chopped pistachio nutmeats
4 cups flour *(pack it down in the measuring cup
   when you measure it)*

½ cup white *(granulated)* sugar for later
15 to 30 red or green maraschino cherries cut into
   quarters

Melt the butter in a microwave-safe bowl or measuring cup. It'll take about 90 seconds on HIGH. *(You can also melt it in a pan on the stove if you prefer.)*

Pour the butter into a mixing bowl and add the sugar. Mix well and let the mixture cool to room temperature.

Mix in the beaten eggs. Add the molasses and mix well. *(If you spray your Tablespoon measure or your ⅛ cup measure with Pam or another nonstick cooking spray, the molasses won't stick to it when you measure.)*

Add the salt, baking soda, and vanilla. Stir everything together and then mix in the finely-chopped pistachios.

Add the flour in one-cup increments, mixing after each addition.

Form the dough into 1-inch balls with your fingers and place them on a cookie sheet that has been sprayed with Pam or another nonstick cooking spray. Form 12 dough balls for each standard-size cookie sheet.

Spray the flat bottom of a water glass with Pam or another nonstick cooking spray. Dip the glass in a bowl of white sugar and flatten the balls on the cookie sheet. Dip the glass into the sugar after every ball you flatten.

Place a quarter cherry in the center of each cookie. Press the cherry down with the tip of your finger.

Bake the cookies at 350 degrees F. for 10 to 12 minutes. Let the cookies set up on the sheet for one minute, and then remove them to a wire rack to finish cooling.

Yield: 8 to 10 dozen delicious cookies, depending on cookie size.

Chapter
Three

"So how was it?" Hannah's partner, Lisa Herman Beeseman, asked when Hannah came in the back door of The Cookie Jar at a quarter past eight.

"Not as bad as I thought it would be." Hannah hung her jacket on the rack by the back door and headed for the miniscule shower enclosure that was attached to the bathroom. "As a matter of fact, it was almost fun once the class started."

Lisa looked shocked. "I never thought I'd hear you say that exercise was fun!"

"I didn't say *fun*. I said, *almost fun*. I'll take a quick shower and then I'll set things up in the coffee shop."

"It's all done," Lisa called after her.

Hannah stopped in her tracks and turned around to stare. Lisa was diminutive, only five feet tall, and Hannah was willing to bet that she didn't weigh in at much over a hundred pounds, but her young partner was tireless when it came to getting things done. "You finished the baking *and* set everything up in the coffee shop?"

"Yes."

"What time did you get here anyway?"

"Five thirty. Herb had to run out to highway patrol headquarters for an early meeting, and I didn't feel like sitting at the kitchen table drinking coffee alone."

"What kind of meeting?"

"I'll tell you all about it right after your shower. You're not going to believe what Mayor Bascomb is thinking about doing now!"

Hannah made short work of her shower. Lisa's husband, Herb Beeseman, was their small town's only law enforcement officer, and he reported directly to the mayor. If anyone knew what Mayor Bascomb was planning to do next, it was Herb.

When Hannah emerged wearing jeans that she thought might be a wee bit looser in the waist, a mug of strong black coffee was waiting for her at the stainless steel work island. She sat down on a stool, took a huge swallow of coffee, and gave a sigh of contentment. "Okay. Tell me what our esteemed mayor has up his sleeve this time."

"Red-light cameras."

"On what? There aren't any stoplights in Lake Eden."

Lisa just smiled. "You're right. There aren't any . . . yet."

"He's at it again!" Hannah groaned and put her head in her hands. "Don't tell me he's still fixated on putting in a light at the end of Main Street?"

"No, he's not."

"Well, thank goodness for that!" Hannah took another sip of life-enhancing caffeine, but before she even swallowed, a dreadful thought crossed her mind. "He's given up the idea of having one at the end of Main Street, but he wants to put one somewhere else?"

"That's right."

"I'm afraid to ask, but . . . where?"

"Third and Main. Remember that traffic survey the varsity baseball team did last summer?"

Hannah had seen several members of the baseball team, equipped with folding chairs and beach umbrellas, staking out various corners in Lake Eden to count the cars that passed through the intersections. "I remember, but I thought it was just an excuse to pay for their new uniforms from the city budget."

"So did everybody else, but it seems Mayor Bascomb had

a double agenda. He asked Herb to tally up the results last week, and the most heavily trafficked corner in town is ours."

"But we don't *need* a stoplight. As far as I know, there's never been an accident on our corner."

"True, but he's not doing it as a safety measure. Herb says to look at it from his point of view. People are used to driving right through our intersection without stopping. And that means when they put in a stoplight, it'll take a while for them to get used to it. They'll drive on through the red light the first couple of times, and the red-light camera will catch them. Then Herb will watch the tapes, issue a ticket to any drivers who run it, and the city will have another source of revenue. That'll provide more money for our school and all the programs at the Community Center, and Mayor Bascomb will look good."

Hannah thought about that for a second, and then she nodded. Lisa's husband was a smart man. "What's next? Shaving another five miles off the speed limit in town?"

"Herb and I talked about that, but he doesn't think it'll happen. Mayor Bascomb would have to order new speed signs, and they're expensive."

"So when is the stoplight going in?" Hannah asked the important question.

"Herb doesn't know, but he's hoping never. He thinks it's a dirty trick to play on everybody in Lake Eden. Of course he can't tell Mayor Bascomb that."

Hannah noticed the small smile that flitted across Lisa's face. "You and Herb have a plan to quash the mayor's spying stoplight?"

"Maybe," Lisa said, and then she clamped her lips shut.

Hannah knew she wouldn't get any more information from Lisa. Her partner could be stubborn. "Well, good luck to you, and let me know if there's any way I can help."

"I will." The phone on the kitchen wall rang, and Lisa hurried over to answer it. She spoke for a few moments, and then she turned to Hannah. "It's Mrs. Janowski and she wants to know if we can make some birthday cookies to serve at Calvin's party. She reserved the banquet room at The Corner Tavern and they're having it there. She said she planned to bake a cake, but Calvin wants cookies instead."

"Ask her what kind of cookies Calvin likes," Hannah instructed. She listened while Lisa asked, and she was surprised to see a frown cross her partner's face.

Lisa covered the mouthpiece and turned to face Hannah. "She says anything that resembles a cheeseburger will be a big hit with Calvin. Cheeseburgers are his favorite food. That's one of the reasons they're having the party at The Corner Tavern. She's ordering platters of cheeseburgers and fries served with chocolate milkshakes."

"Oh, great!" Hannah said, and her meaning was clearly at odds with her choice of words. Cookies shaped like cheeseburgers? She was about to tell Lisa to suggest something else when she remembered Ellen Wagner, her college roommate from North Dakota. Ellen had gone home on semester break and come back with pictures of her niece's birthday party, along with a sample of the cookies her sister had served. Hannah had greatly admired the cookies, sweet little bites of goodness fashioned from store-bought ingredients that closely resembled miniature cheeseburgers.

"What shall I tell Mrs. Janowski?" Lisa prompted.

"Tell her yes, we can do it."

Lisa looked clearly astounded. "We can make cookies that look like cheeseburgers?"

"You betcha!" Hannah said, using her former roommate's pet phrase. She'd made a copy of the photo and stuck it in the recipe file she'd brought back to Lake Eden from college. As far as she knew, the photo was still there, and even if it wasn't, she could probably re-create the cookies if she worked at it. "When is Calvin's party?"

Lisa repeated the question, and she didn't look happy as

she turned back to Hannah. "After school on Friday. That's only four days away."

Hannah groaned. "Okay. It's really short notice, but tell her we'll do it."

"Hannah says it's really short notice, but we can do it," Lisa repeated, but then she gave Hannah a wink and went on. "It'll take some experimenting to get them just right and we may have to work overtime. That means we'll have to charge you double our standard decorated cookie price. Will that be all right?"

Hannah's mouth dropped open. She hadn't told Lisa to say that!

"Okay, we're all set then. We'll deliver ten dozen cheese-burger cookies to The Corner Tavern on Friday before three for your party. And thank you very much for the order."

"You'll have to charge her *double*?" Hannah asked when Lisa had hung up the phone.

"That's right. It's something we've never made before, and she ought to pay for that. Besides, she agreed so fast she practically made my eyes swim. It didn't bother her a bit, Hannah."

"But don't you think that's taking advantage of people?"

"No. It's a special order, and we'll have to work hard on it. People have to pay for special orders. It's only right. We charge too little anyway. Our cookies are the best. We use only the finest ingredients, and everybody knows you have to pay for quality."

"Yes, but things are different here. Lake Eden's a small town and people don't have much money, and . . . I'd feel really bad if they didn't get top value for their money."

"That is the most ridiculous thing I've ever heard!" Lisa put her hands on her hips and stared hard at Hannah. With her small stature and her chef's apron rolled up several times in the middle and held in place with the ties wrapped twice around her waist, she might have seemed ridiculous, but her determination made her a force to respect. "The people from Lake Eden go out to the mall and pay almost five dollars for one little cup of designer coffee and a cookie that tastes like cardboard. And don't say they don't, because I've seen them do it! If they can afford to do that, they can certainly afford to pay the same price for a cup of great coffee with free refills and a cookie that tastes even better than their grandmothers used to make!"

Hannah thought about that for a moment. "I suppose you're right, but . . ."

"You really ought to let me start pricing things around here," Lisa interrupted her. "We're a business, not a charity. I know you think it's your duty to treat the whole world, but it's not. And if you keep devaluing your talent by under-charging, you're going to go broke!"

Hannah just stared at the partner who had turned into a dynamo. It seemed as if Lisa had been thinking about this for a while. But as she watched, Lisa appeared to have second thoughts, because she put her hands over her face and sighed.

"I'm sorry, Hannah," she said, and her voice quavered slightly. "It's just that I get so mad when I see people taking advantage of your good nature."

Hannah thought about that for a minute. Lisa really did have a point. Several other people in her life had pointed out that she hadn't raised her prices in three years, when every other business in town had done so several times. She'd never claimed to be a businesswoman. She simply enjoyed baking for people and seeing how happy they were when they munched on one of her cookies. Perhaps it was time to let a real busi-nesswoman take over the nuts and bolts of the business. She could still enjoy baking and watching people taste her cre-ations, but she wouldn't have to agonize over pricing and mak-ing a profit.

"It's a done deal," Hannah said, smiling at Lisa.

"*What's* a done deal?"

"You take care of the business stuff from now on. I'll come up with new recipes and figure out what to bake every day."

Lisa looked a bit dumbfounded at this news. "But . . . are you sure you want me to handle the pricing and everything?"

"Better you than me. I'm not very good at it, and I know it. But before you leave the kitchen for the rarefied air of high finance, do me a favor, will you?"

"Sure. What is it?"

"Bake a Chocolate Chip Mega Cookie for Sue Plotnik. She's been depressed lately, and Phil wants us to cheer her up. And that reminds me, do we have any extra Oatmeal Raisin Crisps we can package up for Janice Cox at Kiddie Korner? I need to go see her today." Hannah stopped speaking and began to frown. "Let me rethink that. Maybe I shouldn't give so many cookies away."

"Wrong. You should give extra cookies away. Everybody knows we don't sell day-old, and giving them away goes under the promotion category. I'll check with Stan to make sure I'm right, but if I keep track of fair price for day-old cookies, we can deduct it from our taxes."

"I've never done *that* before!"

"That doesn't mean you can't do it now. I'll bet you never even thought to mention it to Stan."

Hannah gave a little shrug. "You're right. I don't think I mentioned it. I just assumed that . . ."

"Never assume," Lisa interrupted her. "Assumption is the mother of a compound word I'm not going to say. Just let me keep track and see if we can use the deduction."

"Okay," Hannah said, giving her partner a smile. It was going to be a lot more fun letting someone else handle the finances.

"Why do you have to see Janice? Andrea's not thinking about putting Bethie in preschool this early, is she?"

"No, Grandma McCann is still living in, and I wouldn't be a bit surprised if she stayed for a couple more years."

Lisa got out one of the stainless steel mixing bowls and began to round up ingredients for Sue's cookie. "Herb ran into her at the Red Owl the other day, and she said she really likes living in town, especially now that it's winter. She told him that wintering on a farm is hard when your family's grown up and moved away, and you're all alone out in the country."

"I can understand that! My grandparents lived on Grandma McCann's road, and sometimes it took almost a week to get it plowed. They were stuck there, come whatever, and if there's a really bad winter storm, the phone lines go down."

"Then you'd be stuck in a house all alone with no way to get out and no phone you could use to call for help. That's really scary!"

"You bet it is, but that's not the worst of it."

"Really? What's worse than that?"

"No cable and no satellite dish. The cable company doesn't run out that far, and her farm is down in a low spot, so a dish won't work without building an expensive tower. Andrea told me that Grandma McCann just loves the movies on the romance channel, and the only place she can get the romance channel is at Andrea and Bill's house."

CHOCOLATE CHIP MEGA COOKIES

Preheat oven to 350 degrees F., rack
in the middle position.

2 cups white *(granulated)* sugar
1 cup softened butter *(2 sticks, 8 ounces, ½ pound)*
2 teaspoons vanilla extract
2 beaten eggs *(just whip them up in a glass with a fork)*
1 teaspoon molasses
1/2 teaspoon salt
1 teaspoon baking soda
1 cup chopped walnuts *(or any other nut you prefer—nuts are optional)*
2 cups chocolate chips *(a 12-ounce package)*
2 1/2 cups flour *(not sifted—pack it down in the cup when you measure it)*

Hannah's 1st Note: You can mix these cookies by hand or use an electric mixer on slow speed.

Place the sugar in a large mixing bowl. Add the softened butter and vanilla extract, and stir until the resulting mixture is light and fluffy. Add the beaten eggs and mix well.

Mix in the teaspoon of molasses. *(To measure molasses or any other sticky liquid, spray your measuring spoon or cup with Pam or another nonstick spray before you measure.)* Stir until the mixture in your bowl is a uniform color.

Add the salt and the baking soda, and mix until they're thoroughly incorporated.

Hannah's 2nd Note: You have alternatives if your family doesn't like or can't eat the chopped nuts. You can use a cup of finely shredded coconut in place of the nuts, or a cup of rolled oats, or a cup of crushed breakfast cereal (measure after crushing), or even a cup of chopped dried fruit like raisins or apricots.

Add the nuts or their alternative and stir them in. Then add half of the chocolate chips and half of the flour. *(You don't have to be exact—the object is to add the flour and the chocolate chips in two parts so they won't glob up when you stir them in.)* Stir until the chips and flour are thoroughly incorporated.

Add the rest of the chips and the rest of the flour. Mix thoroughly. Let the dough rest while you prepare the pans.

You will use two and only two pans for this recipe. *(They're called "mega" cookies for a reason!)* Use two 9-inch or 10-inch pie pans—glass, metal, or disposable, it really doesn't matter. If you must, you can use three 8-inch pie pans, but the cookies will be much thinner and you'll have to reduce the baking time by 5 minutes.

Line your pie pans with a big square of aluminum foil, pressing the foil down to conform to the bottom and sides of the pie pan and leaving the four corners sticking up.

(You'll use them later to remove the cookies from the pie plates.)

Once the pie pans are lined on the inside, spray the foil with Pam or another nonstick cooking spray.

Divide your cookie dough in half *(or thirds if you used three 8-inch pie pans.)* Form each half into a large ball. Place the balls in the center of your pie pans and smush them down with your impeccably clean hands. Continue to flatten the dough balls until they're spread all the way out to the sides of the pan, and the tops are fairly smooth.

Bake the "mega" cookies at 350 degrees F. for 40 minutes *(35 minutes if you made three cookies instead of two.)* Test for doneness by using a time-honored method devised by Hannah's Grandma Swensen. Press the back of a spoon down on the center of the cookie. If it sinks in and comes out gooey and squishy, the cookies need more baking. Try them again after 5 minutes. If it leaves only a slight indentation, your cookies are done.

Remove your cookies from the oven and cool them in their pans on a wire rack for 15 minutes. Then grasp two diagonal corners, lift the cookies out of their pans and continue to cool them on the wire racks until they reach room temperature.

When the cookies are thoroughly cool, carefully peel off the foil. They're wonderful just as they are, but you can add to the enjoyment by decorating them if you wish.

Lisa uses a pastry bag to make little stars around the edge of her cookies, and then she personalizes them with a name written across the center. If you're like me and you prefer not to use a pastry bag, you can buy little tubes of frosting in the grocery store and write a message and a name with them in your choice of frosting color.

Chapter
Four

Hannah was in the kitchen refilling the large cookie jars they kept behind the counter in the coffee shop to display the day's wares. She'd just put the lid back on the Raisin Drops when Lisa pushed open the swinging door that separated the coffee shop from the kitchen. "Mike's here," she announced. "Do you want me to send him back here?"

"Sure." Hannah watched as Lisa crossed the floor and picked up two of the full cookie jars to take to the coffee shop. From day one, Lisa saw what needed to be done, and she did it without being asked. It was only one of the many characteristics that made her such a perfect partner.

Once Lisa was gone, Hannah took off the food service gloves she wore to handle cookies and reached up to smooth her hair. She knew it wouldn't do much good. She could feel her unruly curls popping back up again the moment she removed her hand.

"Hi, Hannah." Mike Kingston came in as if he owned the place, but Hannah didn't mind. His self-confidence and assertiveness were two of the things she liked best about him. Of course she also liked his rugged good looks and the way he made her heart pound against her rib cage whenever he walked into the room. His towering height was impressive too. Hannah wasn't petite and at over five feet, eight inches tall, she appreciated a man she could look up to, a man who made her feel dainty and feminine. This was a rare treat for the daughter Delores claimed was a throwback to her rotund paternal grandmother, not exactly petite either, but the best farmwife, cook, and baker that Hannah had ever known.

"I heard you went out to Heavenly Bodies this morning," Mike said by way of a greeting as he seated himself on a stool at the workstation.

Hannah was so surprised she almost dropped the mug of coffee she'd just poured for him. How did Mike know that? She was about to ask him how he'd heard when she glanced at the clock. It was ten forty-five, and Andrea had most certainly called Bill at work the moment she'd gotten home from the gym. And since Mike had a meeting with Bill every morning to go over the night's crime reports, what Hannah had come to think of as her secret exercise regime was no longer a secret at all.

"I suppose everyone in town knows," Hannah said, delivering Mike's coffee and two of his favorite Twin Chocolate Delights on a napkin.

"Maybe not everybody. Stan Kramer and his wife are on vacation, and I think Irma York's off visiting her cousin in Brainerd."

"Thanks a *lot*." Hannah tried not to show how amused she was. There were times when Mike was really pretty funny.

"So what if people know you're working out at Heavenly Bodies? That's certainly nothing to be ashamed of. I'm proud of you for trying to get in shape."

Trying to get in shape. The phrase ricocheted around in Hannah's mind like a marble in a blender. It was the word *trying* that bothered her the most. *Trying* meant that she wasn't in shape. And it also insinuated that she might not succeed in her attempt to get there. That might not be far from the truth considering her track record for starting an exercise program and then dropping it after a couple of days, but voicing it constituted an insult from the man who'd once asked Hannah to marry him. She was about to object to

Mike's turn of phrase when he popped to his feet like a marionette that had been jerked upright by invisible strings.

"I almost forgot. I've got something in the cruiser for you. Hold on just a second and I'll get it."

Hannah held on. She held on to her coffee cup and she also held on to her temper. She really shouldn't be angry with a man who'd brought her a present . . . unless, of course, the present was also something insulting, like a bathroom scale, or a diet book.

In a very few moments, fewer than it would have taken Hannah to run through the coffee shop, get something out of a parked car, and retrace her steps to the kitchen, Mike was back.

"Here," he said, thrusting a huge, gift-wrapped package into her arms. "It's for you and Moishe."

All traces of Hannah's earlier pique dissipated. It didn't matter what the present was. It was sufficient that Mike had thought enough of her pet to get something for Moishe. She supposed that was why Andrea got all dewy-eyed when a guest brought a "little something" for Tracey or Bethie. It was a case of *Love me, love my kid.* Or in Hannah's situation, it was *Love me, love my cat.*

"Thank you, Mike," Hannah said in a voice that came close to emulating Moishe's best purr.

"You're welcome. Open it now and see if you think the Big Guy'll like it. I got it out at the pet store in the mall."

The box was wrapped in bright yellow paper with brown animal footprints all over it. It reminded Hannah of the time Moishe had knocked over a bottle of chocolate syrup and decorated her kitchen floor with a similar design. She squelched her urge to pluck the elaborate bow from the top and rip off the paper. She'd found out the hard way that people got upset when they paid extra for gift wrapping and she destroyed it in nanoseconds before their very eyes.

"This is really nice paper," Hannah said, paying homage to Mike's thoughtfulness, "and the bow's nice, too."

"Forget the wrapping and open it. I'm due back at the station in fifteen minutes."

Hannah smiled. Mike was a man after her own heart. She pulled off the bow, shredded the paper with one well-placed fingernail, and uncovered the box. It said *Kitty Valet* in big red letters, and Hannah was still puzzled after she opened the box and drew out two plastic bowls and two see-through cylinders.

"They're self-feeders," Mike explained. "One's for food and the other's for water. When Moishe eats food from the bowl, it creates a space and the food in the cylinder drops down to fill it. As long as you fill up the cylinders in the morning, Moishe can't run out of food or water." Mike stopped and frowned slightly. "At least I don't *think* he can."

"It should work, Mike," Hannah said, although, if she were a betting person, she'd lay odds on her cat. Moishe had been a found cat, abandoned on the winter streets of Lake Eden. There might not be food tomorrow, so if there was food today, you'd better eat it all. Immediately. If there were a way to empty both the bowl *and* the feeder tube, Moishe would do it.

"So do you want to go out to dinner tonight? I'm off at five. We could go eat something that's on your diet. Whatever that is." Mike was silent for a moment. "What's on your diet?"

"A six-ounce portion of fish or lean meat, a small garden salad with two tablespoons of dressing, and a smidgeon of carbohydrate that translates to half a dinner roll without butter, a miniscule baked potato with nothing but salt, or one four-inch celery stick dipped in a teaspoon of mustard."

"What was that last thing?" Mike asked in disbelief.

"One four-inch celery stick dipped in mustard, but I was just kidding." Hannah shook her head in disgust. "It's really hard to go out to dinner when I'm trying to get in shape for Mother's launch party. Why don't you come over at six, and I'll cook something that both of us can eat."

"That sounds great," he said with a smile, but then his smile faded. "Will dinner have calories?"

"Yours will, mine won't."

Mike took a moment to digest that before answering. "Okay then. See you at six at your condo."

Hannah was sadly out of breath by the time she arrived at the Lake Eden Community Center. She'd obeyed her fitness guru's maxim and walked instead of driving her cookie truck. She pushed open the outer door, crossed the small enclosure that accommodated double doors and kept the temperature of the lobby constant in both summer and winter, and entered the lobby. As she walked down the hallway toward Janice's classroom, she caught sight of herself in one of the mirrors that dotted the walls. Her cheeks were rosy red, but that wasn't from exertion. A cold north wind was blowing. It had picked up snowflakes from the light, loosely packed blanket that had fallen during the morning and showered them against her face. That really hadn't bothered Hannah at all. It was quite refreshing. But during the last five minutes of her walk, the wind had picked up in velocity to bombard her with what had felt like icy needles.

"Hi, Hannah." Janice Cox stepped out into the hall as Hannah approached. "Does that box contain what I think it does?"

"Of course it does. I couldn't come into a classroom of kids without cookies, could I?"

"No, I don't think you could. But you didn't come over just to bring us cookies. What's up?"

"I need to talk to you about that teacher's assistant position. Is it still open?"

"It sure is. I can't afford to pay very much, and the two people I interviewed wanted more hours than I could give them. It's only from noon to four, Monday through Friday."

"That's just perfect!"

Janice cocked her head to the side and stared at Hannah. "Perfect for you?"

"No, not for me. It's perfect for Sue Plotnik. Phil works the swing shift at Del Ray, and he sleeps until midafternoon. She'd get home about the time he was getting up."

"I'd love to hire Sue. She'd be absolutely perfect, but she's way overqualified. Most of her time would be spent reading to the kids, helping them blow their noses, and cleaning up messes."

"She's the mother of a two-year-old. That's what she does now."

"You've got a point." Janice took a couple of steps toward the table where six children were busily tracing around their hands. "Linda? Please get a tissue from the box on my desk and give it to Bradley before he drips on the paper. And Heather? Don't color your thumb. That's the head."

"Thanksgiving turkeys?" Hannah guessed.

"That's right. We tried pilgrims last year, but the kids really like the turkeys better." Janice gave a little sigh. "Do you really think Sue would be interested in something like this? I talked to her after church on Sunday, and she mentioned that she was only a few credits short of her teaching degree."

"That's true, but she can't go back to finish college until Kevin's in school. She doesn't want to leave him with a baby-sitter, and Phil wouldn't like that either. Could she bring him along with her if she worked for you?"

Janice took a minute to think about that. "I don't see why not. I'm not set up for kids who need two naps a day and aren't potty trained, but it'll only be for four hours, and the older kids will love having a toddler coming in every afternoon to visit. Shall I call Sue tonight and make her an offer?"

"Yes. Do it before Phil leaves for work. And I'll stack the deck by talking to him when he drops by The Cookie Jar this afternoon."

"I hope Sue decides she wants the job. It would be just . . ." Janice stopped in midsentence and rushed across the room to rescue a container of paint that was about to tip over. "Leave the paints in the center of the table, honey." She gave the little blonde at the easel a smile to show that she wasn't angry, and then she hurried back to Hannah. ". . . great," she said, picking up right where she'd left off. "It would be just great to have Sue here for four hours every day. If you talk to her, tell her that unless I grow another pair of arms and learn how to be in two places at once, I really need her here to help me out!"

"Good afternoon, dear!"

Hannah looked up to see the perfectly coiffed, perfectly poised woman who'd just taken a seat at the counter. Delores Swensen was wearing a buttercup yellow wool suit with a white silk blouse under the jacket, and the combination was stunning with her dark brown hair and flawless makeup. Even though Delores admitted to being over fifty and Hannah knew for a fact that she was a decade older than that, she was still one of the most attractive women in Lake Eden. "Hi, Mother," she said.

"Do you have time for coffee, dear? I have something I need to discuss with you."

"Yes, if you can wait. Lisa's due back from her coffee break in five minutes."

Delores glanced at the dainty silver watch on her wrist.

It was decorated with diamonds around the face, and Hannah knew it was from Cartier. Her father had presented it to her mother on their twenty-fifth wedding anniversary, and he'd joked that it cost almost as much as the first house they'd bought in Lake Eden.

"I really don't have much time, dear," Delores declared, "but since it's not a private matter, I'll just catch you between customers. If that's all right with you, that is."

"It's fine with me." Hannah reached out with the coffee carafe and refilled Earl Flensburg's coffee cup. The county tow truck and snowplow driver was sitting on her mother's right. She went quickly down the counter, refilling cups for

Mayor Bascomb, Doug Greerson, and Florence Evans, who owned the Red Owl grocery store. "What's this about, Mother?"

"It's about my book launch party."

Hannah stifled a groan. Delores was a founding member of the Lake Eden Gossip Hotline, and nothing escaped her. Naturally her mother had learned about Andrea's membership at Heavenly Bodies and how Hannah was going along as a guest so she could lose enough weight to fit into her dress for the launch party. "It's not about my dress for the party, is it, Mother?" Hannah simply had to ask.

"Of course not. I'm very happy to hear you're doing . . ." Delores paused and Hannah knew she was attempting to be discreet, ". . . *what* you're doing, but that's another matter, dear. What we need to discuss now are the refreshments."

Hannah gave a little sigh. She hadn't even thought about the refreshments yet. "Well . . . I haven't actually started planning . . ."

"Oh, good!" Delores interrupted her. "I want to give you my input, dear. I know I told you I wanted to serve Regency desserts."

"That's right." Hannah felt like holding her breath. Coming up with desserts that were authentic to the time period of her mother's novel was not easy.

"Well, I know how much work that is, and I'm rethinking the whole concept."

"Rethinking," Hannah repeated, hoping her mother wasn't going to come up with something even more difficult.

"Perhaps we *don't* have to serve Regency desserts. What do you think?"

"Serve cream puffs," Earl Flensburg jumped in, not even pretending that he hadn't been listening to their conversation.

"Why should Delores serve cream puffs?" Florence wanted to know.

"Because they're my favorite dessert. And I know Delores likes them, too. Isn't that right, Delores?"

Delores began to smile. "Actually . . . it is. I *love* cream puffs. But how did you know that, Earl?"

"I still remember the birthday party you had in second grade. Your mother brought about a dozen boxes of little tiny cream puffs, and they were all filled with something different."

"I remember that!" Delores looked as pleased as punch.

"Grandma Zimmerman baked miniature cream puffs?" Hannah was amazed. As far as she knew, her maternal grandmother hadn't set foot in the kitchen.

"Of course she didn't bake them." Delores gave a little laugh. "You know she never cooked. Aunt Bertha took care of all of our meals. She made the best cream puffs I've ever tasted."

"Me, too," Earl echoed.

"Do you have her recipe?" Hannah asked.

"No, dear. I'm not even sure she used one. But the puff part wasn't what made them so good."

"It was the filling!" Earl jumped in. "I still remember the ones I had. One was apple, one was blueberry, one was strawberry, and the fourth was chocolate."

"You had *four*?" Delores asked, and Hannah noticed that Earl looked slightly embarrassed.

"Yeah. I know we were only supposed to have two, but Alvin Burkholtz went home sick that morning, and I figured I'd eat his."

"You weren't the only one to eat Alvin's cream puffs," Delores said with a little laugh. "Mother always brought plenty of extras, and I'm almost positive there weren't any left. But all this talk about cream puffs is irrelevant. I want to serve a dessert that has something to do with my book. And cream puffs don't have anything to do with Regency romances."

"Sure they do." Earl obviously wasn't willing to give up

the fight yet. "They're light and fluffy. And romances are light and fluffy, too . . . aren't they?"

"Well . . . I like to think my story has more to offer than that, but perhaps you're right." Delores turned to Mayor Bascomb. "What do you think, Ricky Ticky?"

Mayor Bascomb looked a bit startled by the use of his childhood nickname, but Delores had been his babysitter one summer, and that gave her certain privileges. "I think cream puffs are completely appropriate, Delores. They're sweet and that's what romance is."

"You're certainly an expert on that!"

Delores's comment fell like a stone into a widening pool of silence. Everyone at the counter had heard rumors about the mayor's peccadilloes, but Delores was the only one who ever mentioned it.

"I think cream puffs are just perfect," Florence said, jumping in to break the tense moment. "They're not something you have every day. A cream puff is a special dessert for a special occasion."

"That's true, but . . . I'm just not sure . . ."

"I think we've all missed the most important part," Hannah interrupted her mother's objection. "At first glance, cream puffs might look insubstantial, but just like Mother's book, the inside is surprisingly complex and completely satisfying."

Mayor Bascomb's mouth dropped open, and he turned to stare at Hannah. "Wow! That was brilliant, Hannah. Have you ever thought about going into politics?"

Delores joined in the laughter at the counter, and after it was over, she was still smiling. "You talked me into it. We'll serve mini cream puffs at the launch party." And then she turned to Hannah. "You can do that, can't you, dear?"

"Yes, Mother." Hannah hoped she didn't look stressed. Her *To Do* list was growing longer and longer. In addition to doing her own work at The Cookie Jar, she had to re-create the cheeseburger cookies for Calvin Janowski's birthday party, find a good mini cream puff recipe for her mother's book launch party, attend class at Heavenly Bodies with Andrea each morning, stick to her diet and lose enough weight to fit into the dress her mother had given her, and talk Sue Plotnik into going to work for Janice at Kiddie Korner. It was more than most people had to do in a month, and she had to accomplish it all in only two weeks. It was a good thing there hadn't been any murders in Lake Eden lately. She was way too busy to help Mike investigate, even if he performed an about-face and asked her!

Chapter
Five

"My mom used to make cream puffs." Lisa looked sympathetic after Hannah had told her about the book launch party.

"Do you have her recipe?"

"It's probably in one of her recipe boxes. I'll look tonight, I promise."

"And I'll look for that photo of those cheeseburger cookies," Hannah exchanged promises, "right after I make dinner for Mike."

"You're fixing dinner for Mike?" Andrea, who was sitting at the counter talking to them both, looked confused. "I thought he was pulling a double."

"He is," Hannah told her. "He called me a couple of minutes ago and said he'd only have forty-five minutes once he got to my place."

"That's not much time for dinner," Lisa commented.

"What are you making?" Andrea asked, and Hannah noticed that she looked a bit worried.

"Something quick and easy. And something substantial with plenty of calories. Whatever it is, it's got to carry him through another eight-hour shift."

"Substantial? Calories?" The worried expression on Andrea's face intensified. "And you're going to eat dinner with him?"

"Of course. But stop looking so worried. I'm having a diet meal. I promise I won't even touch anything that's left on his plate when he leaves."

"That's good!" Andrea gave her an approving nod. "Did he tell you why he's pulling a double?"

"No. I just assumed that somebody was out sick."

"Not exactly. Bill called me earlier and told me all about it. Rick Murphy's taking compassionate leave, and everybody's taking turns filling in for him."

"What's wrong?"

"His wife's in the hospital. She went into labor last night, and she almost lost the baby. Doc Knight's got her on strict bed rest."

Lisa sighed deeply. "I hope they weren't fighting about Ronni Ward."

"You heard about that," Hannah commented. She wasn't surprised, but if the news had reached The Cookie Jar, people were definitely talking. No wonder Bridget had been so angry with Ronni at Bertanelli's!

"Of course I heard. All I have to do is walk around with the coffee carafe and I hear everything that's happening in Lake Eden. I heard all about Bridget confronting Ronni only ten minutes after it happened."

"How?" Hannah was curious.

"A couple of Jordan High seniors were talking about it. The girls were here, and one of the boyfriends was texting his girlfriend on her cell phone."

Hannah winced. She wasn't sure which offended her more, the fact that all the Jordan High kids were sending text messages with improper spelling and no punctuation, or the fact that *texting* was fast becoming accepted as a word.

"I heard her telling her friends about Mrs. Murphy and Ronni," Lisa went on. "There was something about a food fight and how they'd better not go out there for pizza for a while, but I'd been standing there for too long and I had to move on."

"Invisible waitress trick," Hannah said to Andrea. "It works every time."

The bell on the door jingled, and all three of them turned to see who'd come in. Hannah gave a little wave as she recognized the man under the hooded parka with fur that hid most of his face.

"Hi, Phil."

"Hi, Hannah. It's snowing again, in case you hadn't noticed." Phil hung his parka on the coatrack by the door, but before he could take an empty seat at the counter, she hurried over to take his arm.

"Follow me, Phil. I've got something special boxed up for you in the kitchen."

Once she'd settled Phil at the stainless steel workstation and presented him with a cup of coffee and two Minty Melts, she poured coffee for herself and joined him. It would take a bit of finessing, but it was the perfect opportunity to bring up the subject of Janice's job opportunity at Kiddie Korner.

"These are really good cookies, Hannah." Phil wiped his mouth with the napkin. Then he picked up his second cookie and took a large bite. "They remind me of peppermint schnapps."

"Really?" Hannah was puzzled. "But peppermint schnapps tastes like peppermint. It doesn't taste like chocolate . . ." Hannah hesitated as she realized she'd never actually tasted peppermint schnapps. "It doesn't taste like chocolate, does it?"

"No, but it should. It would be a lot better that way."

Hannah waited until Phil had taken the last bite. Then she whisked away the napkin and slid one of her distinctive bakery boxes in front of him.

"Is that it?" he asked her.

"Yes. Take a peek and tell me what you think."

Phil opened the box and stared down at the giant-sized cookie inside. When he looked up he was grinning from ear to ear. "That's perfect, Hannah!"

"Lisa and I thought so. The roses around the edge were

her idea, and she wrote on the words. She said that any wife who got a cookie that said *I Love You* in chocolate frosting from her husband couldn't possibly be down in the dumps."

"I really hope Lisa's right." Phil gave a little sigh. "I just hate to see her this way. She used to smile and laugh all the time."

"She'll smile and laugh again," Hannah said, crossing her fingers for luck. "But that cookie's not all I have up my sleeve. I think Sue needs a break from your condo and from Kevin, so I found her a job."

"A job?!" Phil began to frown. "But she'd never agree to go back to work. Neither one of us wants Kevin to grow up with a babysitter!"

"Oh, there's no need for a babysitter," Hannah said, reaching out to pat Phil's hand. "Kevin gets to go right along when Sue goes to work."

"You're talking about an employee nursery like some of the big companies run?"

"Not at all. I'm talking about a teacher's aide job at Kiddie Korner. Janice Cox needs a helper, and it's only Monday through Friday in the afternoons. Sue would work from noon to four, and Kevin would come along to play with the other kids in Janice's class."

Phil leaned back and blinked. "That sounds ideal for Sue. But isn't Kevin too young for Kiddie Korner?"

"Yes, he is. Janice would never take him as a regular student, especially for all day. But she thinks it would be good for the other kids to have a toddler around in the afternoons. It would be like a play date for Kevin, but with older children."

Phil took another sip of his coffee. "That sounds good, Hannah. I know Sue likes Janice. They talk after church practically every Sunday. I'm sure she'd like to help Janice out, and it would be something new she could do with Kevin, something that gets her out and away from the condo."

"Exactly. Did I mention that there's a salary?"

"Sue gets out of the house, Kevin gets new friends, *and* there's a salary?"

Hannah laughed at the utterly amazed look on Phil's face. "That's right. I don't know how much the salary is, but it's something. And whatever it is, Sue can have a little money of her own."

"Egg money."

"Exactly. I know you earn good money, Phil. And I know you tell Sue that it's her money, too. I've heard you say it. But Sue might like to have a little something of her own to spend."

"I can understand that. I'd feel that way if Sue had the job and I stayed home with Kevin. It would be a little strange to have to ask my wife for money to buy her a birthday present."

"That's exactly what I mean." Hannah gave him a big smile. "Janice told me she'll call Sue tonight and make her a formal offer . . . if it's okay with you, that is."

"You bet it's okay. When would Janice want Sue to start?"

"Yesterday. She's really shorthanded all by herself. I know she's been advertising the position, and a few people have applied, but most of them want full-time work."

"Well, part-time is perfect for Sue."

"That's what I thought."

"I'm going to do my best to talk Sue into it." Phil got to his feet and picked up the box with Sue's cookie. "Not that she'll need much encouragement from me. This is just perfect for her."

"Tell her I'll see her down at Kiddie Korner one of these days. I promised I'd bring more cookies."

"Okay. Thanks again, Hannah. You really ought to hang out a shingle and charge for solving problems right along with your cookies."

MINTY MELTS

Do not preheat oven yet. Dough
must chill before baking.

1 ½ cups melted butter *(3 sticks, ¾ pound)*
2 ½ cups white *(granulated)* sugar
2 beaten eggs *(just whip them up with a fork)*
1 teaspoon baking soda
½ teaspoon salt
1 teaspoon peppermint extract
3 drops red food coloring *(or more if needed)*
4 cups flour *(there's no need to sift it)*

½ cup white sugar for later

Hannah's Note: In the original recipe, these cookies are
partially dipped in chocolate. If I don't feel like dipping and
drying all those cookies, I take a little shortcut you might
want to try someday. Right before I mix the flour into the
cookie dough, I add a 12-ounce (2 cups) package of miniature chocolate chips. (If they don't have the mini-chips in
your store, you can use regular and chop them up in smaller
pieces with a knife or in a food processor.) Once the flour
is mixed in, chill the dough and bake according to the original directions.

Another trick we use at The Cookie Jar is to make half
of the batch pink and the rest green for a pretty mix of
cookies on the platter.

Melt the butter in a large microwave-safe bowl. Add the sugar and stir. Let it cool slightly. Then add the beaten eggs, baking soda, salt, and peppermint extract, stirring after each addition.

Add the red food coloring, stir it in, and then check the color of the dough. It should be bright pink. If the color's too pale, add another drop or two of food coloring and stir it in thoroughly.

Add flour in one-cup increments, stirring after each one. The dough will be quite stiff.

Cover and refrigerate for at least two hours. *(Overnight is fine too.)*

Preheat the oven to 350 degrees F., rack in the middle position.

Place the ½ cup of white sugar in a small bowl.

Spray two cookie sheets with Pam or another nonstick cooking spray. Or use parchment paper to line the two cookie sheets.

Roll the chilled dough into walnut-sized balls. Roll the balls in the sugar so that the whole ball is coated.

Place the dough balls on the cookie sheet, 12 to a standard-size sheet. Press the balls down just a little with a metal spatula *(or the palm of your impeccably clean hand)* so they won't roll off when you carry them to the oven.

Bake for 10 to 12 minutes. They'll flatten out the rest of the way all by themselves.

Let the cookies cool for 2 minutes on the cookie sheet, and then move them to a wire rack to finish cooling. Once the cookies are cool, transfer them to sheets of wax paper and prepare to dip them in chocolate. *(If you used parchment paper, you can frost them right on that.)*

CHOCOLATE DIP

2 cups chocolate chips *(12 ounces)*
1 stick butter *(½ cup, ¼ pound)*

Melt the chips and the butter in a microwave-safe bowl on HIGH for 90 seconds. Stir to make sure the chips are melted. If not, heat in 20-second increments until you can stir them smooth.

Hannah's Note: Keep this dip fairly hot so that it's thin and it won't glop up when you dip in the cookies. If it cools and thickens too much, just return it to the microwave for 10 seconds or so to heat it so it's thinner.

Dip the cookies, one by one, so that one-third to one-fourth of the cookie is chocolate coated. Place the cookies back on the wax paper *(or the parchment paper)* faceup to dry and harden the chocolate.

When the chocolate dip is dry *(approximately 1 hour)*, store the cookies between sheets of wax paper in a cool place.

Yield: approximately 8 dozen *(depending on cookie size)* pretty and tasty cookies.

These cookies can be frozen in single layers between wax paper.

 # Chapter
Six

"What'll it be, Hannah?" Florence stood behind the meat counter with a little white cap perched on her head. It reminded Hannah of the doilies her great-grandmother had used on the candle stands of the old pump organ that had stood in her parlor. "I've got a really nice pork roast."

"It looks wonderful, but I don't have time to cook it. Mike's coming over at six for dinner."

"Does Norman know that?"

Hannah bit back a sharp retort and reminded herself that in a town the size of Lake Eden, everybody knew everybody else's business. "I don't know if he does or not." And then, because she was tired from her long day and more than a bit out of sorts, she zinged one in. "I guess you like dentists more than cops right now, right?"

Florence just looked at her for a moment, and then she started to laugh. "You nailed that, Hannah! I'm partial to Norman right now because he replaced one of my fillings for free."

"So if you'd been robbed and Mike had recovered the money, you would have been partial to him?" Hannah pressed her point.

"Maybe so. In fact, I'm almost sure of it. And I guess that means they're interchangeable?"

"Not interchangeable, but equal. You like them equally and you can't choose between them in the big picture."

"You're right. But in the small picture, they keep bobbing up and down. One's on top on one day, and the other's on top on the next day." Florence stopped speaking and gave Hannah an assessing look. "Is that how *you* feel about them?"

"It's like my mother taught me . . . a woman never discusses her age or her love life." She paused to let that sink in, and then she went on. "Unless, of course, she's with a friend. And since you're a friend, that's *exactly* how I feel."

"Then you should wait, Hannah. One has to be the clear winner."

"I think you're right. But let's get back to the real problem. What am I going to make for dinner?"

"Sausage. That cooks in no time at all, especially if you get the precooked kind. Fix sausage and potato pancakes, and some of your cookies for dessert."

"Sausage it is," Hannah decided, "but potato pancakes aren't quick and easy."

"Yes, they are. Pick up a package of frozen hash browns. They're already grated. Just chop them up so they're in smaller pieces and follow your favorite recipe."

"Good idea!" Hannah began to smile. "What else?"

"Get applesauce and don't forget the sour cream. You can serve those on the side. I'll wrap up your sausage while you go and get the rest. And pick up some ice cream. You can serve it for dessert, along with some of the cookies you always carry around in your truck."

"Sausage tonight," Hannah announced to the cat that hurtled himself into her arms the moment she pushed open her door.

"Rowwww."

"I knew you'd like that. And Uncle Mike is coming for dinner." Hannah stopped and stared down at Moishe, who was staring up at her with startled yellow eyes. "Did I really call him Uncle Mike? I did, didn't I?" She kicked the door shut behind her and placed her resident feline on top of the couch so that she could shrug out of her parka. "Sorry, Moishe. I must be hanging around Andrea too much."

Moishe said nothing. He was a smart cat. Hannah went back outside, picked up the Kitty Valet boxes and the sack of groceries she'd propped up outside her door so that she'd be able to catch him, and carried them inside. She tossed the boxes on the couch and carried the sack to the kitchen. The ice cream went into the freezer, the sausage and the chicken breast that would constitute the meat portion of her dinner went into covered pans in the oven, the hash browns sat on the counter waiting for her attention, and the kitty crunchies came out of the bag in her broom closet.

"I know you're hungry. Just hold on a second," Hannah said as she scooped up a generous portion and put it in the bottom of Moishe's empty food bowl to cover the grinning portrait of Garfield, whose cartoon countenance appeared every time the bowl was emptied. Another generous scoop ensured that Hannah would have time to mix up the potato pancakes. Once Moishe's water bowl was filled, she was free to continue the preparation of Mike's dinner for at least ten minutes, maybe fifteen, or until her cat ran out of essentials.

The hash browns went into the food processor and were more finely chopped by the steel blade. Hannah imagined her Great-Grandmother Elsa spinning in her grave because she'd used *boughten* hash browns, but that couldn't be helped. Two large eggs sans shells had found their way into a large mixing bowl. Hannah whipped them up until they were fluffy and then added onion powder, season salt, black pepper, and two tablespoons of cracker crumbs. She stirred everything up, covered it with a paper towel just in case feline interest escalated, and turned back to her food processor. Once the hash browns had been removed to a cutting board and patted dry with paper towels, she spooned them into her mixing bowl, gave everything an encompassing stir, re-covered the bowl with the kitty deterrent towel, put on a fresh pot of coffee, and headed off to the bedroom to change clothes for Mike's arrival.

She wasn't a moment too soon. When Hannah came out of the bedroom wearing her favorite forest green top and clean jeans, she heard the doorbell ring. Mike was here. She had to hurry. She opened the door, ushered him in, gave him a cup of coffee, and settled him on the couch with the Kitty Valet boxes to assemble the contents while she went into the kitchen to finish preparing their meal.

Heating the butter and olive oil didn't take long. Hannah gave the contents of her mixing bowl a stir, decided the batter was neither too dry nor too wet, and began to scoop tiny pancakes into her largest frying pan. She flattened them slightly with a metal spatula so that the shredded potatoes would form a single layer, and then she opened the oven to check the progress of Mike's sausage and her skinless, boneless, chicken breast.

The sausage was heated through, and it smelled delicious, the chicken breast less so. Hannah returned it to the oven hoping that some of the sausage flavor might migrate behind the closed, sealed door, and turned her attention to dishing up the sour cream and the applesauce.

"Almost ready," she called out to Mike once she'd checked her pancakes, found them browned nicely, and flipped them over. "What would you like to drink?"

"I'd like a Cold Spring Export, but I'll settle for coffee. I'm on duty tonight."

"I know. What's the latest? Are Jessica and the baby going to be all right?"

"They think so, but it'll be touch and go for another couple of days. Bridget and Cyril are keeping Rick's oldest, and Rick's staying at the hospital with Jessica."

Hannah bit her tongue. She really wanted to ask if Mike knew the truth about Rick and Ronni, but that would be fishing for gossip. It wasn't her business. She didn't need to know. But oh, how she wanted to!

"Rick said they'd been fighting about Ronni. Jessica got really upset, and he thinks that's why she went into premature labor. He feels horribly guilty about it."

He ought to if what I heard is true, Hannah thought, but of course she didn't say it. She said nothing and waited for the floodgates to open and Mike to go on.

"Nothing happened, you know. Ronni told me that. She said Rick had a little crush on her, but she handled it without hurting his feelings."

"Oh?" Hannah said, but she thought something different. *And just how did she do that?* her mind queried.

"She told him he was very attractive, but she never dated married men," Mike answered her unspoken question.

I'll bet! Hannah's mind said sarcastically, but her mouth said, "That's good."

"I thought so. But you know how young guys are. They think with their . . . uh . . . *libido* and not with their brain."

"Right." Hannah removed the sausage from the oven, cut it into serving-size pieces and paired it with the six small potato pancakes she'd fried for Mike. Once she'd grabbed the coffee carafe to pour more into his mug, she headed out to the coffee table to deliver his dinner.

"That sure smells good," Mike commented, staring down at the plate Hannah placed before him. "What kind of sausage is that?"

"Polish. I got it from Florence, and she said it's handmade at a tiny sausage factory near Red Wing. And those are potato pancakes. Help yourself to sour cream, or applesauce, or both."

"Thanks, Hannah." Mike clearly wanted to dig in, but he looked up at her instead. "What are you having?"

"Chicken breast and salad, but don't worry about me. I've got all night to eat. Just start and I'll fry you up another batch."

"Okay," Mike said, forking a piece of sausage and popping it into his mouth. "You're the best, you know? Sometimes I wish you'd taken me up on that marriage proposal. Then I could eat like this every night."

That was the reason he'd asked her to marry him? Hannah's eyebrows approached lift velocity. But she wasn't being fair, and she curbed her impulse to make a sharp retort as she headed off to the kitchen to fry up another batch.

LAZY POTATO PANCAKES

3½ cups frozen hash brown potatoes
2 eggs *(2 extra large or 3 small)*
¼ cup grated onion *(or ½ teaspoon onion powder)*
1 teaspoon season salt
½ teaspoon black pepper
2 Tablespoons cracker crumbs *(matzo meal or flour will also work)*
⅛ cup butter *(¼ stick, 1 ounce)* for frying
⅛ cup good olive oil for frying

Toppings for the Table:
sour cream
applesauce
cherry sauce***
blueberry sauce***
apricot sauce***

*** Recipes for cherry, blueberry, and apricot sauces are included right after the instructions for frying Lazy Potato Pancakes.

Hannah's 1ˢᵗ Note: Great-Grandma Elsa used to make these in a cast iron frying pan she called a spider. She peeled and grated her own potatoes and put them in a bowl of cold water, salt, and lemon juice so they wouldn't turn brown. I added the word "lazy" to the title of her recipe because when I'm in a hurry, I use frozen hash browns.

Place the frozen hash browns in the bowl of a food processor. Use the steel blade, and process with an on-and-

off motion until the potatoes are finely chopped. *(If you don't have a food processor, you don't have to go out and buy one to make these. Just lay your frozen potatoes out on a cutting board in single layers, and chop them up into much smaller pieces with a chef's knife.)*

Leave the potatoes in the food processor *(or on the counter)* while you . . .

Crack the eggs into a large bowl and beat them with a fork or a wire whip until they're fluffy.

Stir in the grated onion *(or the onion powder if you decided to use that)*, and the salt and pepper.

Mix in the cracker crumbs.

Let the mixture sit on the counter for at least two minutes to give the crumbs time to swell as they soak up the liquid.

If you used a food processor, dump the potatoes on a cutting board. *(If you used a chef's knife, they're already there.)* Blot them with a paper towel to get rid of any moisture. Then add them to the mixture in the bowl, and stir them in.

If the mixture in your bowl looks watery, add another Tablespoon of cracker crumbs to thicken it. Wait for the cracker crumbs to swell up, and then stir again. If it's still too watery, add another Tablespoon of cracker crumbs. The resulting mixture should be thick, like cottage cheese.

Place the ¼ stick of butter and the 1/8 cup of olive oil in a large nonstick frying pan. *(This may be overkill, but I spray the frying pan with Pam or another nonstick cooking spray before I add the butter and olive oil.)* Turn the burner on medium-high heat.

Once the oil and butter are hot, use a quarter-cup measure to drop in the batter. Don't try to get all of the batter out of the measuring cup. Your goal is to make ⅛ cup pancakes, and if you don't scrape out the batter, that's approximately what you'll get.

Keep the pancakes about two inches apart, and cover the bottom of the frying pan with them. Flatten them very slightly with a spatula so the potatoes spread out and don't hump up in the middle.

Fry the pancakes until they're lightly browned on the bottom. That should take 2 to 3 minutes. You can tell by lifting one up with a spatula and peeking, but if it's not brown and you have to do it again, choose another pancake to lift.

Once the bottoms of the pancakes are brown, flip them over with your spatula and fry them another 2 to 3 minutes, or until the other side is brown.

Lift out the pancakes and drain them on paper towels. Serve hot off the stove if you can, or keep the pancakes warm by placing them in a pan in a warm oven *(the lowest*

temperature that your oven will go) in single layers between sheets of aluminum foil.

Serve with your choice of sour cream, applesauce, cherry sauce, blueberry sauce, or apricot sauce.

Yield: Approximately 24 small pancakes, depending on pancake size.

CHERRY, BLUEBERRY, AND APRICOT SAUCES

1 small can pitted cherries, blueberries, or apricots
1 small jar cherry, blueberry, or apricot jam

Hannah's 1st Note: It doesn't really matter how large the can of fruit or jar of jam is. If you want a lot, buy large cans and jars. If you don't want so much, buy small cans and small jars.

Drain the can of fruit, reserving the juice. You may need it later to thin your sauce if it's too thick.

Place the canned fruit in a food processor with the steel blade or in a blender. *(If you're using cherries, it's a good idea to squeeze them a little when you put them in to make sure they're all properly pitted.)*

Process or blend until the fruit is pureed. Transfer it to a bowl and let it sit on the counter while you . . .

Heat the fruit jam. You can do this by removing it from the jar and placing it in a microwave-safe bowl to heat in the microwave. You can also put the jam in a small pan over medium heat on the stove and stir it until it's melted. *(If there are whole cherries in your cherry jam, you might want to cut them up a little. Then again, big pieces are nice, too. The same goes for some apricot jam—it may have large pieces, too.)*

Add the melted jam to the bowl with the pureed fruit. Mix it all up thoroughly. Let it sit on the counter to cool, and then check for consistency. If you think it's too thick to drop onto the top of a hot potato pancake, stir in a little of the reserved fruit juice.

Store your sauce in the refrigerator in an airtight jar or container, but remember to take it out to warm to room temperature an hour before you plan to serve your pancakes.

Hannah's 2nd Note: You can make sauces from almost any canned fruit. I've used peach, raspberry, and pear. I've also served my Lazy Potato Pancakes with rhubarb sauce, but I don't think you can buy canned rhubarb. If you live in Minnesota, you won't have to buy it, or make your own, for that matter. I've got a whole cupboard full of rhubarb sauce and jam that my customers canned and gave me last summer.

Lisa said she tried pineapple sauce (that's Herb's favorite fruit) and it was wonderful. Since she couldn't find pineapple jam at the Red Owl, she used apple jelly.

Chapter Seven

Hannah was sitting on the rug in the middle of her living room floor when the phone rang. Scraps of paper were scattered all around her in little piles that Moishe assumed were his duty to destroy, and it took her a minute to find the receiver. Once she had, she punched the proper button and answered. "Hi, this is Hannah."

"Hello, Hannah. It's Norman."

Hannah started to grin. As if she wouldn't recognize Norman's voice! But it was proper phone etiquette, and she guessed that was important. "Hi, Norman. What's happening?"

"My electricity's out, and I'm calling you on my cell phone. I was wondering if you'd let me come over and watch some movies with you. I rented *Sabrina*."

"The original? Or the remake?"

"Both. I wanted to compare them. How about it, Hannah? I'm sitting here all alone in the dark."

"Where's Cuddles?"

"She's spending the night at the clinic. There's a mouse in my office, and when I tried to take her home tonight after work, she wouldn't let me put her in her carrier."

"She wouldn't *let* you?" Hannah was amused by his choice of words.

"That's right. She stuck all four legs straight out in different directions so she wouldn't fit. I could get her front legs in, but not her back legs. And then, when I finally managed to get her to bend her back legs so I could push them in, she pulled out her front legs and I had to start all over again. I've put her in her carrier before, and she's always been very cooperative. I don't know why it didn't work this time."

Hannah laughed. She couldn't help it. "It didn't work because you tried to force her and she didn't want to go. You can't force a cat. Even a very good-natured cat like Cuddles will fight you every inch of the way."

"What should I have done then?"

"You should have left enough food and water for the night, locked up the clinic, and driven home without her."

"And I shouldn't have tried to put her in the carrier in the first place."

"Exactly right. It's very dangerous to come between a cat and her mouse."

"Tell me about it! I've got scratches on both arms. I've had a rough day, Hannah. Can I come over so you can make things all better?"

"Of course you can come, but I'm going to extract my pound of flesh."

"Feeling carnivorous are we?"

"Feeling just plain hungry is more like it."

"Then Mike was right when he told us that you went on an exercise regime and a high-protein, low-fat diet to lose weight?"

Hannah was about to confirm it when she realized Norman had used the word *us*, as in plural. "Who's *us*? Don't tell me he mentioned it in front of your patients!"

"Of course not. I don't allow anyone except relatives in the treatment rooms and that's only when the patient is a child. Mike came in while I was having lunch at Hal and Rose's Cafe. And by the way, he told us all that he's very proud of you."

Hannah gave a little groan of dismay. "I wish he'd be a little less proud and a lot more silent. Now everybody in Lake Eden is going to ask me how my diet's going."

"So you *are* on a diet?"

"Yes, at least until Mother's book launch party."

"Have you eaten dinner yet?"

Hannah thought briefly about the skinless, boneless chicken breast waiting for her in the kitchen, and decided that Moishe could have it for breakfast. "No, not yet."

"Then I'll stop at The Corner Tavern and get us steaks to go. You want yours rare, right?"

"*Extra* rare. Tell them it's for me. They know how I like it."

"Can you have a baked potato on the side?"

Hannah hesitated and decided to skip it. For the calories she'd save, she could take one small bite of the cookies she was planning to assemble for Calvin's birthday party. "I'd better pass on the potato. Just bring me a small dinner salad, no dressing."

"You got it. Anything else?"

Hannah glanced down at the photograph in her lap and flipped it over to reread the list of ingredients that were written on the back in pencil. "Yes, but you can't get what I need at The Corner Tavern. Do you have time for a stop on the way?"

"I've got nothing but time. Where do you want me to go?"

"Pull in at the Quick Stop and pick up a box of vanilla wafers and some chocolate-covered cookies."

"Sure. What kind of chocolate-covered cookies?"

"It doesn't really matter as long as they're round and flat on the top and the bottom, and they're covered in melted chocolate. I'm not sure what brand Sean and Don carry, but I know they've got them."

There was a lengthy silence, and then Norman cleared his throat. "Am I helping you break your diet?"

"No, you're not. I need to make something for a catering job, and they're on the list of ingredients. I'm curious, though.

Would you bring me the cookies if I told you I was going to break my diet and eat them?"

"That's a difficult question." Norman was silent for another long moment, and then he cleared his throat again. "Is this some sort of a test?"

"Maybe. As a matter of fact, I'm pretty sure it is."

"Then there's a correct answer?"

"I think so, but I'm not sure what it is. And if I don't know the right answer, I won't be able to tell if you get it wrong."

"There's an example of ironclad logic."

"I'm nothing if not logical. Just think about it, Norman. If I said I was going to break my diet and I really needed you to bring me cookies, would you do it?"

Norman gave a deep sigh, a sigh so powerful that she imagined she could feel the air move next to her ear. "I'd do it, Hannah. I mean, you're an adult and you know what you want. I trust in your ability to make your own decisions. And if you wanted to break your diet, I'd put on *Sabrina* and sit on the couch to eat cookies with you."

"I love you, Norman," Hannah said, a delighted smile spreading over her face. "You never try to tell me what's good for me."

"I love you, too. And I know telling you what to do is a lost cause. You never listen, anyway. I'll see you in about forty-five minutes with steak and salad and two kinds of cookies."

By the time Norman arrived, Hannah was hard at work doing some preparation work for Lisa Colleene's Mini Cheeseburger Cookies. She'd used green food coloring to dye a bowl of shredded coconut the shade of green that came closest to the color of lettuce. She'd also mixed up a thick buttercream frosting that she'd split up into two small bowls. She'd already tinted the frosting in one bowl yellow, and now she was adding red food coloring to the frosting in the other bowl.

"What are you making?" Norman asked, taking two

plates from Hannah's cupboard and gathering the silverware they'd need.

"Cheeseburgers. That's why I need the cookies."

Norman turned around to stare at her and then he said, "I'm so hungry, I'm hearing things. I thought you said you needed the cookies to make cheeseburgers."

Hannah grabbed a stack of napkins and a bottle of diet salad dressing. "I did, but I'll explain it all later. Let's go eat before Moishe decides to tunnel through the carryout packs and help himself to our steaks."

Other than the infrequent request for the saltshaker, the pepper grinder, or another napkin, no conversation took place in Hannah's living room until they'd become members of the clean plate club. Hannah tossed Moishe a final scrap of the filet Norman had brought for her and gave a satisfied sigh. "Thank you, Norman. That was just what I needed. How about some coffee? It's all ready to go."

"Sounds good. I'll take care of the dishes while you make it."

Hannah poured water into the well of the coffeemaker while Norman handled their dishes and silverware. After he'd rinsed them and stacked them in Hannah's dishwasher, he walked over to examine the Kitty Valet that Mike had set up next to Moishe's old food bowl. "So *this* is Moishe's new self-feeding system. I wasn't sure what Mike meant when he told me about it. Does it work?"

"I don't know. So far, he hasn't gone near it. The instructions said to leave out his old food and water bowls for the first few hours to give him time to get used to it. Then you're supposed to pick up the old bowls and he'll switch to the new."

"In theory."

"Right. In theory."

"I can see how it works, but what if Moishe doesn't like it? Can you take it back?"

Hannah gave a little laugh. "Not really. They say that it's fully returnable as long as the plastic wrapping on the tubes is intact. And you have to remove it to put in the food and the water."

"So once you try it out on your cat, you can't return it."

"Exactly. It's a win-win situation for the manufacturer."

Just then Moishe padded into the kitchen and stopped by his Kitty Valet feeding system. He sniffed at the food, sniffed at the water, and then he walked on past.

"Mike may have wasted his money." Hannah watched as her cat lapped at the water in his old bowl.

"Maybe he'll try the new bowls once the old ones are empty," Norman said, following Hannah as she carried two mugs of fresh coffee to the kitchen table. "Now that we've eaten, I've got a question. You were kidding about using cookies to make cheeseburgers, weren't you?"

"Not really. I'm making a dessert that looks exactly like a mini cheeseburger, but it's assembled from store-bought cookies, shredded coconut, and frosting."

"Really?"

"That's right. I got the recipe from my college roommate's sister. Do you want to help me make a batch? Then we can sample them for dessert." Hannah thought about the eight-ounce fillet she'd eaten and the small dinner salad that hadn't been very small at all. "Correction. Then *you* can sample them for dessert."

"It's a deal," Norman agreed, "but don't expect too much from me. I'm not a baker like you are."

"There's no baking involved. All we have to do is stack the cookies and glue them together with the right color of frosting."

In an effort to keep from getting in each other's way, Hannah and Norman formed an assembly line. She started by covering the slightly rounded top of a vanilla wafer with red frosting. Then she handed the cookie to Norman. He stuck on the chocolate-covered cookie and covered the top of it with yellow buttercream frosting, letting a bit drip down over the sides. Hannah took the cookie back, sprinkled on green coconut to resemble shredded lettuce, and clamped another vanilla wafer on top, rounded side up.

"They're cute," Norman said when they'd run out of hamburgers, or in their case, cookies. "I never thought that yellow frosting would look like cheese, but it does."

"And the coconut looks like shredded lettuce."

"Exactly. And the red frosting you made is the exact color of ketchup. They're all done now, aren't they?"

"Not quite. We still have to brush the tops with egg white and sprinkle sesame seeds on the tops of the buns."

Once the cookies were finished, Hannah and Norman watched the older version of *Sabrina* while the egg whites dried. Then Norman tasted a cookie, and pronounced it perfect for a children's party.

"I don't think I can stay awake for the second *Sabrina*," Hannah said with a yawn. "It's been a long day. Why don't you call home and see if your answering machine picks up?"

Norman looked perplexed for about half a second. "That's clever, Hannah. If the machine picks up, my power's back on. If it doesn't, it's not."

"Right. And if your power's still out, you can stay here for the night." Norman's face brightened and she hurried to explain. "The bed in the guest room's all made up."

Norman gave a little sigh as he picked up the phone, and Hannah knew he'd hoped for a different outcome. He punched in his number, listened for a moment, and then he hung up the phone. "Power's back on," he said, getting to his feet. "I'd better go. I've got an early appointment tomorrow. Do you want to keep the *Sabrina* we didn't watch?"

"I don't know when I'd watch it. Maybe you can rent it again when both of us have more time." Hannah stood up too, and gave him a little hug. "Thanks for dinner and the movie."

"Thank *you* for the cookies. They're going to be a big hit at the birthday party."

"I hope so." Hannah pulled him down for a good night

kiss. And when it ended, she opened the outside door for him. "See you tomorrow, Norman. Lisa's looking for her mother's recipe for cream puffs. If she finds it and you drop in around two, you can sample the mini cream puffs we're making for Mother's book launch party."

"I'll do that. Thanks, Hannah."

Norman gave a little wave and went down the stairs. Hannah watched him step over the planter that separated the buildings and walk off to the visitors' parking lot. When she stepped back inside and closed the door behind her, she gave a little sigh and went over to the couch to pet Moishe. If she'd offered to share her bedroom, Norman would have stayed regardless of the status of his electricity. Of course she hadn't. There was no way anyone was going to place her in the Ronni Ward category. But Norman had left, and now she felt lonely.

"Come on, Moishe. It's time for bed." Hannah flicked off the lights and headed to the bedroom. "It's going to be an even longer day tomorrow."

Five minutes later, her teeth were brushed, her face was washed, and she was dressed in the oversized sweats she always wore for pajamas when the mercury dipped below freezing. She climbed under the covers and gave a long sigh. Alone again.

She was in the throes of feeling terribly sorry for herself when Moishe jumped up on the other pillow and started to purr. It was such a comforting, soothing sound that it made Hannah smile as she drifted off to sleep.

MINI CHEESEBURGER COOKIES

DO NOT preheat oven—these cookies don't need to bake.

FOR THE BUNS:
12-ounce box round vanilla wafers *(I used Nilla Wafers)*

FOR THE HAMBURGER PATTIES:
approximately 3 dozen slightly larger round chocolate-
covered cookies *(I used 2 packages of Keebler Fudge Shoppe Caramel Filled Cookies—18 cookies to a package)****

FOR THE SHREDDED LETTUCE:
½ cup shredded coconut *(pack it down when you measure it)*
green food coloring

FOR THE CHEESE AND THE KETCHUP:
½ cup salted butter *(1 stick, 8 ounces, ¼ pound)* at
room temperature
¼ cup milk *(2 ounces)*
1 teaspoon vanilla extract
16-ounce *(1 pound)* box powdered sugar *(approximately 3½ cups)*
yellow food coloring
red food coloring

FOR THE TOP OF THE BUN:
¼ cup sesame seeds
1 egg white

*** *Keebler also makes Fudge Shoppe Grasshopper cookies in a 10-ounce package (mint—40 cookies), Keebler Fudge Shoppe Fudge Filled Cookies in a 9.5 ounce package (18 cookies), and Fudge Shoppe Peanut Butter Filled Cookies in a 9.5-ounce package (18 cookies.) Any of these cookies will work, but if you use the peanut butter cookies, make sure none of your guests has a peanut allergy.*

Prepare your shredded "lettuce" first. It will need time to air dry. Dump the coconut into a large plastic Ziploc bag. Hold the bag open and add three drops of green food coloring to the coconut. Squeeze out some of the air and seal the bag.

Toss the coconut around inside the bag. Squeeze it, play catch with it, roll it around on the counter, whatever. The object is to evenly color the coconut. Once it's a uniform color, decide if it's the color of lettuce. If it's too light, add a few more drops of green food coloring and repeat the mixing process until you think it's right.

Line a cookie sheet with wax paper and dump out the green-coated coconut. Use a spoon to spread it out as evenly as you can. Let it sit out on the counter to dry, stirring it around every so often.

Once the coconut is dry, it's time to assemble your cookies.

Line another cookie sheet with wax paper. Lay out 40 vanilla wafers, rounded side up.

In the bowl of a stand mixer, or simply in a medium-size mixing bowl, combine the softened butter, milk, vanilla extract, and powdered sugar. If you're using a stand mixer, beat on LOW for 2 minutes. If you're using a handheld mixer, beat on LOW for 3 minutes. If you're mixing by hand, use a wooden spoon and beat like crazy for 4 minutes, or until the frosting is smooth, with no lumps.

Divide the frosting into two parts, using your original bowl and another bowl. Add three drops of yellow food coloring to the first bowl and mix it in thoroughly. If it's not bright yellow, add a few more drops of food coloring, mixing them in until it is. This frosting will be the cheese for the Mini Cheeseburger Cookies.

Add three drops of red food coloring to the second bowl and mix it in thoroughly. If it's not bright red, add a few more drops, mixing them in until it's the color of ketchup.

With a rubber spatula or a frosting knife, spread the curved side of a vanilla wafer with red frosting. Pile it up around the rims of the wafers so it will form flat beds for the "hamburgers."

Place a chocolate-covered cookie, faceup, on top of the red frosting on the wafer. Press the chocolate-covered cookie down slightly so it'll stick to the frosting.

Frost the top of the chocolate-covered cookie with yellow frosting. Use just a bit too much so it'll drip over the sides of the "hamburger" like melted cheese.

Sprinkle on some green coconut "lettuce." It'll look more realistic if you let a few strands stick out on the sides.

Clamp on the second vanilla wafer, rounded side up. Now your Mini Cheeseburger Cookie is complete, except for the sesame seeds on the bun.

Repeat until you run out of "buns" or "hamburgers."

Whip up the egg white in a small bowl. Use a pastry brush to brush the tops of the vanilla wafers. Sprinkle on a few sesame seeds, and you're finished.

Let the cookies dry thoroughly. Once dry, they will keep just fine in a loosely covered container until it's time to serve them.

Hannah's Note: There's a photo of the Mini Cheese-burger Cookies on Jo Fluke's Web site. The address is: www.MurderSheBaked.com, and the photo is on the "Recipe" page.

Chapter Eight

Morning came much too early for Hannah. She was experiencing the loveliest dream, all about frothy milkshakes in peach, strawberry, blueberry, and lemon, dancing Viennese waltzes with dozens of handsome chocolate-dipped biscotti. It was a wedding, or perhaps it was a book launch party. She really couldn't tell which. The guests, in formal clothing, were chatting merrily, eagerly waiting their turn to capture their favorite refreshment as it dipped and whirled past. Of course she knew it was a dream. Milkshakes couldn't dance, with or without chocolate-covered biscotti, but the beauty of dreams was that they were impervious to logic.

"Weird," Hannah mumbled, opening her eyes. But once she'd glanced at her radio alarm, she realized that it wasn't as strange as it had seemed at first. Instead of pushing the button for alarm, she'd hit the button for wakeup music, and the local classical music station was playing Strauss.

Hannah reached out to shut off the alarm before electronic beeping rudely interrupted "The Skater's Waltz." At least she *tried* to reach out to shut it off, but a bolt of pain that had her gasping for breath shot up from her wrist and found a home in her shoulder.

"Must have slept wrong," Hannah mumbled, turning on her side and attempting to reach out with her other arm. But that arm hurt almost as much as the first one had! Was she having a heart attack? What were the symptoms? Pain . . . yes, one of the symptoms was pain. She remembered Hank Olson, the bartender at the municipal liquor store, telling them about the symptoms of his heart attack. She definitely had shooting pains going up both arms, but if she recalled Hank's description correctly, his arm pains had reached all the way to the center of his chest, squeezing and constricting like a steel band.

Not a heart attack, then. Her chest felt fine, not squeezed at all, and she wasn't light-headed, sweaty, or nauseated. But something was definitely wrong. Every time she moved, she hurt. Had she contracted some dreadful disease that would render her paralyzed and helpless in her bed?

Michelle would cry when she learned of her terrible malady. Hannah was sure of that. Michelle loved her. And Mother did too . . . but in her own way. Delores would be a trifle put out that Hannah couldn't cater her book launch party, but she'd do the right thing. She'd arrive at her eldest daughter's bedside, appropriately dressed of course, and lay a cool hand on Hannah's fevered brow. *If only I'd ordered a larger dress size,* she'd sob into a lace-edged handkerchief. *Dear, dear Hannah starved herself until her immune system collapsed to try to please me!*

No, Mother, Andrea would contradict her, her voice quavering with emotion. *Immune systems don't go down in a day and a half. She must have picked up some virus at Heavenly Bodies, and that means it's all my fault. I talked her into going out there with me, and it was just too much for her. You can't take an overweight person who's never exercised and expect miracles to . . .*

Hannah wasted no time cutting off Andrea's imaginary conversation, since it wasn't at all flattering. A dying woman didn't need criticism about her weight and lifestyle. She wanted sympathy, appreciation for what she'd accomplished, a few sterling accolades. But something Andrea had said struck a familiar chord, something about never exercising and . . .

If you're not in the habit of exercising regularly, some of you may wake up stiff and sore in the morning. Roger, their fitness instructor, had addressed the whole class, but he'd been looking straight at her. *If that happens, simply stretch your arms and legs gently until you feel more comfortable.*

Hannah sighed and met the gaze of the cat who sat on the pillow next to her head. Perhaps it was her imagination, but she thought he looked worried. "It's okay, I'm just stiff and sore. I can get your breakfast, no problem."

The gaze never wavered, but Moishe moved closer. He inched over until he was near enough to rub his head against Hannah's face, and his rough tongue shot out to lick her chin.

"I love your kitty kisses," Hannah said, reveling in the un- accustomed display of affection from her feline roommate. "That's so sweet. Just let me stretch first, and then I'll get you something you'll like."

She tackled her arms first, raising them slowly and painfully above her head. She brought them down again, very slowly, and gave a sigh of relief. Stretching hurt, but it hadn't killed her. She stretched her arms again, very slowly, and it didn't hurt quite so much. Perhaps there was something to this after all!

Her legs were next. She carefully bent, extended, pointed her toes at the ceiling and then relaxed. The first time was agony, but after four stretches per leg, she felt capable of get- ting out of bed.

The rest was easy, especially since Moishe followed along at her heels, batting at the hem of her robe. In her efforts to stay ahead of him, she must have been stretching out what was supposed to be stretched, because by the time she arrived at the kitchen, she felt almost human again.

Garfield's face grinned up at her from the bottom of

Moishe's food bowl. He'd eaten it all during the night and she had just turned toward the broom closet to fill it up again, when she remembered that the instructions on the Kitty Valet had said to let your pet empty his old bowl once and then put it away so that he would switch to the new, improved feeder.

"Here you go, Moishe," Hannah said, picking up the Garfield bowl and hedging her bets by tossing a few fish-shaped salmon-flavored kitty treats into the Kitty Valet bowl. "That's your new bowl. Try it, you'll like it."

Never one to turn down his favorite treat, Moishe approached the bowl with the feed tube and extracted one fishy treat with a well-placed claw. Once that was gone, he extracted another and, as Hannah watched in amazement, he started to chow down on the kitty crunchies in the bowl.

"You like it!" Hannah said, pouring herself a life-giving mug of coffee from the pot that brewed automatically every morning, and then grabbing the phone to punch in the sheriff's department number. Mike would be pleased when she told him that Moishe was using his gift. When the desk sergeant answered, she asked for Mike's extension and waited until he picked up.

"It's Hannah," she said, "I just called to say . . . he likes it! Moishie likes it!" And then she waited to see if Mike had been watching the oldie but goodie commercials KCOW television had been rerunning.

"*Moishie* likes . . . oh!" Mike gave a little laugh. "I get it. It's a takeoff on Mikey, the little brother who'd eat anything on those cereal commercials. Does that mean Moishe's eating out of his new Kitty Valet?"

"That's exactly what it means. I picked up his regular bowl, just as it said to do in the instructions, and tossed in a couple of treats to get him started. Now the treats are history and he's chowing down on his regular food."

"It's nice to get good news for a change."

"What's the matter?"

"Rough night. A blue spruce jumped out in front of Wade Hoffman's car at sixty miles an hour."

"Wade Hoffman?" Hannah began to frown. "Wasn't he Ronni Ward's fiancé?"

"Yeah. Wade's passenger said he was despondent and he'd been drinking heavily. The passenger tried to get the keys, but Wade insisted on driving."

"Were they badly hurt?" Hannah hated to ask, especially before she'd had her second cup of coffee.

"Wade got the worst of it. He'll be in a body cast for six months. His passenger got off lucky with just a broken arm."

"Who was his . . ." Hannah stopped in midquestion as she heard a loud beeping noise on the line.

"I've got to go, Hannah," Mike broke in. "I'm expecting a callback from Doc Knight and that's probably him now."

The line went dead, and Hannah hung up the phone. She'd been about to ask Mike who'd been riding in the passenger seat, but that could wait until later. Right now she had to get into her awful yellow-and-black exercise outfit and meet Andrea at Heavenly Bodies.

"So how are you feeling now?" Andrea asked, leaning back in the Jacuzzi. They'd finished their workout routine and were relaxing before class began.

"I'm a lot better. The muscles I didn't know I had aren't screaming anymore. Now they're just groaning a little." Hannah stopped speaking and listened intently for a moment. "I hear something ringing."

"It's probably my phone. It's in my purse in the dressing room."

"Why is it there, and not here?"

"Because I don't want to answer it. It's Mother, and she's probably just checking to make sure we're out here exercising."

"How do you know it's Mother?"

"Because nobody else would call me this early. It's hours before I usually get up."

"It could be Grandma McCann with an emergency."

"It's not. She has her own special ring tone, and so does Bill. If it's not Mother and it's something important, whoever it is will leave me voice mail." Andrea glanced up at the clock on the wall. "We'd better dry off and get dressed for class, Hannah. Roger should be coming in any minute."

But Roger didn't come in, even though the class was all assembled and waiting for him. Laura Jorgensen was in the front row looking good in a bright green exercise outfit. Hannah had found out yesterday that Laura wanted to lose ten pounds before her wedding to Drew Vavra, Jordan High's head coach, in June.

Donna Lempke, an unmarried woman in her early thirties, was in the same boat. She'd told Hannah that she had a brand-new swimsuit she'd bought two years ago, but she'd gained weight around the middle, and last summer she'd been afraid to wear it. This summer would be a different story if Roger's class worked for her.

Cheryl Coombs, who ran the cosmetic counter at Cost-Mart, had another goal in mind. She'd lost weight recently, and now she was attempting to tighten and tone up. Her daughter, Amber, was also in the class. Hannah wasn't sure if it was a mother-daughter project, or Cheryl just wanted to keep an eye on Amber to make sure she didn't run off to meet her boyfriend, Richie Maschler, before school started.

Vonnie Blair, Doc Knight's secretary, was a perfect size five. She wasn't interested in losing weight or toning up her muscles. Vonnie was interested in Roger, their fitness coach.

Gail Hansen, on the other hand, was a forty-year-old woman with a purpose. Always buxom, even as a young teenager, she was now engaged in a pitched battle to keep certain parts of her anatomy from engaging in a downhill race toward her waist.

Immelda Giese, Father Coultas's housekeeper, had admitted to Andrea that she was there for the company. Father was so busy he didn't have much time to talk, and Immelda was a gregarious person. She wore a solid black sweat suit as a concession to her employer's occupation, and talked to her neighbor, Babs Dubinski, during the entire class.

Babs readily admitted that she was there to lose weight, no ifs, ands, or buts about it. She said she needed to keep up with her grandchildren and she couldn't play softball in the park with them if she didn't get in shape.

The last two members of the class were Loretta Richardson and Trudi Schuman. They were practically inseparable. They'd been best friends in high school, settled in houses across the street from each other when they were married, and helped to raise each other's children. Trudi had three boys, and Loretta had three girls, but so far the kids hadn't gotten together in any meaningful way. They'd opened a store together right across the street from Hal and Rose's Cafe. It was called Trudi's Fabrics because Trudi's husband had put up most of the money. Loretta needed to tone up more than Trudi, but they drove out to class together, showered and dressed for work when it was over, went into town to have breakfast at the cafe, and then opened the shop at nine.

Andrea glanced at her watch. It was the new high-impact resistant, waterproof, easy-read dial watch she'd bought for the express purpose of exercising. "He's almost ten minutes late," she announced.

"Maybe he's not coming," Loretta said in what Hannah thought was a hopeful tone. It was no secret that Loretta didn't enjoy exercising.

"He'll be here," Immelda said. "Roger has a real sense of duty. He'd call to notify someone if he couldn't come in."

Vonnie looked worried. "I hope he's all right. The roads were slippery this morning."

"He'll be fine," Andrea reassured her. "He drives a Range Rover, and Bill says they're the safest vehicle on the road."

Babs Dubinski gave a little laugh. "That's because Bill wants one. Marvin was in the dealership looking at a used one for Shirley and the kids, and Bill was there pricing the new models."

Hannah glanced at Andrea. From her surprised expression it seemed that Bill hadn't mentioned a word about wanting a new Range Rover.

"Somebody's coming!" Vonnie said, glancing toward the door.

Hannah listened to the sound of footsteps. Someone was coming down the hall. Then the door to their exercise classroom opened, and Ronni Ward stepped in.

"Sorry about that," she said, throwing her coat over the handlebars of a stationary bike and stepping up on the platform the instructors used so that the whole class could see and copy their movements.

"Where's Roger?" Andrea recovered enough to ask.

"He's in the hospital getting a cast on his arm. He was in an accident last night."

Suddenly things clicked for Hannah. Mike had mentioned an accident involving Ronni's ex-fiancé, Wade. And in class yesterday, Roger had told them that he taught fitness classes a couple of evenings a week at a gym in Elk River. He must have been talking about Wade's gym, and that meant Roger was the injured passenger in Wade's car.

"Let's get started," Ronni said, giving them all a perky smile that Hannah immediately labeled as phony. "I'll be taking over this class for the next two months, and we'll be doing things my way. I know Roger was pretty easygoing with you, but my goal is to get results." She glanced around the room, and her gaze landed on Vonnie. "What are *you* doing here? You don't need to lose weight."

"I just wanted to shape up a little," Vonnie said, and a blush rose to her cheeks.

Ronni referred to her clipboard. "You're enrolled in three of Roger's classes, and you have private sessions with him twice a week. I think I know what you're after, but take it from me, you don't stand a chance. Roger likes them a lot younger and a lot prettier.

"And here we have . . ." Ronni referred to her clipboard again. "Babs. You're over fifty, aren't you, Babs?"

"Well . . . yes."

"Don't you think Babs is pretty childish for somebody who's got grown kids?"

Babs looked flustered. "I don't know. I never thought about it. I've been Babs all my life."

"It looks like you've been heavy all your life, too. Let's get a few pounds off that stomach of yours. It looks like you're hiding a ten pound rump roast under your shirt."

Ronni referred to her clipboard again. "And here's Immelda, the nun."

"I'm not a nun. I'm the housekeeper for Father Coultas."

"Nice of him to give you his black sweats. Maybe if you lose some weight and dress like a woman, you can be more than just his housekeeper."

Ronni turned away, not a bit concerned about the expression of outrage on Immelda's face, and zeroed in on Gail Hansen. "You're getting pretty top heavy there, Gail," she said. "If somebody shoved you forward, you'd bounce.

"And there's the quilting ladies," Ronni went on. "Didn't Roger tell you that you'll never lose weight if you go to Hal and Rose's after class for pancakes and eggs with a side of sausage?"

Hannah glanced around the room. Those who hadn't been bitten by Ronni's sharp criticism looked nervous wondering if they'd be next. It was time to put a stop to this before someone really got hurt. Ronni turned to face Andrea, but before she could open her mouth, Hannah stepped in.

"Are you going to lead us through our exercises, or just insult us?" she asked.

"The cookie lady steps up to the plate!" Ronni gave a little laugh. "I wondered how long it would take for somebody to talk back. Get mad, ladies. Get mad and do something to improve your image. If I noticed how bad you look, so does everybody else. Now watch me, and let's do some bends and stretches."

Hannah bent and stretched with the rest of the class, and as she did, she watched her classmates. Vonnie was blinking back tears, Immelda still looked outraged, Gail was clearly humiliated, Trudi and Loretta were just beginning to get over their embarrassment, and Babs had her fists clenched so hard, the knuckles she undoubtedly wanted to slam into Ronni's face were turning white.

"How to win friends and influence people," Hannah said in an undertone to Andrea. "If she treats all her classes this way, I'm surprised someone hasn't decked her."

Chapter
Nine

"I can't believe Ronni was so awful!" Lisa just shook her head after Hannah told her what had happened at Heavenly Bodies. "I always knew she didn't care that much for other people's feelings, but I thought she was just self-centered. Now I'm changing my mind. I think she might actually enjoy hurting other people."

"That was my impression. She looked really pleased when Vonnie got tears in her eyes."

"And Vonnie's so sweet. How can they keep Ronni on as a fitness instructor if she treats all her classes like that?"

"She doesn't, at least that's what Andrea told me. She said that Ronni's entirely different when she teaches a men's class. Then she compliments them on how well they're doing, and encourages them to do more. The guys all think she's great."

"That figures." Lisa got up to bus their coffee cups, but she turned back for one more comment. "I'm glad Herb doesn't have a membership out there. I trust him completely, but I'd still wonder if the BowFlex machine was the main attraction."

Hannah laughed. Marriage had been good for Lisa. Before she'd teamed up with Herb, Lisa had been shy, easily embarrassed, and a very private person. Now that she was happily married, she was much more open about her feelings, and she'd gained enough self-confidence to say what she thought.

She still blushed at the drop of a hat, but Hannah found that trait endearing.

"I almost forgot," Hannah said, gesturing to the box she'd placed on the kitchen counter. "I found Lisa Colleene's recipe for Mini Cheeseburger Cookies. Norman and I made some last night. They're in that box if you want to take a look."

Lisa hurried over to the box and lifted the lid. She stared down in silence for a moment, and when she turned back to Hannah, there was a huge smile on her face. "They're just darling!" she said.

"I think so too. That's why I saved the photo and the recipe."

"I can try one, can't I?"

"Of course. They're just two different kinds of store-bought cookies held in place with buttercream frosting."

Lisa popped a cookie into her mouth and chewed. Then she nodded and swallowed. "You're right. It's not the taste that's so special. It's the fact they look like cheeseburgers. The kids at the party will just love these, but I think we'll have to double Mrs. Janowski's order. They're pretty small."

"Good idea," Hannah said, and then she started to frown. "Don't double the price again, though."

Lisa laughed. "I won't. But I might just have to point out what wonderful value she's getting for her money."

Hannah studied the recipe Lisa had found for Emmy Herman's cream puffs. It seemed to be simple enough, and she wondered why she'd never tried to make cream puffs before. There were only five ingredients in the puff part, and she had plenty of water, butter, salt, flour, and eggs.

It didn't take long to mix up the first batch. Hannah spooned them onto parchment paper, the way it said to do in the recipe, and popped them into a four-hundred-degree oven. In less time than it took her to refill the display cookie jars they kept behind the counter in the coffee shop, her first-ever batch of cream puffs was ready to come out of the oven.

They were golden brown, puffed up high, and beautiful. Hannah went off to call Lisa to take a look. Several people stopped her to chat, and at least ten minutes passed before she switched aprons with Lisa and sent her partner off to the kitchen to take a look.

Lisa was back almost immediately, but she didn't look happy. She was shaking her head slightly as she approached the counter to take back her apron.

"What's wrong?" Hannah asked her.

"I'm not sure, but I think you'd better go look for yourself. Maybe Mom left something out of the recipe."

When Hannah pushed through the swinging door to the kitchen, she saw why Lisa had looked unhappy. The cream puffs weren't puffed any longer. They'd collapsed and now they resembled . . . she didn't really want to think about what they resembled, but she'd stepped over a few the last time she'd walked through a cow pasture.

When something didn't work, she wanted to know why. Hannah broke one puff open and stared at the wet strands of dough inside. Steam was the culprit and she knew what to do about that. It was the final step in Bernadette's Popover recipe. She should have released the steam by poking the puffs with the tip of a sharp knife right after she'd taken them out of the oven.

While she was at it, there was another change she could make in Lisa's mother's recipe. Hannah picked up a pen and wrote in an additional ingredient. She'd add a little safeguard to help with the rising and stabilize the puffs. Baking powder should do it.

Tasting was next. Hannah broke off a little piece of puff and sampled it. She could taste the egg, and the dough was slightly salty, but that was about it. Perhaps real cream puff aficionados wanted a perfectly bland puff to show off their fillings, but Hannah didn't see why the outside shouldn't taste as good as the inside. A little sweetness would help, and there was no sugar in Emmy Herman's recipe.

Since she didn't think it would disturb the balance of wet and dry to add a bit of sugar, Hannah wrote in a second ingredient, a tablespoon of white granulated sugar. She was about to add some cinnamon or nutmeg, but she reconsidered. The puffs would have various flavors of fillings. Not all of those fillings would be enhanced by her choice of spices.

Hannah spent the next hour making another batch of cream puffs from her revised recipe. She pierced the side of each puff when they came out of the oven, placed them on a cooling rack away from any drafts, and sat at the stainless steel workstation, sipping a cup of coffee and waiting to see if disaster would strike twice.

Ten minutes passed, and the puffs were still high and golden. The baking powder had worked! She was about to go out and get Lisa when her partner stuck her head into the kitchen.

"Look at these, Lisa," Hannah fairly crowed.

"They're beautiful. I'm almost sure they rose higher than Mom's ever did."

"Really?"

"I think so. Did you change the recipe?"

"Just a little. I added baking powder and sugar. And I pierced them to let out the steam when they came out of the oven. Your mother's recipe is a good one, Lisa. I'm going to call them Emmy's Cream Puffs."

Lisa shook her head. "I think you should name them something else, Hannah. Mom's recipe was just a jumping-off place for you."

"Well . . . maybe you're right," Hannah conceded. "But I made a batch of your mother's vanilla custard, and I didn't change a thing. I'll name that Emmy's Vanilla Custard if it's okay with you."

"It's fine with me," Lisa said with a smile.

"I thought we could have a taste test with different fillings if we have enough customers willing to sample them for us."

Lisa laughed. "Are you kidding?! Get busy and fill them.

It's just about time for the midafternoon rush, and I can guarantee we'll have plenty of customers ready to taste them."

Hannah didn't know when she'd felt so good. Delores and Carrie had come in, and both of them had gone into raptures over the cream puffs. Her mother had pronounced them even better than the ones her Aunt Bertha had baked. Now Hannah was in the kitchen making a third test batch. They were mini cream puffs, the bite-size kind she wanted to serve at her mother's book launch party. She'd just opened the three cans of pie filling Florence had hand-delivered from the Red Owl in return for a dozen Walnuttoes, when Lisa appeared in the doorway.

"Mike's here," she said. "Do you want me to send him back?"

"Sure." Hannah sliced the top from a mini puff and spooned in strawberry pie filling. She alternated between the three flavors, strawberry, lemon, and blueberry, placing them on a platter with the ones she'd already filled with Emmy's vanilla custard and the rich, homemade chocolate pudding that her great-grandmother had made. Hannah had just replaced the tops like jaunty berets on top of the cream puffs and dusted them with powdered sugar when Mike walked into the kitchen.

"Hey, Hannah. What are those?"

"Mini Cream Puffs. I'm testing them out for Mother's book launch party."

"Need any help?"

Mike looked hopeful, and Hannah gave a little laugh. "Sure. Which do you like best, strawberry or blueberry?"

"Blueberry."

"Okay." Hannah picked up a blueberry mini cream puff and set it on a plate. "Now choose between lemon and vanilla."

"Vanilla, as long as there's lots of vanilla."

"There is." Hannah set a mini puff filled with Emmy's Vanilla Custard on the plate. Then she added her final choice, a puff filled with her great-grandmother's homemade chocolate pudding.

"They're pretty," Mike said when she delivered them with a steaming mug of coffee. "It's almost a shame to eat them."

"But you'll make the sacrifice?"

"You said it!" Mike popped a puff into his mouth, and an expression of bliss crossed his face. He chewed, swallowed almost reluctantly, and followed that with a gulp of coffee.

"Good?" Hannah asked him.

"Better than good. I really like the blueberry. And there's something else I like, too."

"What's that?"

"You filled them up full, and I can see what kind they are. The blueberry was peeking out at me. It's not the box of assorted chocolates thing, you know?"

Hannah knew exactly what Mike meant. Unless you remembered the candy maker's code for swirls that meant one type of filling and lines and squiggles that designated others, you could be disappointed in the chocolate candy you chose.

"Here goes the vanilla." Mike picked up the mini puff and turned to look at Hannah. "You made the filling, right?"

"Right. It's Lisa's mother's recipe for vanilla custard."

"Oh, boy!" Mike popped the confection into his mouth and made a little sound of satisfaction. When he'd finished it, he took another swallow of coffee and sighed. "That was *really* good. And this is chocolate?"

"It's not just any chocolate. It's the richest chocolate pudding I've ever made."

"I think I love you," Mike said as he picked up the last mini cream puff and popped it into his mouth. He was smiling as he finished it, licked his fingers, and drank more of his coffee. "Correction," he said. "I *know* I love you."

"Actually, you love my great-grandma Swensen. It's her recipe for chocolate pudding."

"But she's not here, and you are. How much would you charge for a tray of those?"

Hannah shrugged. "I'm not sure. I wasn't really planning on offering them for sale."

"Well, what are you going to do with those?" Mike pointed to the array of mini cream puffs arranged on the counter.

"I'll freeze some so I can see how they thaw. That's important to know for Mother's book launch party. And the rest I guess I'll . . ."

"Eat," Mike interrupted her.

"Not on your life! The only thing I've tasted is the dough from the first batch, and that was only a crumb."

Mike looked pleased. "Good for you! So they're not even tempting you?"

"Oh, they're tempting me, all right!"

" 'Course they are. Tell you what . . . I need something special for a birthday. I was going to run to the Red Owl and pick up a cake, but those cream puffs would make it a really special party. How about selling me half of what you have there? You can keep the rest for freezing and whatever else you want to do with them."

"Deal." Hannah started arranging the cream puffs on a platter. "Bring back the platter, okay?"

"You got it. This is going to make for a really special birthday."

Hannah placed the last cream puff and covered the platter with plastic wrap. "If you're not going to serve these right away, refrigerate them. They should be fine for hours. Whose birthday is it anyway?"

"Somebody at the gym." Mike handed her some folded money and picked up the platter. "Just let me know if that's not enough. Now I'd better get going or I'll be late. I'll call you and tell you how it goes, Hannah. Everybody's going to just love these."

HANNAH'S VERY BEST CREAM PUFFS

Preheat oven to 400 degrees F., rack
in the middle position.

1 cup water
½ cup *(1 stick, 8 Tablespoons, ¼ pound)* butter
¼ teaspoon salt
1 Tablespoon white *(granulated)* sugar
1 cup flour *(pack it down in the measuring cup and
    level off with a knife)*
1½ teaspoons baking powder
4 extra large eggs *(at room temperature)*

Spray a cookie sheet with Pam *(or any nonstick cooking
spray that doesn't contain oil or butter),* or line it with a
sheet of parchment paper. *(You'll need 2 cookie sheets for
mini cream puffs.)*

Place the water in a heavy saucepan. Cut the butter into
small pieces and add it to the water. Sprinkle in the salt
and the sugar.

Turn the burner on medium to melt the butter.

While the water is heating and the butter is melting,
measure out the flour and place it in a bowl. Add the baking powder and stir it in with a fork.

When the butter has melted, turn up the heat and bring
the water to a full rolling boil. Turn the burner to low and
dump in the flour mixture all at once, stirring it in quickly
with a wooden spoon. After a few moments of vigorous

stirring, the dough will clean the sides of the saucepan and begin to "ball up." *(This takes about 30 seconds.)* Pull the saucepan from the heat and turn off the burner.

Let the dough sit on a cold burner or on the counter to cool for 20 minutes.

When the dough has cooled, break an egg and add it to your dough. Beat it in with a wooden spoon. Continue to beat vigorously until the egg is fully incorporated and the dough is smooth. Add the remaining eggs, one at a time, beating after each addition until each egg is incorporated and the dough is smooth again.

Hannah's 1st Note: Total time for beating in the eggs by hand is about 5 minutes. A hand mixer also works, but the dough gets caught inside the beaters and you must poke it out with a rubber spatula after each egg has been added to the dough.

Test your dough by lifting out a spoonful and dropping it on top of the rest of the dough. If it stays on top and maintains its shape, it's ready to bake. If not, beat it some more until it does.

Drop the dough by large spoonfuls onto the cookie sheet. Make 12 mounds of dough, and if they need shaping, do so with damp fingers. Don't crowd the puffs. They should be at least 3 inches apart. *(If you want to make mini puffs, drop small spoonfuls on the sheets, 15 to each sheet.)*

Bake at 400 degrees F. for 45 to 50 minutes for the large puffs. *(Mini puffs bake 30 to 35 minutes.)* **DON'T OPEN THE OVEN TO PEEK!** Finished cream puffs should feel firm to the touch and be golden brown.

Remove the cream puffs from the oven and pierce the side of each one with the point of a sharp knife. *(This isn't necessary for the mini puffs.)* Cool the puffs on the baking sheet, careful to keep them away from drafts.

Cut off the top third of each puff for the lid. Remove any filaments of dough inside the bottoms and fill the puffs with sweetened whipped cream, Emmy's Vanilla Custard, Great-Grandma's Chocolate Pudding, ice cream, or any flavor of pie filling. Overfill a bit so the lids sit jauntily on top of the filling. Dust each one with powdered sugar and serve. If you want messy but yummy, you can drizzle a bit of chocolate sauce or icing over the tops.

Hannah's 2nd Note: You can make these puffs a day ahead and store them, tightly covered, in a dry place like a kitchen cupboard. You can also fill them, wrap them tightly, and freeze them. Just thaw frozen cream puffs, dust them with powdered sugar, and serve.

Yield: 12 large cream puffs or 30 mini cream puffs.

EMMY'S VANILLA CUSTARD

½ cup white *(granulated)* sugar
⅛ teaspoon salt
¼ teaspoon freshly ground nutmeg
⅓ cup flour *(not sifted)*
1 cup whole milk
1 cup heavy cream
2 beaten eggs
2 teaspoons vanilla extract
1 ounce *(⅛ stick)* butter

Combine the sugar, salt, nutmeg, and flour in a saucepan off the heat. Stir well.

Gradually stir in the milk and the cream. Blend everything together off the heat.

Turn the burner on medium high heat and cook, stirring constantly, until thickened. *(This takes about 10 minutes on my stove.)*

Remove the saucepan from the heat, but LEAVE THE BURNER ON.

Break the eggs into a small bowl and quickly beat them with a whisk until they're well mixed.

Stir several Tablespoons of the hot mixture into the bowl with the eggs. Whisk until it's incorporated.

Slowly pour the eggs into the saucepan with the hot mixture, whisking it all the while.

Return the saucepan to the heat and stir for 2 to 3 minutes, until the mixture is very thick.

Remove the saucepan from the heat *(you can turn off the burner this time)*. Add the vanilla, stirring it in quickly. Add the ounce of butter and stir it in until it's melted.

Let the mixture cool and use it to fill your cream puffs, or pour it into bowls while it's hot, chill it in the refrigerator, and serve it with a little sweetened whipped cream for a lovely dessert.

Yield: 4 servings of pudding, or filling for 6 to 8 cream puffs.

GREAT-GRANDMA'S CHOCOLATE PUDDING

2 cups whole milk
2 cups heavy cream
1 cup white (*granulated*) sugar
4 squares unsweetened chocolate (*I used Baker's*)
9 eggs yolks, beaten
2 teaspoons vanilla extract
2 ounces butter

Separate 9 eggs into whites and yolks. If you plan to make Angel Kisses Cookies or Angel Pillows Cookies with

the whites, save them in a tightly covered container in the refrigerator. *(Each recipe calls for 3 egg whites so you can make a triple batch of either one.)* Beat the yolks and set them aside.

Combine the milk, cream, and sugar in a heavy saucepan off the heat. Unwrap 4 squares of unsweetened chocolate, break them into two parts at the indentation, and add them to your saucepan. *(Breaking them up causes them to melt faster.)*

Heat the mixture over medium high heat on the stove, stirring constantly until little whiffs of steam start to escape and you think it's about to boil.

Pull the saucepan from the heat, but don't turn off the burner. This next step will take only a moment or two.

Give the beaten egg yolks a final stir, and add approximately 2 Tablespoons of the chocolate mixture to the egg yolks, stirring it in quickly. *(This is called tempering, and it's important—without it you could have pudding with scrambled eggs inside.)*

Off the heat, slowly pour the egg mixture into the chocolate mixture in the saucepan, stirring all the while. When it's incorporated, put the saucepan back on the heat.

Cook, stirring constantly, until the mixture comes to a full boil. *(This took about 3 minutes for me on my stove.)*

Pull the saucepan off the heat, and this time you can turn off the burner.

Quickly stir in the vanilla. Then stir in the butter and continue to stir until the butter is melted.

Let the pudding cool and use it to fill cream puffs, or . . .

Pour the pudding into 8 bowls and cool in the refrigerator. Top with sweetened whipped cream and serve it for a delicious dessert, or . . .

Pour the pudding into a cookie crumb, shortbread crumb, or graham cracker crumb pie shell. *(You can buy them already prepared at the store if you don't want to make your own.)* Chill and top with sweetened whipped cream for dessert.

Yield: enough filling for 12 to 18 cream puffs, 8 servings of dessert pudding, or a chocolate pie.

Chapter Ten

Never had a cat looked so innocent. Hannah stood next to the Kitty Valet and met Moishe's guileless gaze. "I know your new feeder is lots of fun, but please don't eat all your kitty crunchies while I'm at work today. Save some for tonight, and maybe even tomorrow. The instructions say that it stores enough food for three days. And that's for a family with *two* cats! I know you love to eat, Moishe, but you're going to get sick if you keep on emptying the whole thing every time I leave."

He was purring! Her cat was purring! Hannah sighed deeply and gave up lecturing. Chances were that Moishe didn't understand a word she was saying. And even if he did, he'd ignore her advice the second the door closed behind her.

"Okay, I'm gone," she said to the cat, who probably wasn't listening anyway. "I'll be home around six, and I want to see some food left in that bowl."

As she walked down the covered staircase to the parking garage, Hannah was frowning. She was worried about Moishe. He'd always been a big eater, but last night when she'd come home from work, she'd found the Kitty Valet that contained his food completely empty.

Even though her feline friend hadn't been sprawled on his back on the rug groaning, Hannah had still called his vet. It just couldn't be good for Moishe to eat *that* much food! But once she'd answered several questions that Dr. Bob had asked about Moishe's behavior, he'd assured her that once the novelty of unlimited food without human intervention had worn off, Moishe's eating habits would return to normal.

It was cold this morning, five below zero according to Jake and Kelly on KCOW Radio, and Hannah wished she'd asked Andrea to pick her up. Her sister's Volvo had heated seats, a welcome luxury in the Minnesota winter. She wondered, idly, how much it would cost to install them in her cookie truck but decided it would probably be several times more than she could afford.

The radio helped her to keep her mind off the cold. Hannah listened to one more pseudo news item on *The News at O'Dark-Thirty*, something about a pet horse who came inside the farmhouse whenever he smelled cookies baking. That didn't sound so unusual to Hannah, especially if the cookies were carrot cookies. And thinking about carrot cookies reminded her that she'd promised to bake Terry's Carrot Cake Cookies for Grandma Knudson, who was trying to convince her grandson, the reverend, that they were an excellent way for him to get his vegetables.

Another fifteen shivery minutes later, and Hannah arrived at the Tri-County Mall. She had a standing appointment to meet Andrea so that they could do their workout routine before class started. She pulled up by the back door at Heavenly Bodies, greeted Andrea, who was just pulling into a parking space, and they went in together.

The only good thing about exercising early in the morning was the absence of noise. The incessant beat of the workout music, the buzz of conversation, the clatter of weights, and the occasional grunt and groan were silenced. The only sound was her own labored breathing as she went through her exercise routine.

Never a big fan of muscle aches and pains, Hannah found this morning's workout particularly grueling. Perhaps it was because Andrea performed every bend and stretch so effortlessly. She even made her mile on the machine Hannah had nicknamed the *Walk to Nowhere* look like fun.

"So how's Moishe's feeder working out?" Andrea asked, not a whit out of breath despite the fact she was currently duplicating the rigors of cross-country skiing.

"Fine," Hannah answered, choosing a one-syllable word so that her sister couldn't hear her pant. They could talk about the fact that Moishe's feeder was working a little *too* well later, when she could breathe.

"How long has it been now? Two days?"

"Yes."

"And he hasn't pried the tops off yet?"

"No."

"Well, give him time. He's defeated every other attempt you've made to regulate his food."

"Right." Even though she'd uttered only one syllable, Hannah gasped a bit. Luckily, Andrea didn't seem to notice. Perhaps it was because she'd increased the resistance on her skiing simulator. Hannah could see the little graphic that showed her sister skiing up a thirty percent slope. That was twenty-eight percent steeper than anything Hannah had attempted.

Andrea was silent, and Hannah was grateful. It gave her time to catch her breath. This twenty-minute workout wouldn't be so bad if she had half the morning to do it. Unfortunately, they were pressed for time. Ronni Ward would be arriving soon for their Classic Body Sculpting class, and that wasn't a pleasant thought.

"You're through, Hannah," Andrea announced, stepping off her ski simulator and taking a seat on what looked like a stationary bike.

"I am?" Hannah slowed to a halt. She'd been so busy thinking about how much she disliked Ronni, the last five minutes of her workout had practically flown past. She glanced up at the clock on the wall and then turned to her sister. "We've got twenty-five minutes until class. Do you want me to get you something cold to drink?"

"That sounds good." Andrea gave a little sigh. "Class used to be fun, but now I'm dreading it. I really wish that Ronni was out of the picture."

"Me, too. Do you want to skip class today?"

"No way. If we skip, she's won. And I won't give her the satisfaction. Just get our drinks and go relax by the pool. I'll join you as soon as I finish."

Hannah headed off at a fast clip before her sister changed her mind and thought of other exercises that she should do. Since no one was manning the counter at the Snack Shack, the large area with a fountain in the center surrounded by scores of round tables for eating, drinking and socializing, she fed quarters into a vending machine to get a bottle of zero-carb, zero-calorie strawberry-flavored water for Andrea and a bottle of zero-carb, zero-calorie peach-flavored water for herself. Then she headed down the red-carpeted hallway to the Aqua Therapy room.

The scent of chlorine rolled out to greet her as Hannah opened the door to the area containing the pool and the Jacuzzi. There was the stale odor of sweat in the air, and despite the antiperspirant she'd slathered on earlier, Hannah suspected that she might be contributing to the aroma. Whatever the cause, it was certain that the plug-in room fresheners, specifically designed to mask unpleasant odors, failed to triumph over the potent mix.

The pool looked inviting, with wooden deck chairs arranged in patterns at the shallow end and potted trees dotting the periphery. Hannah removed her shoes and socks and took a seat on the concrete lip of the pool so that she could dangle her feet in the water. They were sore after her trek on the motorized belt of the *Walk to Nowhere* machine. The pool heater had just kicked in. The pool wouldn't reach the proper temperature until Aqua Therapy classes started at noon, but that didn't matter to Hannah. The cold felt good. She opened her bottle of water, took a sip, and sat there feeling righteous about finishing her workout.

Her drink was slightly fizzy, and it tasted a little like peach. Hannah supposed that was all one could ask of a product that was less than a dollar fifty and had no carbohydrates or calories. She sat there for at least five minutes, trying to figure out how the manufacturer could make something taste like peach without actually using peach, but then she realized that her toes had stopped tingling and were numb from the cold.

It was time to warm up. Hannah grabbed her towel and headed to the Jacuzzi to thaw her icy feet, but the first thing she saw when she climbed up the steps to enter the lattice-work gazebo was something that stopped her cold. There was a red-colored smear on the floor that looked a lot like blood.

Visions of cut feet or skinned knees ran through Hannah's mind, but then she spotted a lump of red near the end of the smear. She walked closer to take a look. It was a smeared, crushed strawberry! Someone had broken the rules. Although plastic bottles or boxes of drinks were allowed in the pool area and the workout rooms, food was only allowed at the tables in the Snack Shack.

The gazebo was a tropical paradise with hanging plants and potted palms. A bar ran the length of one latticework wall. During regular hours, an employee who sold bottled water manned it. A half-dozen stools were arranged in front of the bar. They provided seating for those who'd tired of the steaming water, but wanted to wait for friends who were still enjoying the heat of the tub. Several stools had been tipped over and Hannah wondered why no one had righted them.

There was something shiny on the floor next to the far end of the bar. Hannah walked over for a closer look and immediately wished she hadn't. It was her silver platter, the very same platter she'd used for Mike's birthday cream puffs, and it was upside down in front of the flowering hibiscus that thrived in the moist heat.

With the same sinking feeling she experienced every time she came across a bad accident on the road, Hannah lifted one handle and surveyed the smashed cream puffs it had held. Blueberry and lemon filling had overlapped in a puddle of gooey green. There were bits of pastry mixed into a glutinous mash of strawberry and vanilla filling, but there were no chocolate cream puffs. She supposed she should be happy that her great-grandma's pudding had been such a success, but she felt sick at the cream puff carnage she saw. Mike had told her it was a birthday party at the gym. She'd just assumed he meant the gym at the sheriff's department, but he'd obviously been talking about Heavenly Bodies. It was clear that the birthday party had gone awry, and from the tipped stools, she guessed that the partygoers had left in a rush. That made her very curious. She had to ask Mike what had happened.

Hannah shivered. Her feet were still cold. She'd clean up the cream puffs and reclaim her platter later, but right now she needed to thaw her frigid digits.

The switch that operated the Jacuzzi was behind the bar. Hannah turned on the heat, activated the jets, flicked on the underwater lights, and headed over to the tub. She was about to dip her toes in the water when she realized that there was something in the center of the Jacuzzi.

The surface was roiling and bubbling so furiously that visibility was limited. Hannah waited until the object resurfaced again, and when it did, she was puzzled. It looked like one of the red-and-black exercise outfits worn by the female instructors at Heavenly Bodies. Had one of them dropped her clothes in the Jacuzzi?

That didn't make much sense, and the moment she realized it, Hannah felt the hair on the back of her neck stand up in exactly the same way Moishe's did when he encountered something that frightened him. She braced herself and reached out to grab the material, intending to pull it out of the water to examine it more closely. But instead of grasping nothing but spandex, she felt something under the material, something firm, something muscled, something decidedly human.

"Uh-oh," Hannah breathed, fighting the impulse to turn tail and run. The only thing that kept her feet rooted to the spot was the thought that Andrea could walk in at any moment. She had to find out who was wearing that red-and-black exercise outfit and spare Andrea from what could very well be a gruesome sight.

Taking a deep breath for courage, Hannah tugged until the solid mass turned from back to front. She took one look and swallowed hard as she stared down at blond hair, a perfect figure, and lifeless blue eyes with a deep indentation between them.

"Hannah?" Andrea called out from the doorway. "Are you going in the Jacuzzi?"

"No," Hannah said, standing up quickly and blocking the sight as best she could. "Go out to the security station and tell whoever's on duty to call Mike at the sheriff's station."

"But why?"

"Just do it, Andrea. And don't come any closer."

Andrea gasped. "Don't tell me there's someone . . ."

"Don't think, just do it!" Hannah ordered, and she gave a relieved sigh when Andrea turned and ran down the hallway.

Even though she tried to keep her gaze on the tropical wallpaper, or the flowering plants, or the colorful tile that covered the floor, Hannah's eyes were drawn to the sight she didn't want Andrea to see. It was Ronni Ward, and she was quite dead. It seemed that someone else had wanted her out of the picture even more than they had!

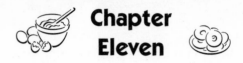 **Chapter
Eleven**

Lisa's initial expression of shock turned to one of worry after Hannah finished telling her about finding Ronni's body. "How awful for you!"

"Actually, it was more awful for Ronni."

"I guess that's true, but I don't really care about Ronni. I care about you." Lisa reached out to touch her arm. "You need some chocolate, Hannah. There's a pan of Brownies Plus cooling on the kitchen counter. Go have one."

Hannah was sorely tempted. She loved Brownies Plus, and chocolate would certainly make her feel better. But better sense prevailed and she shook her head. "I'd love to have one, but I won't. There's no way Ronni Ward's going to spoil my diet . . . dead or alive."

"Okay, but at least go back and have a cup of coffee. I'll open up the coffee shop. The news hasn't broken on KCOW yet, but when it does we'll be crowded."

Hannah sighed as she headed to the kitchen. Lisa was right. They would be chock full of customers when the news broke. And every one of them would want to know all about how Hannah had found Ronni's body. At least this time she wouldn't be asked, or even allowed, to investigate. Mike would be so upset, he'd want to catch Ronni's killer himself. And if what she'd heard about Ronni's flirtations was true, she had no doubt that at least sixty percent of the Winnetka County sheriff's deputies would feel the same way.

Hannah was grating carrots for the Carrot Cake Cookies she'd decided to bake. Baking always made her feel better, and finding Ronni's body in the Jacuzzi hadn't exactly started her day on a high note.

Since she couldn't use her food processor to grate carrots as finely as she needed them, Hannah was doing it by hand. Her tool was a standard, four-sided box grater, and it took a while to grate enough. She was only halfway through when there was a knock on the back door.

"Mother," Hannah muttered, coming close to grating her knuckle right along with her favorite root vegetable. Delores had probably heard about Ronni's death, but that wouldn't be her main concern. Delores would be much more upset about Hannah's finding another body.

"Might as well face her now," Hannah said, even though there was no one to hear her. She put down her grater and the half-done carrot, wiped her hands on a towel, and hurried to open the back door.

"Hi, Hannah."

Hannah blinked, and then she smiled. "Hi, Norman. Why didn't you come in the front way?"

"Because I didn't want anyone to see me. Let me in. I'm on a mission."

Hannah stepped aside, and Norman came in. They parted ways three steps inside. He headed for the work island and sat down on a stool, while she headed for the kitchen coffee pot to pour him a mug.

"What's all this about a mission?" she asked, delivering the java along with two Brownies Plus on a napkin.

"In a minute." Norman took a bite of his brownie and a sip of coffee. "These are the best brownies I ever had!"

"Thanks. They're Diana Dickerson's recipe." Even though she was brimming with curiosity, Hannah waited until Norman had eaten both brownies and reduced the coffee in his mug by half. "The mission?" she reminded him.

"Somebody told me your slay-dar is working overtime."

"My *what*?"

"Slay-dar. It's like radar, except that you find murder victims."

"Cute," Hannah said, being entirely truthful. It *was* a cute thing to say. "So you heard the news on KCOW?"

"Not exactly. Mike just left my dental clinic, and he told me all about it. He wants me to tell you that Bill's put him on leave until Ronni's murder is solved."

Hannah just stared at Norman for a moment. Then she shook her head. "I don't understand. Mike's the head detective. Bill needs him to solve the case . . . doesn't he?"

"He does, but Mike can't work it. It's in the rulebook. You can't be assigned a case where you have . . . uh . . . a personal relationship with the victim."

"Personal relationship," Hannah repeated. "Does that mean what I think it means?"

Norman took a sip of his coffee. When he answered, he looked down at the mug, not at her. "I don't know. Mike didn't volunteer that information, and I didn't ask."

Right. Sure, Hannah's mind said, *and that's why you won't meet my eyes.* Norman was a terrible liar. His mother, Carrie, had mentioned it numerous times. She said that even as a little boy, he looked guilty when he wasn't telling the truth. And here he was, trying to lie to her to spare her the steamy details.

"You know more than you're telling me," Hannah said, facing him squarely. "But don't you know that if you tell me about Ronni and Mike's relationship, I'll probably think less of Mike?"

"I know that," Norman said quickly, and then he looked a bit chagrined. "*If* there's anything in the details to warrant it, that is."

Hannah grinned. Norman had almost fallen into a trap, but he'd caught himself in time. "Okay. But if I think less of

Mike, I'll probably gravitate your way." She stopped and frowned as a most unwelcome thought occurred to her. "You two are still in a kind of competition for me . . . aren't you?"

"I can't speak for Mike, but I am. It's just that . . ." his voice trailed off.

"What?" Hannah prodded him.

"Mike and I are friends. And friends don't divulge each other's confidences. At least *I* don't." Norman stopped speaking and looked worried. "Am I being a real chump?"

"No, you're being Norman. And the fact you won't take advantage of Mike's situation makes me like you even more."

A slow smile broke out over Norman's face. "Well!" he said, as pleased as Hannah had ever seen him. "That's good. Now can we get down to business? Mike gave me a list of things he wanted to tell you."

"Hold on. Why isn't Mike here, telling me all this himself?"

"Bill made him swear he wouldn't have anything to do with the official investigation. He can't even call his detectives to see how they're doing. And right after Mike agreed to that, Bill made him promise that he wouldn't speak to you about anything concerning the case. Mike's getting around that by talking to me and having me tell you what he said."

"Like a reverse Cyrano?" Hannah couldn't help asking, since they'd watched the old black-and-white movie just last week.

"I guess it's a bit like that, but it's not about love. It's about murder. You *are* going to try to find out who killed her, aren't you?"

"Of course I am. The killer ruined at least a dozen of my mini cream puffs."

"Good. I'll tell Mike you're in, then. He's going to tell me what to do to work the case, and I'll tell you what he says."

"Solving murder by proxy?" Hannah began to frown. "I don't think I can do that. Mike and I solve murders in different ways. He has a lot more resources than I do."

"Not this time."

Hannah thought about that for a minute. "I guess that's true if he can't contact anyone at the department. But I don't want Mike to tell me what to do. I need to do things my own way."

"He said you'd say that. And he said to tell you that you could still do things your own way if you do them his way, too. That way you'll have two different procedures, and you should solve the case twice as fast."

Hannah gave a little laugh. "His logic is faulty, but it would be interesting to see how Mike would manage the case. He didn't mention that running parallel investigations would be double the work for me, did he?"

"Not to me. But I can help you, Hannah."

"How about your dental patients?"

"That's not a problem. Doc Bennett's been asking if I need him to fill in. I think he's trying to earn a little extra for Christmas. I'm pretty sure he wants to go on a cruise to the Caribbean."

"Really?"

"A whole stack of travel brochures can't be wrong. He left them on my desk the last time he filled in for me."

"Cruises are expensive."

"I know, and I'd like to provide a little of the financing. I'll call him the minute I get back to the clinic and ask him to come in. Then I can take time off to help you."

"That would be fun," Hannah said, but she quickly sobered. "I guess *fun* is a strange word to use when we're talking about murder. But I *do* like working with you, Norman."

"And I like working with you." Norman got up and carried his empty coffee mug to the counter by the sink. "If Doc Bennett can come in, I'll see you later today, Hannah."

"Wait!" Hannah hurried to the counter and packed up six Brownies Plus bars for Doc Bennett. "Doc Bennett loves Brownies Plus. Tell him I gave you a half-dozen for him and he'll run all the way down to your clinic."

BROWNIES PLUS

Preheat oven to 350 degrees F., rack
in the middle position.

6 one-ounce squares semi-sweet chocolate *(or three-quarters cup chocolate chips)*
1 cup butter *(two sticks, ½ pound)*
2 cups white *(granulated)* sugar
4 beaten eggs *(just whip them up in a glass with a fork)*
2 teaspoons vanilla extract
1½ cups flour *(pack it down in the cup when you measure it)*
5 to 7 three-ounce chocolate candy bars *(I've used Nestle's Treasures Cappuccino Truffle Bars, Hershey's Symphony Bars, and Nestle's Crunch Bars—the number of bars depends on how many inches of your pan they cover.)*

A SHORT CUT: Lisa got this recipe from Diana Dickerson. Diana says that if you don't feel like making your brownies from scratch, use two packages of brownie mix, the kind that makes an 8-inch by 8-inch square. Use two bowls, one for each package, and prepare the brownie batter by following the directions on the box. Once the batter is mixed, use the contents of one bowl for the bottom layer and the contents of the other bowl for the top. Diana's favorite candy bars to use are Hershey's Symphony Bars.

Prepare a 9-inch by 13-inch cake pan by lining it with a piece of foil large enough to flap over the sides. Spray the foil-lined pan with Pam or another nonstick cooking spray.

Microwave the chocolate squares *(or chocolate chips)* and butter in a microwave-safe mixing bowl for one minute. Stir. *(Since chocolate frequently maintains its shape even when melted, you have to stir to make sure.)* If it's not melted, microwave for an additional 20 seconds and stir again. Repeat if necessary.

Stir the sugar into the chocolate mixture. Feel the bowl. If it's not so hot it'll cook the eggs, add them now, stirring thoroughly. Mix in the vanilla extract.

Mix in the flour and stir just until it's moistened.

Spoon half of the batter into your prepared pan. Smooth it out with a rubber spatula.

Unwrap the candy bars and place them on top of the batter. Make a single layer, and try to cover as much of the batter as you can. You may have to break a couple of the bars to fill in the gaps.

Spoon the remaining batter on top of the candy bars, and use the rubber spatula to smooth it out.

Bake at 350 degrees F. for 30 minutes.

Cool the Brownies Plus in the pan on a metal rack. When they're thoroughly cool, grasp the edges of the foil and lift the brownies out of the pan. Put them facedown on a cutting board, peel the foil off the back, and cut them into brownie-sized pieces.

Place the squares on a plate and dust lightly with powdered sugar if you wish.

Hannah's Note: These brownies freeze well if you leave them in one large piece. When they're cool, just lift them out of the pan, fold the foil over the top, and slip them into a freezer bag. When you want to serve them, let them thaw on the counter, cut them into pieces, and dust with powdered sugar.

Chapter Twelve

"Oh, Hannah! How could you?!" Delores marched into the kitchen, coming close to mowing Hannah down. "Didn't I raise you better than that?"

"Than what, Mother?" Hannah was ninety-nine percent certain she knew what Delores was talking about. The news must have broken on KCOW Radio, and Delores knew that her eldest daughter had found yet another murder victim.

"You know perfectly well what I mean. You found another body. Everyone in the Tri-County area knows you did. Why you decided to go in that gazebo and look in the Jacuzzi is beyond me!"

"But it's not beyond me. Andrea and I were going to hop in the Jacuzzi until it was time for our class. She was still exercising, and I got there first."

"Well . . . I guess I should be grateful for *that!*" Delores looked slightly mollified. "At least you're used to things like that by now. Your sister's the sensitive type. It would have devastated poor Andrea."

"Right," Hannah said. What Delores said was true. Andrea had never been able to handle things that were, to use their mother's word, *unpleasant.* But if Andrea had discovered Ronni's body, would it have been *unpleasant* for her? Perhaps she would have taken one look at Ronni's lifeless countenance and let out a cheer of victory.

"Anyway," Delores sat down on a stool at the workstation. "I know she was in the Jacuzzi. They said all that on KCOW. I want you to tell me something nobody else knows so that I can tell my friends. There's got to be some advantage to being the mother of . . . of a body finder!"

Hannah thought back to the murder scene. It probably wouldn't be politic to mention the smashed mini cream puffs, especially since Delores wanted them served at her book launch party. She didn't want to mention the tipped stools at the bar, either. It could be something the police might use to weed out suspects. She needed a tidbit of information that was shocking enough for the Lake Eden gossip hotline, but not gross enough to upset Delores.

"I had to turn her over," Hannah said, lighting on something titillating enough for her mother, but not something the police were likely to keep under their hats.

"You *did*?" Delores gave a little shiver, and Hannah knew it was more of excitement than fright.

"At first I thought someone had dropped their exercise outfit in the hot tub. Then I recognized that it was one of the outfits that the female staff wore, and I went to fish it out."

"Oh, my!" Delores shivered again. "And you actually turned her over?"

"I did. I reached out and grabbed the outfit, and that's when I realized that someone was wearing it."

"Oh, my!" Delores repeated, and her voice was slightly breathless.

"I think turning her over was instinctive. I didn't really think about it, I just did it. I don't know if I thought she was still alive, or I could help, or what. I just rolled her over, looked at her face, and saw that she was Ronni Ward."

"The anchorman on the news team said she suffered a blow to the head." Delores stopped and cleared her throat. "Could I have a cup of coffee, dear? Black, of course. Hearing about something like this always makes me a little shaky."

And caffeine will certainly help with that! Hannah thought, but of course she didn't say it. Instead she brought her mother two newly frosted Carrot Cake Cookies along with the mug of coffee.

"Thank you, dear!" Delores took a sip of her coffee and sighed deeply. "I needed that. What are these cookies? They're pretty."

"They're Terry's Carrot Cake Cookies. She's a friend of Lisa's from Wisconsin. I mixed them up when I got back from the gym, and I just finished frosting them when you came in. I know they're not chocolate, but they're good."

"Not everything has to be chocolate, dear. Of course that would be nice, but there's room for other flavors." Delores picked up a cookie and bit into it. "Cream cheese frosting?" she asked after she'd taken another bite.

"Yes. So what do you think?"

"They're perfection, dear. And they do taste just like carrot cake." Delores finished one cookie and took a bite from the second. "Now tell me more about Ronni's appearance, dear."

"While you're *eating*?"

Delores thought about that for a moment, and then she shook her head. "Perhaps not. Just let me finish this cookie, and then we'll talk."

Hannah waited, her mother chewed, and the second cookie disappeared. "What else do you want to know?" she asked.

"Was there much blood?" Delores gave another little shiver and raised her coffee cup to her lips.

"No, Mother. She was facedown in the water, and the wound was washed clean."

"Do you think she . . . suffered before she died?"

Hannah gave a little shrug. "I hope not, but I really don't know. Only Doc Knight would be able to tell that."

"I wonder how he could tell."

"I think it would be pretty simple. If she didn't die instantly or bleed out, she probably drowned. If she bled out, he could tell by the amount of blood left in her body. If she drowned, there would be water in her lungs."

"That's enough, dear. Let's not talk about it anymore." Delores took another sip of her coffee. "Will you let me know when you find out?"

"What makes you think I'm going to find out?"

Delores looked shocked. "Well, you're going to investigate, aren't you? You simply have to, Hannah!"

"Why do I have to, Mother?"

"Because we all have to work to catch Ronni's killer before my launch party!"

I should have known it had something to do with you, Hannah thought, but she remained silent. Verbalizing that sentiment would only hurt her mother's feelings. The book launch party, the very first for Delores, was an important event in her mother's life. "Okay, Mother," Hannah said instead. "I'll do my best to catch Ronni's killer. But I don't really understand how it could possibly hurt your party if the case is still open."

"Use your head, dear. Everybody will be talking about Ronni's murder and how the killer hasn't been caught yet. And no one will pay the least bit of attention to my book!"

So it was competition for the limelight. Now Hannah understood. Everyone should be focused on Delores's book and nothing else. She was about to say that people were coming because they liked Delores and wanted to read her book, but her mother had a point. Everyone would be speculating about Ronni if her killer hadn't been apprehended.

"You see what I mean, don't you, dear?"

"I do, but don't worry, Mother. I'll catch him long before then."

"You're certain you can?"

"Absolutely." Hannah crossed her fingers and hoped her

words would be prophetic. She now had triple incentives to solve the case. She wanted to prove that she could do it alone in her own way, she wanted to catch the person who'd dumped her beautiful cream puffs on the floor of the gazebo, and her mother was depending on her to do it. "Nothing's going to spoil your party, Mother. You have my word on that."

Delores gave a relieved smile. "Thank you, dear. I certainly feel better now. You're very good at investigating. I've said so to everyone I know. Is there anything Carrie and I can do to help?"

"Yes. You can help a lot if you're willing to make some phone calls for me."

"Of course we are! Just tell us what to do. But before you do, give me another one of those cookies. I'm not sure if it's the cookie or the frosting, but they're addictive."

Hannah got up, plucked a cookie off the counter, and carried it to her mother. She couldn't remember the last time Delores had eaten three cookies in one sitting, and that meant Terry's Carrot Cake Cookies were an unqualified hit. Then she cleared her throat, trying to think of a polite way of saying it. "You've probably heard that Ronni was flirting with various men around town."

"Much more than flirting, the way I hear it, dear. Say *involved*. It's a much better word. And do stop trying to spare my sensibilities. I know what Ronni was."

"You do?" Hannah still wasn't sure her mother actually knew what was going on.

"Of course I do! I wasn't born yesterday, you know. And here's one you don't know, dear. Did you know that Mayor Bascomb is putting in that indoor swimming pool and hot tub that Stephanie always wanted?"

"No. I had no idea. That must be terribly expensive."

"Oh, it is." Delores took another sip of her coffee in preparation for delivering her punch line. "But it's not as expensive as divorce."

"I didn't know that!"

"I know, dear. I have my ear to the pulse of Lake Eden. Now what, exactly, do you want Carrie and me to troll for."

Hannah laughed. She couldn't help it. Her father had been an avid fisherman and Delores was using fishing terms again. "I want you to troll for trouble. Find out who Ronni was flirting . . ."

"Involved," Delores interrupted her.

"Right. Find out who Ronni was involved with and how it affects or affected their lives. I don't need dates, or times of . . . assignations, or anything like that. I just need to know who might have wanted to . . ."

"*Put a period to Ronni's existence,*" Delores interrupted to finish the sentence for her in Regency romance phrasing.

"Anybody who might have wanted her dead for *any* reason. If you hear something that's not about . . . uh . . ."

"Sex, dear. Say sex. It's the word you want. Let's not equivocate here."

"Okay, Mother. If you hear something that's not about sex, that might be important, too."

"What's not about sex?"

"Mother!"

"I'm sorry, dear, but you're beating around the bush. Say what you mean. And before we go any further, I have to tell you something I heard from a very good source."

"What's that, Mother?"

"Mike. I heard that he was involved with Ronni. He's a *bounder*, dear. He's always going to have a roving eye. I know he's handsome, and I know he's appealing, but he's never going to be true to you. Norman will. He's a much better bet for a husband."

Hannah just blinked. Delores had never been so frank with her before, and she wasn't quite sure what to say.

"I realize that I'm overstepping my bounds here," her mother went on. "I do it all the time, and I can't seem to stop, especially with you. I used to be able to control it much better when I had a love life of my own, but now that Winthrop's gone, there's no one to diffuse my concern. And . . . I think I may have a control issue."

Hannah's mind went on red alert. *A control issue? Overstepping her bounds?* That wasn't her mother's usual terminology. Either she was seeking professional psychiatric help, or . . . "Are you listening to Doctor Love on KCOW talk radio?"

"Yes, dear. But how did you know . . ."

"Did you ever call in?"

"No, of course not. I'm not the type to do something like that."

Hannah relaxed slightly. Delores would never take the chance that someone might recognize her voice on the air. "Did you read, *Love Is Right Around the Corner*?"

"Pop psychology," Delores dismissed Doctor Love's newest book, the one she plugged on every show.

"But you read it."

"Well, yes. But how did you . . . ?"

"Control issue," Hannah said, before her mother could finish the question. "That's Doctor Love's favorite diagnosis. She also likes to talk about overstepping bounds, and diffusing concern."

"But Doctor Love is right. I *do* have a control issue, especially when I try to run your life. If I'm not careful, you're going to hate me for it."

Hannah shook her head and said what was in her heart. "I couldn't hate you, Mother. I love you too much."

"Oh!"

Delores looked as if she was about to break into tears, and Hannah knew that would embarrass them both. As a family, they'd always kept their emotions under control and private. "Okay, let's get back to business, here," Hannah changed the subject quickly. "You're going to help me catch Ronni's killer . . . right?"

"Right." Her voice quavered a bit, but Delores took a deep breath and managed to pull herself together. "You said you want Carrie and me to find out who Ronni was involved with and how it affects or affected their lives."

"Exactly right."

"We'll do that, dear. Anything else?"

"Just be alert for anyone who hated Ronni enough to kill her. You uncover the motive. I'll check it out and see if there's an alibi."

"We're all set, dear." Delores got up and walked around the stainless steel island to give her eldest daughter a hug. "I'm proud of you, Hannah. And I love you very much. I know I don't tell you that enough."

"Thank you, Mother. Was that Doctor Love?"

"Yes. Most of the time she's full of hot air, but that's some of her very best advice."

TERRY'S CARROT CAKE COOKIES

DO NOT preheat oven yet—this
cookie dough has to chill for at least
2 hours before baking.

1 cup butter *(2 sticks, ½ pound)* at room temperature

2 cups white *(granulated)* sugar

3 eggs, beaten *(just whip them up in a glass with a fork)*

1 cup unsweetened applesauce

2 teaspoons pure vanilla extract

1 teaspoon baking soda

1 teaspoon baking powder

4 teaspoons cinnamon

½ teaspoon freshly grated nutmeg

1 teaspoon salt

20-ounce can crushed pineapple *(very well drained)*

1 cup golden raisins

1 cup chopped walnuts *(measure after chopping)*

3½ cups flour *(pack it down in the cup when you measure it)*

1 cup coconut *(chopped a little finer than it comes out of the bag)*

3 cups finely grated carrots

Terry's tips for her recipe:
1. When she drains her crushed pineapple, Terry uses a wire mesh sieve and presses the pineapple against the mesh to remove as much liquid as possible.

2. When she's in a hurry and doesn't want to grate her own carrots, Terry buys shredded carrots and then chops them up a bit finer in her food processor with the steel blade, or with a chef's knife on a cutting board.

3. Terry says she uses a medium cookie scoop (approximately 2 Tablespoons) and puts 12 cookies to a sheet. She always uses parchment paper instead of a bare cookie sheet. She rinses her cookie scoop after every 4 or 5 cookies so the dough won't stick to the scoop.

Hannah's Note: These are a lot easier to mix if you use an electric mixer. You can also do them by hand, but it does take some muscle.

Beat the butter, sugar, and eggs together until all three ingredients are thoroughly incorporated and the mixture is smooth, fluffy, and light yellow in color.

Make sure your applesauce is well drained. You don't really want to add liquid here. *(I pat off any excess liquid with a paper towel before I add it to my bowl.)* Add the applesauce to your bowl and mix in thoroughly.

Mix in the vanilla extract.

Blend in the baking soda, baking powder, cinnamon, nutmeg, and salt. Mix it well, until the dough is smooth and is a uniform color.

Mix in the pineapple, golden raisins, and walnuts.

Blend in the flour, about a rounded cupful at a time. You don't have to be exact—the point is to add the flour in three parts so that you don't try to mix it all in at once. If you add the whole 3½ cups at once and then try to beat it, it'll spill out all over your counter and floor! *(The next time you come into The Cookie Jar, you can ask me how I know this.)*

Remove the bowl from your mixer. You'll have to do this next part by hand. Coconut and shredded carrots tend to bunch up inside your beaters and will cause a real mess. *(You can ask me how I know this, too!)*

Stir in the coconut. When it's incorporated, stir in the shredded carrots. Mix well to make sure everything is blended.

When the dough is all mixed, it will be thick and rather sticky, much like very thick cake batter. That's why you have to chill it. It would be impossible to work with without "hardening" it in the refrigerator.

Cover the dough with plastic wrap, and chill it in the refrigerator for at least 2 hours. *(Overnight is fine, too.)*

When you're ready to bake, preheat the oven to 350 degrees F., rack in the middle position.

Prepare your cookie sheets by lining them with parchment paper *(the best method for this cookie)* or spraying them with Pam or another nonstick cooking spray.

Use two spoons to drop the dough onto the cookie sheet, 12 cookies to a standard-size cookie sheet. Each cookie should contain about 2 Tablespoons of dough.

Wet your fingers and shape the dough into rounds if needed. This won't make them taste any different, but they'll look more uniform.

Bake at 350 degrees F. for 12 minutes. Leave the cookies on the cookie sheet for a minute, and then remove them to wire racks to cool. When they've cooled, frost them with Terry's Cream Cheese Frosting.

Yield: approximately 10 dozen yummy cookies

TERRY'S CREAM CHEESE FROSTING

8 ounces cream cheese at room temperature
1 stick *(½ cup, ¼ pound)* butter at room temperature
2 teaspoons pure vanilla extract
1-pound box of confectioner's *(powdered)* sugar *(3 ½ to 4 cups)*

Mix the cream cheese and butter together until they're smooth and blended to a uniform color.

Mix in the vanilla.

Blend in confectioner's sugar in one-cup increments until the resulting frosting is smooth and creamy.

Hannah's Note: This frosting is a win-win proposition. If it turns out to be too thick to spread, mix in a few drops of milk or cream to thin it. If it turns out to be too thin, mix in a little more confectioner's sugar to thicken it.

Chapter Thirteen

"Yes, I did find her. And yes, she was in the Jacuzzi." Hannah poured more coffee for a table of women who'd come in for the express purpose of getting more information from her. "I really can't tell you any details. The sheriff's department is investigating her death, and they should be circulating an official press release very soon."

"Hannah?" Lisa motioned her over to the counter.

Hannah made her apologies to the table of ladies and hurried to her partner's side. "What is it?"

"More cookies. We only have a dozen left, and that's with the new prices."

"New prices?"

Lisa nodded. "You told me to handle the financial end of things, and that's what I'm doing. We're going to make a good profit today."

"That's the only thing I ever felt like thanking Ronni for," Hannah said, frowning slightly.

"I feel exactly the same way. Anyway . . . do we have any more cookies left in the freezer?"

"I don't think so, but I'll go look. If we don't, do you want me to bake some?"

"Yes, if you can think of something quick."

"How about some Boggles?"

"They should work, since the dough doesn't have to chill."

Lisa glanced at the clock. "It's almost time for the lull between lunch cookies and afternoon cookies, but I don't think
it'll be much of a break today. Everybody's coming in to see
you. They'll wait if I promise them fresh cookies and your
firsthand account of finding Ronni."

"But I can't give them very much information. About all I
can tell them is that she was dead in the hot tub."

"You don't have to give them details of the crime scene.
Just tell them about your reaction when you found her."

"My reaction?"

"You know. Say something like this . . . *I was all ready to
climb into the water when I realized that there was something in the Jacuzzi. But nobody else was there except Andrea, and she was still exercising. I had a really strange
feeling, the kind you get when you think something is wrong.
My heart was pounding like a trip hammer, and . . .*"

"Hold it," Hannah interrupted her. "What's a trip hammer?"

"I don't know, but that's what they always say. Anyway . . .
*My heart was pounding like a trip hammer, and my palms
were damp, but I just had to move closer. One step and then
another, and I stared down into the bubbling water to see
what it was.*"

"That's good," Hannah said, giving her a smile. "What's
next?"

"Let's see. You could say, *I caught sight of it almost immediately. It was red and black, and that's when I realized it
could be . . .*" Lisa stopped and frowned. "No, make that,
*and that's when I realized it had to be one of the exercise out-
fits the female staff wore. But what was it doing in the Jacuzzi?
Was one of the instructors using the hot tub as a washing machine? Had someone accidentally dropped it there as they
passed by on their way home? Or had someone tossed it in
there deliberately to play a prank on an instructor?*"

"That'll have them sitting on the edges of their chairs,"
Hannah complimented her partner. "What next?"

"*I still felt that prickling sensation. As a matter of fact, it was getting stronger. But I just had to find out what was going on, so I stepped right up to the rim of the tub and grabbed it to haul it out.* Now this is when you pause for a minute to build up the suspense. And then you say, *I came very close to screaming when my hand encountered something I wasn't expecting, something that had once been living, and breathing, and teaching classes at Heavenly Bodies. And even though I didn't really want to, I grabbed that someone, whoever she was, and rolled her over. One look at her still beautiful but lifeless face, and I realized it was my very own fitness instructor, Ronni Ward!*"

Hannah just stared at Lisa for a long moment. And then she asked, "Have you been reading a lot of murder mysteries lately?"

"Well . . . actually, I have. Marge drops them off from the library. When Herb works late, I read. It keeps my mind off missing him."

"Well, you ought to try writing one. You're pretty good. I have only one suggestion to give you."

"What's that?"

"You tell that story for me. You're much better at it than I am. Just say I'm in the kitchen baking, but I told you everything, and I said it was okay for you to repeat it."

Lisa began to smile. "I can do that. It'll be fun for me, and besides, it'll give you a break to bake and think about the case. If you take it, that is. You *are* going to take it, aren't you?"

"Absolutely. I don't want the killer to get away with something like this!"

"You're right, Hannah. Murder is awful."

"Oh, it's not murder that's the problem." Hannah gave a little grin to show Lisa that she was kidding. "Whoever killed Ronni smashed my cream puffs. And to add insult to injury, since I'm on a diet for Mother's book launch party, I didn't even get the chance to taste one!"

* * *

Hannah had just finished mixing up the dough for the Boggles when there was a knock on the back door. She hurried to answer it, assuming it was Norman, but instead came face-to-face with her very agitated sister.

"Andrea. Come in." Hannah took her sister's coat, hung it on the pegs by the back door, and led her to a stool at the workstation. "You're shaking. Don't tell me there's been another murder!"

"No, but it's almost as bad as that. I need to calm down, Hannah. Do you have any chocolate?"

"You've come to the house of endorphins, the source of the Dark Chocolate River, the heart of the Milk Chocolate Valley, and the foothills of the White Chocolate Mountains." Andrea gave a wan smile, acknowledging the attempt at humor, but Hannah noticed that her sister was still shaking. "Hold on a second. I'll get you chocolate you'll never forget."

Two minutes later, four Brownies Plus from a catering order and a full mug of coffee sat in front of Andrea. Three minutes later, only two Brownies Plus remained. Another minute and a half, and Andrea was wiping her face and sipping her coffee. That was when Hannah figured it was time to speak. "So tell me what's wrong," she said.

"Everything. Remember Shawna Lee?"

"How could I forget?" Hannah gave a deep sigh. Shawna Lee was the last woman who had trifled with Mike's affections. Or perhaps Mike was the trifler and Shawna Lee was the triflee. Then again, both of them could have been triflers . . . or triflees. Hannah just wasn't sure.

"Well, it's Shawna Lee all over again!" Andrea pronounced.

"Because of Mike? I already know Bill took him off the case."

"That's part of it, but it's even worse than that. It's Section Fourteen, Article Six of the Winnetka County Sheriff's official rulebook. A detective must be excused from duty or reassigned at the sheriff's discretion in the case of personal involvement with the victim. When Shawna Lee was murdered, Bill had to take two detectives off the case."

"I know that."

"Well, this time Bill had to take off *three* detectives!"

"Three detectives were personally involved with Ronni?"

"Yes. And that includes Lonnie."

"Uh-oh," Hannah breathed. "Michelle's going to be livid."

"That's what I thought. I called her to break it to her gently, but she already knew because Lonnie called her just as soon as it happened. She's going to take a midterm early and catch the bus this afternoon. It'll get in at the Quick Stop at five forty-five tonight."

"Uh-oh. We'd better meet her and check for weapons. She probably wants to grind Lonnie into little pieces and use him for hamburger."

"Wrong."

"Wrong?" Hannah stared hard at her sister.

"She told me they were testing their relationship by dating other people."

Hannah shook her head. "You're kidding!"

"No, I'm not. Remember at Lisa and Herb's family reunion when Michelle told us she wanted to be free to date some professor of hers if he asked?"

"I remember."

"Well, she must have worked that out with Lonnie. At least he felt free enough to take Ronni dancing last Saturday night. And before you say it, I know he's at least five years younger than she is . . . I mean five years younger than she *was*."

"This isn't good," Hannah said, covering her face with her hands. She sat there for a moment, taking it all in, and then she dropped her hands. "So what's Michelle's attitude about all this?"

"It was hard to tell. She was hurt. I could hear that in her voice. But she was the one who said they should try dating other people. I really don't think she expected Lonnie to go out with anybody."

"That figures. I wouldn't expect him to go out with anyone, either. I know he loves Michelle. But I suppose she told him she was going to do it, so he felt he had to follow suit. It was probably a case of male pride. Is Michelle going to stay with Mother?"

"I don't think that's a good idea. Mother's really busy with her business. She told me that the Christmas rush for antiques is already starting at Granny's Attic, and she's got all sorts of things to do before her book launch party. She feels she won't be able to give Michelle the attention she needs, and she told me that she's not very good at dealing with problems when it comes to affairs of the heart."

"Affairs of the heart? Is that what Mother said?"

"Yes. I thought it was a nice way of putting it."

"Doctor Love," Hannah said.

"On KCOW Radio?"

"Yes," Hannah affirmed it, and then she got back to the subject at hand. "Michelle is welcome to stay with me."

"I think that would be best. Bill loves Michelle, but there's going to be a procedural problem since Lonnie's a murder suspect."

"What?!"

"Lonnie admits he went out to Heavenly Bodies after he finished his shift at ten. He wanted to tell Ronni he had to cancel the date they'd made for the movies on Friday night. He told Bill he was only there for twenty minutes or so, but there was something wrong with the security system, and the cameras didn't record him leaving. He also admitted to Bill that they exchanged angry words about something personal."

There was that word *personal* again. Whenever people didn't want to talk about something, they used that word. It was usually an evasion, an excuse to hide some fact they didn't want anyone to know. Perhaps Lonnie did have something to hide, but somehow Hannah doubted it.

"Anyway," Andrea continued, "I came here to tell you that Bill's also excused himself from the case."

Hannah's mouth dropped open and she clicked it shut again. "But what's going to happen if all the top detectives are off the case?"

"He's got two guys who just passed the detective exam, but they've never worked an actual case before. Bill figures they can do some of the legwork, but he needs someone to direct the investigation. He's calling in Stella Parks from the Cities to take Mike's place temporarily. She's coming in tonight."

"Who's Stella Parks?"

"She heads up the detective division that Mike used to run in Minneapolis. He worked with her and recommended her for the job when he left. Bill met her when he went to that law enforcement conference in Miami. He says she's tough as nails, brave as a lion, and she has a mind like a steel trap."

"That's three clichés in a row. Does she deserve them?"

"I think so. Bill talked about her, and I got the impression that she's a real force, if you know what I mean."

Hannah knew exactly what her sister meant. If Detective Parks was that tough, she might be able to handle the case. She'd check with Mike to find out more about her. But Stella Parks wasn't the issue, now. Her main concern was Andrea and how she felt about Bill's excusing himself from the case.

"So are you upset about Bill?" Hannah asked, wondering if she should duck just in case Andrea threw something.

"Of course I am, especially since he doesn't have an alibi."

"He wasn't home with you?"

"He was home, but not until almost three in the morning. He told me that he was driving around checking on a backlog of skip traces. You know what skip traces are, don't you?"

"I think so. People who have a court date but don't show up?"

"That's right. A couple of bail bond companies contract

with the sheriff's department to locate the skip traces and bring them in. The department gets paid for every skip trace they apprehend, and that gives them extra revenue. They use the skip trace money for additional overtime, and personal equipment, and things like that."

"Did Bill find any skip traces?"

"No, and that's the problem. Nobody was home. And that means he doesn't have an alibi."

"But not having an alibi doesn't necessarily mean that you're a suspect."

"That's true."

"You need a motive to be a suspect. I mean, somebody would have had to see Bill with her in a compromising situation before . . ." Hannah stopped abruptly as tears welled up in Andrea's eyes. "No!"

"Yes. Bill says it was nothing, that they walked out of Heavenly Bodies together about a week ago. The wind was blowing, and Ronni got something in her eye when he was walking her to her car. Bill leaned over her to see if he could tell what it was. He didn't even think about how it would look to anyone passing by, but someone saw them and drew the wrong conclusion."

Hannah got up and gave her sister a big hug. "It's okay, Andrea. I'm sure it happened exactly the way Bill said it did."

"So am I but I wouldn't put it past Ronni to do something like that deliberately to cause trouble between Bill and me. That's why I want you to solve the case fast and prove that my Bill had nothing to do with it."

Chapter Fourteen

"Espionage is thirsty work," Norman said, as Hannah opened the back door at The Cookie Jar.

"I've got coffee."

"Coffee's good." Norman stepped inside the kitchen and gave her a hug.

It felt so good to be in Norman's arms that Hannah just stayed there for a long moment. She felt safe and secure, and very loved. She also wondered whether she felt thinner to him. Of course it had only been a couple of days and a weight loss that Norman could notice by just hugging her was unlikely. Not only that, it didn't really matter. She didn't have to lose weight to attract Norman. He loved her just the way she was.

"That was nice," Norman said, smiling down at her as she stepped back, out of their embrace.

"Yes, it was." Hannah gave him an answering smile. "Have a seat and I'll pour some coffee for you."

"Hi, Andrea," Norman greeted her as he took the adjoining stool.

"Hi, Norman. What's all this about espionage?"

"Oh, um . . ." Norman glanced at Hannah for help.

"You can tell her. Andrea's going to be helping us investigate. So is Michelle. She'll be coming in on the bus around six, and she's staying in my guest room."

"I'll pick her up and bring her out to your condo. How about Chinese? We can stop for that on the way. And after we eat, we can discuss the case."

"Sounds good." Hannah turned to Andrea. "Can you join us?"

"Sure. Bill has to stay late to meet Detective Parks and hand over the paperwork. Now what's all this about espionage?"

"I'm delivering messages from Mike to Hannah about how to work the case. He had to promise not to contact her, not even by phone."

"Bill told me about that." Andrea turned to Hannah with a frown. "And you're letting Mike tell you what to do?"

"Of course not, but I'm not discounting his advice out of hand. He's a trained professional, and he might come up with something that would help us catch the killer."

Andrea glanced at Norman. "How do you feel about delivering these messages from Mike?"

"It's a little strange. I write them down so I get them right. I don't want to put my own spin on something Mike wants me to say to Hannah."

"Good idea. I'll do that, too."

"You're going to write down Mike's messages?" Hannah asked, thoroughly confused.

"No, I'm going to write down *Bill's* messages. I'm supposed to be a go-between, too. Bill can't ask you for help directly. That would be undermining the official investigation. I'm supposed to tell you what he says about solving Ronni's murder."

"So I'm expected to be a marionette detective with Bill and Mike pulling the strings?"

There was silence for a moment, and then Andrea spoke. "I think that's what Bill wants," she said.

"And I think that's what Mike wants," Norman concurred.

"Well then, I guess it's a good thing they can't even call me on the phone."

"Why's that?" Andrea asked her.

"Because I won't have to waste time hanging up on both of them!"

"Something smells good," Lisa pushed through the swinging door that separated the coffee shop from the kitchen.

"That must be the batch of Candy Bar Bar Cookies I have in the oven. I'm glad you brought in that recipe, Lisa. They're really good."

"I know. I got it from my Aunt Lois Meister. She spends every Saturday baking with her best friend, Marcia, and they come up with some real winners."

"Well, let me know if you get any more from them." Hannah glanced at the kitchen clock and frowned. "It's only three thirty, and it's awfully quiet out there."

"That's because we're closed."

"You closed early?"

"I had to. We ran completely out of cookies."

"But we baked extra cookies. There were two batches of Terry's Carrot Cake Cookies and three double batches of Boggles."

"And every cookie sold." Lisa gave Hannah a proud smile. "We made more profit today than we usually make in a week."

"Then that means we can take the rest of the week off," Hannah said and waited for Lisa's reaction. When it came, it was worth the wait. Lisa looked absolutely horrified by Hannah's disregard for their work ethic.

"Just kidding," Hannah was quick to reassure her. "Do you think tomorrow's going to be busy?"

"It won't be quite as busy as today, but it'll be busier than usual, especially if you let me tell another story that's straight from your mouth to mine."

It seemed that Lisa had discovered a second career, and Hannah wasn't about to thwart her. "Okay. I told you everything I know. You come up with something tonight and call me before I leave for the gym in the morning. As long as it's not an outright lie or something the sheriff's department asked me to keep quiet, you're welcome to tell it to everybody who comes in the door."

Evening came early in November. At five thirty on the dot, Hannah flicked off the lights on her cookie truck, locked the doors behind her, and hurried up the stairs to her condo, eager for warmth and light. She inserted her key in the lock, dropped her purse to the floor, and held out her arms as she pushed the door open.

She was not disappointed. An orange-and-white furry ball hurtled into her arms, sending her back two steps. It might have knocked her over if she hadn't been standing with her feet braced apart, but Hannah was well acquainted with Moishe's coming-home ritual. She picked up her purse, carried him inside, and placed him in his favorite position on the back of the couch.

"So you're glad to see me tonight?" she asked him.

"Rowww!"

"And it's not just because you know I'm going to give you one of your favorite treats?"

"Rowww!"

She laughed and scratched him under the chin. Hannah loved the way Moishe answered every question she asked him. She'd counted once, just to see how long he would keep it up. His record was almost forty answers to her questions. "Hold on a second. I'll get something for you."

Hannah headed to the kitchen to fetch the round canister of fish-shaped, salmon-flavored kitty treats. Once Moishe was munching on one and another two sat on the edge of the couch in easy paw reach, Hannah hung up her parka, switched on a few more lights, kicked off her shoes, and carried them back to her bedroom to change into something more comfortable.

It didn't take long to slip into gray sweatpants and a green sweatshirt. She pulled on fleece-lined moccasins and padded back to the kitchen. She had just enough time to feed Moishe, bake another batch of Candy Bar Bar Cookies in her home oven for dessert, and set the round table in the living room with plates, glasses, silverware, and napkins for her sisters and Norman.

"You ate all your food again?" Hannah stared at Moishe's Kitty Valet in disbelief. There was plenty of water left, but the food was all gone. She turned to watch her gluttonous *gato* as he strolled into the kitchen, but he didn't seem appreciably larger, his stomach wasn't distended, and he didn't look uncomfortable. How could he chow down on twelve cups of kitty crunchies and look perfectly normal?

"Not now," Hannah said, coming to a decision out loud. She just wasn't going to worry about her feline food lover tonight. She'd refill Moishe's Kitty Valet, bake the dessert she planned to serve to her company, and settle down on the couch with something to drink until her guests arrived.

By six fifteen, the bar cookies were in the oven and she was sitting on the couch, her feet tucked up under her, sipping a cup of coffee. If she'd been a drinker, it would have been a double Scotch on the rocks. If she hadn't been on a diet, it would have been hot chocolate. As it was, coffee was the only noncaloric hot beverage she could think of to drink . . . unless she wanted to count tea. And she didn't.

Moishe hopped onto the seat of the couch and snuggled up against her legs. Hannah reached out to pet him and sighed in contentment. It was good to be home. It had been a very long day, starting with the gruesome discovery of Ronni's body in the Jacuzzi and ending with the heavier than usual preparations for tomorrow's baking.

A cat's purr was soporific. Hannah had heard that before, and it was true. She yawned widely, closed her eyes, and stroked Moishe's soft fur. In a moment she was asleep, dreaming of walks in the North Woods with her great-grandmother, the deer they'd seen leaping in the distance, the birds flitting from branch to branch, beeping cheerily. Beeping? Birds didn't beep!

"The oven!" Hannah exclaimed, getting up so swiftly she dislodged Moishe. She must have fallen asleep, and her oven timer was beeping. She rushed to the kitchen, opened the oven door, and gave a sigh of relief as she pulled her pan of Candy Bar Bar Cookies out of the oven. They weren't too brown on top. Everything was just fine.

She'd just replaced her oven mitts on the hook next to the stove when the doorbell rang. A glance at the apple-shaped clock on the wall over the kitchen table showed six forty-five. It was a good thing she'd set the table earlier. Company was here, and she'd gotten up from her nap just in time!

CANDY BAR BAR COOKIES

Preheat oven to 350 degrees F., rack
in the middle position.

1 cup softened butter *(2 sticks, ½ pound)*
¾ cup white *(granulated)* sugar
1 beaten egg *(just whip it up in a glass with a fork)*
2 teaspoons vanilla extract
½ teaspoon salt
2½ cups flour *(pack it down in the cup when you measure it)*
5 three-ounce chocolate candy bars *(I used Nestle Milk Chocolate)* * * *

¼ cup white *(granulated)* sugar

* * * Lisa says that when her Aunt Lois and Marcia make these, they use three 7-ounce (or 8-ounce if you can't find 7-ounce) Hershey's chocolate bars. They say to tell you that the 8-ounce bars are a tight fit, but you can do it.

Prepare a 9-inch by 13-inch cake pan by lining it with a piece of foil large enough to flap over the sides. Spray the foil-lined pan with Pam or other nonstick cooking spray.

Mix the butter and the sugar together in a bowl. Continue to stir until the mixture is light and creamy.

Add the egg, and stir it in thoroughly. Mix in the vanilla extract and the salt.

Add the flour in half-cup increments, mixing after each addition. The dough will "ball up" like piecrust, and that's fine.

Pat half of the dough into the bottom of your prepared pan. Smooth it out with your impeccably clean fingers.

Unwrap the candy bars and place them on top of the dough. *(Make 2 rows with 2 candy bars in each row. Break the fifth candy bar in half lengthwise, and use it to fill in the ends of the rows.)*

Pat the remaining dough on top of the candy bars, distributing it as evenly as you can.

Use the back of a table fork to make cross-hatches on the top of the dough, the way you'd do with a peanut butter cookie. The little grooves the fork makes will hold the sugar.

Sprinkle the quarter-cup sugar over the top of your pan as evenly as possible.

Bake at 350 degrees F. for 25 minutes. The bars should be slightly brown around the edges and still quite white on top.

Cool the Candy Bar Bar Cookies in the pan on a metal rack. Feel the bottom of the pan. When you can comfortably place your hand against the bottom and it's not too hot to hold, grasp the foil and lift the bars out of the pan. Cut them into brownie-sized pieces while they're still warm.

Place the squares on a plate and serve. Everyone will love these a bit warm from the oven, but they'll also love them cold.

Chapter Fifteen

She made the attempt, but after ten minutes of hoping that it might get better, Hannah put down her chopsticks. Chinese chicken salad with low-cal ranch dressing just wasn't very good. She should have made her own with raspberry vinegar, a little olive oil, and a good sugar substitute. To disguise the fact that she wasn't eating, she alternated between moving bean sprouts around on her plate and taking notes in the brand-new shorthand notebook she'd started for Ronni's murder.

"What's wrong with Moishe?" Andrea asked as Moishe gave a howl from the kitchen.

"I don't know. I filled his Kitty Valet when I got home, so I know he's got plenty of food and water."

"Rowwwww!" Another yowl hit their ears, louder and more prolonged than the first.

"Something's bothering him," Norman said, getting up from his seat on the couch. "He sounded really upset. I'll go see what's wrong."

Michelle leaned close to Hannah. "Norman loves him," she said.

"Norman loves *Hannah*," Andrea said, correcting their younger sister.

"Where's the yardstick, Hannah?" Norman called out, poking his head around the corner of the kitchen doorway.

"It's either next to the stove, or leaning up against the side of the counter by the window," Hannah told him. "Did Moishe lose his duck's foot again?"

"Yes. It's in that little space between the broom closet and the refrigerator."

"Good luck fishing it out. Sometimes it goes under the refrigerator and I lose it."

"I'll get it. Never fear. Moishe's directing the whole operation for me."

All three sisters laughed. And all three were tempted to get up and go into the kitchen to watch. But they didn't. They just sat there relaxing while Norman took care of the duck's foot.

"If it slips under the refrigerator, do you have to move it to get out the duck's foot?" Michelle asked.

"Yes, and I don't. There's a really short tube running to the icemaker and if it breaks, it's a big plumbing bill. I just leave the duck's foot there and hope for the best."

"But doesn't it smell?" Andrea wrinkled up her nose.

"No. I think maybe it's because there's not much meat on a duck's foot."

"Has Moishe lost more than one under there?" Michelle asked.

"Oh, yes. He gets one every time I have takeout Chinese food and that's a couple of times a month. There must be at least a dozen under there, maybe more."

"Success," Norman reported, coming back into the living room holding a slightly grungier duck's foot. "You've got a loose board back there, Hannah."

"Okay. I'll have someone take care of it."

"I can help you with it one of these days," Norman offered, handing her the duck's foot. "I rinsed off the foot and dried it on a paper towel."

"Thanks," Hannah told him, accepting the webbed prize. "Here you go, Moishe." She turned to her cat and wiggled the duck's foot for him to see. "Follow the flying foot!"

The moment the avian appendage left Hannah's hand,

Moishe was off and running down the hall to chase it. There was a thump as he pounced and then a smothered yowl of triumph as he chomped down on it.

"Back to business," Hannah said, waiting until Norman had resumed his seat. "So what's Lonnie's problem, Michelle? I'm assuming he doesn't have an alibi."

"That's right. He told me he went out to Heavenly Bodies after his shift to cancel their movie date. Her birthday party had already started, and she was drinking."

"Drinking?" Norman asked, picking up on the part of the story that Hannah was about to query.

"Yes, from a martini glass. Lonnie said it was a Green-teani. They carry diet green tea in the Snack Shack. You mix it with vodka and serve it over ice in a martini glass."

"But there's no alcohol allowed on the premises," Andrea said. "It's in the rules. Is Lonnie sure she had vodka?"

"That's what he said. And he also said he was pretty sure it wasn't her first Green-teani of the night."

"She shouldn't have brought in vodka." Andrea still sounded shocked. "I'm sure that's grounds for dismissal and . . ."

"Never mind that now," Hannah told her. "The important thing is that she was drinking and Lonnie was there." She turned to Michelle. "What did he say happened next?"

"They moved the party to the gazebo, and Lonnie went along. That's where he told her he needed to cancel their date for Friday night. And she said, 'Oh, do you have to work a late shift?' Lonnie didn't want to lie to her, so he told her that he just didn't feel right going out with another woman when he was in love with me."

"What did she say to that?" Norman asked.

"Plenty, but Lonnie didn't go into details. He just said that she insulted me and he said something back, and then she said something back, and before he knew it they were shout-ing at each other. He knew he had to leave, but he was so mad, he knocked over a couple of stools on his way out of there."

Hannah thought back to the crime scene. The stools had been made from anodized aluminum, and they had a smooth mirrored surface. "So the crime scene techs might find his fingerprints on the stools?" she guessed.

"That's right. That's why he needs you to catch the killer. Since the camera wasn't working and nobody actually saw him leave, it's the only way to prove he didn't hide out somewhere and kill Ronni when everyone else left. He's in big trouble, Hannah. He told me what he wants me to do, and I promised him I'd help."

Hannah nodded. She could understand that. But then a terrible suspicion dawned. "Wait. Don't tell me Lonnie wants to tell me how to run the investigation."

"Well . . . not exactly. He just wants to make suggestions. He says that Bill is taking a hands-off position." Michelle turned to Andrea. "Is that right?"

"That's right. As Ronni's employer, Bill feels he's a little too close to the situation to be entirely impartial."

Hannah turned to stare at Andrea in awe. It seemed that her sister doubled as a spin doctor. Andrea had spun Bill's departure from the case in the best possible light.

"Anyway," Michelle went on, turning to face Hannah. "With Mike and Rick off the case, Lonnie says there's nobody left who's ever run a murder investigation before. That's why Lonnie wants to give me suggestions for you. Since he can't take an active part in the investigation, he can't talk to you directly. He wants me to be his courier and tell you what he says."

"Wonderful!" Hannah's tone was sarcastic. "That makes three people who want me to be their puppet investigator. Doesn't anyone think I'm capable of catching the killer on my own?"

Norman moved closer and slipped his arm around Hannah's shoulder to give her a little hug. "I do. And look on the bright side. Only three people from the sheriff's department want to give you advice."

"You're right." Hannah gave a little smile. "I suppose it could have been four."

"Uh . . . actually . . ." Michelle stopped speaking and sighed. She couldn't quite meet her sister's eyes when she continued. "Actually, it's four. Lonnie's brother Rick is in on it, too."

When the phone rang at the witching hour, Hannah wanted to ignore it. She did her best to pretend that absolutely nothing was amiss. She rolled over, pulled the blankets up to her chin, and attempted to go back to sleep. But of course she couldn't. She wasn't the type of person who could ignore a ringing phone at midnight.

She picked up the phone, held it to her ear, and answered it in a voice groggy with sleep. " 'Lo."

"Hannah. Wake up, Hannah. I've got to see you, and this is the only safe time. Meet me in your garage by the Dumpster in fifteen minutes."

"What?"

"It's Mike. Wake up! Meet me by your garage Dumpster in fifteen minutes. It's important."

The curtains of sleep began to part and Hannah sat up in bed. "Mike?"

"Yeah. I've got to get off the line now. They could be tracing your calls."

Hannah clicked on the lamp on her bed table. Tracing her calls? Surely not! The isolation from his colleagues must be taking its toll in the guise of paranoia.

There was no way she was going to get dressed to go out at midnight, spend five minutes telling Mike that he was crazy, and then come back upstairs to undress and go back to bed again. She slipped on her robe, the warmest one she owned, and thrust her bare feet into her fleece-lined moccasins.

Her parka was next. Hannah zipped it up to her chin and pulled a wool ski cap over her ears. At least she'd be warm enough. She was just debating the wisdom of brewing a pot of coffee in the eleven minutes she had left when she heard a soft voice at her elbow.

"What is it, Hannah?"

For a moment, Hannah was startled. Then she remembered that Michelle was staying with her. She flicked on the lights and apologized. "I'm sorry if the phone woke you. Everything's okay. You can go back to bed."

"But what *is* it?"

"Mike. He wants me to meet him in the garage."

Michelle stared at Hannah for a moment. Then she giggled.

"What?"

"I guess the bloom's off the rose if you're going out to meet Mike like that."

Hannah glanced at her reflection in the big mirror that hung on her living room wall. The apparition that stared back at her wasn't pretty. "I'm not getting dressed for him. He doesn't deserve it. For all I know he killed Ronni."

"You know better than that."

Hannah thought about that for a moment. "You're right. I do. If Mike decided to kill Ronni, he would have figured out a way to do it so it looked like an accident."

"Exactly right. Do you want me to package up some bar cookies for him? There's about a dozen left."

"Sure. I'll put on the coffee and take him a cup. He doesn't deserve it, but I'll do it anyway."

Once the coffee was ready and the bar cookies were packaged, Hannah zipped up her parka and started down the stairs. Fourteen minutes had elapsed since Mike's call, and she was right on time. She shivered a bit as a gust of wind threatened to whip the knit cap from her head, and she was glad to reach the underground garage where the absence of wind chill caused the air to feel considerably warmer.

"Psssst!"

A shrill hiss greeted her as she approached the Dumpster. Hannah had all she could do not to laugh as Mike stepped out. He was clothed entirely in black and he had a black ski cap on his head, rolled down low to almost cover his eyes.

"Thanks for coming, Hannah," he said.

"I wouldn't have missed it for the world. I'm just sorry my cloak and dagger were at the cleaners."

"Very funny. It's just that I promised I wouldn't see you, and I could lose my job over this."

Hannah nodded to show she understood and moved a few steps away from the Dumpster. Someone had dined on fish . . . several days ago. "I brought you some bar cookies and some coffee."

"Thanks, Hannah." Mike accepted the package of bar cookies and the coffee. "That was really nice of you."

"You said it was important?"

"Yes. I just wanted you to know that there was nothing between Ronni and me. I know it looks bad, but there wasn't."

Why did it look bad? Was there something she'd missed? These and several other questions occurred to Hannah. She wanted to ask them, but she didn't. It was an old interrogation trick she'd learned from him. If you remained silent, a guilty person kept right on talking and trying to explain. The increasingly frantic explanations resulted in inconsistencies. Once the inconsistency is addressed, lies tumble out pell-mell and eventually lead to the truth.

"She was really upset after she broke up with Wade, you know," Mike went on. "She needed a friend, a shoulder to cry on. I guess I knew she was using me, but I didn't mind being helpful."

I'll bet! Hannah said, but not out loud. And she continued to play the waiting game.

"Maybe I let her depend on me a little too much. I mean, maybe I gave her the wrong idea. She was always calling me to come over for something and I went because . . . well . . . we had a lot in common since we both worked for the sheriff's department and all."

Right. Sure. Hannah clamped her lips shut. No way was she going to comment.

"When I said that about looking bad? I know it's going to come out that I slept at her place a few nights. We'd be watching a movie or something, and I'd fall asleep on her couch. She never woke me. She'd just go to bed and let me wake up on my own the next morning. That's all it was. Really."

Ah-ha! Now we're at the crux of it! Hannah's mind crowed with victory, but her stomach felt a little sick. Hearing the truth could be very unpleasant, especially when it was something you didn't want to know.

"I just wanted to get everything straight with you, Hannah. You know how important you are to me."

Important enough to tell me that you spent several nights at Ronni's place? I could stand to be a little less important than that, thank you very much!

"Hannah? You believe me, don't you?"

"Of course," Hannah said, being entirely truthful. She did believe he'd spent several nights at Ronni's place. Perhaps that wasn't precisely what he was asking, but it would have to do for now. "Tell me about Stella Parks," she said.

"Stella? Why are you asking about *her*?"

The way Mike asked the question made Hannah pause. It was pretty obvious he hadn't heard about his replacement. "Bill asked the Minneapolis Police Department if he could borrow her to head up Ronni's murder case."

"I didn't know that. She's a tough cop, and she happens to be a good detective. Stella took over for me when I left the M.P.D. to come here."

"So you think she'll catch Ronni's killer?"

"I don't know. She doesn't know the people, she doesn't know the area, and she didn't know Ronni. She'll run a tight investigation, but she won't have the hometown advantage. And she'll drive my team hard. She'll want to prove she's better than I am."

"Hannah?" a voice called out from the dim interior of the garage.

Hannah came close to groaning. It was Clara Hollenbeck, one of her neighbors. Clara's church groups must have run very late. Hannah turned back to Mike to tell him to va-moose, but he had vanished in the space behind the Dumpster, leaving her to deal with her neighbor. There had to be some way of dealing with Clara . . . but what on earth could it be?

"Were you talking to somebody?" Clara asked, walking up to Hannah's side.

"Myself. I was talking to myself. I do that when I'm . . . um . . . working on a new recipe."

"Are you sleepwalking, Hannah? It's cold out here in the garage, and you're here in your robe and slippers."

"Sleepwalking? No, Clara. No, I'm not sleepwalking. I'm definitely awake."

"But what are you doing out here?"

Hannah saw movement out of the corner of her eye. Mike was slipping out from behind the Dumpster in a crouch, and he was heading for the sloping exit. She just hoped that Clara wouldn't turn around and see him.

"Hannah?" Clara prodded her for an answer.

"I think best when I'm pacing," Hannah said quickly. "A lot of people are like that. And I have to pace out here be-cause . . . I don't want to take the chance I'll wake Kevin and Sue by pacing the floor above them. Now that Sue's working part-time, she needs a full night's sleep."

"I didn't know Sue was working!"

"Yes, part-time at Kiddie Korner."

"That's wonderful. She needs to get out more. What type of recipe is it?"

"Recipe?"

"The one you're working on. The one that's making you pace out here."

"Oh. It's a cookie recipe."

"It's just fascinating to see your mind at work, Hannah!" Clara was clearly intrigued. "What kind of cookie will it be?"

"Watermelon." Hannah said the first thing that occurred to her and risked a glance in Mike's direction. He was halfway up the sloped exit, heading for the bushes at the top that lined the sides of the road.

"That sounds very unusual." Clara frowned. "To tell you the truth, Hannah, I don't think a watermelon cookie would be very good."

Mike was out of sight at last, and Hannah gave Clara a big smile. "You're absolutely right. Watermelon cookies would be dreadful. Thanks for telling me, Clara. Now I don't have to lose any more sleep working on the recipe."

 **Chapter Sixteen**

It was before the crack of dawn, and the sisters were sitting at Hannah's almost-antique Formica-topped table in the kitchen. Hannah was wearing her exercise outfit, and it seemed slightly looser than it had when she'd first started taking exercise classes. That could be her imagination, but she really hoped it wasn't. Michelle was in robe and slippers, and Hannah suspected that after she left, her youngest sister might very well go back to bed.

"So what did Mike say that was so important he had to see you in the middle of the night?" Michelle asked.

"Not much. He said he just wanted me to know that nothing happened with Ronni."

"And you believed him?"

Hannah shrugged. "It doesn't really matter whether I did or I didn't. Mike and I don't have an exclusive arrangement or anything like that."

"But you'd still be hurt if you thought he'd been romantically involved with Ronni."

"Well . . . yes. I wouldn't have any right to be angry with him, but I *would* be hurt."

"That's exactly the way I feel. I hope both our guys are truthful and they weren't really involved with her."

"Me, too." Hannah zooped down the rest of her coffee and stood up to go. "Are you going anywhere today?"

"You tell me."

"What do you mean?"

"I want to help you investigate, and Mother's giving me her car for the week. She's picking me up at nine, and the only commitment I have is to go out to lunch with Carrie and her. I'm perfectly willing to do some legwork for you. Just name it."

Hannah thought fast. "If it's ready, please get the phone list from Mother and bring it to me at The Cookie Jar. Andrea and I are staying at Heavenly Bodies for a while after class to nose around, so we won't be there until ten or eleven. Once we have the list, we can check alibis for any suspects that Mother and Carrie unearthed."

"Okay. Anything else?"

"You can help Lisa bake a batch of Don't Ask, Don't Tell Cookies."

"What are those?"

"A recipe based on Chocolate Sauerkraut Cake."

"That's one of my favorites. Do the cookies taste like the cake?"

"Almost exactly." Hannah shrugged into her parka and picked up her gloves. "I'll see you later. Describing those cookies is making me hungry. I'd better get out to Heavenly Bodies before I gain weight just thinking about them."

Within two minutes of entering the back door of The Cookie Jar, Hannah and Andrea were seated at the work island, sipping mugs of freshly brewed coffee. It was shortly after eleven in the morning, and Michelle had just told them that she didn't have the list of suspects.

"Mother didn't give you the list?" Hannah was surprised. Delores was always efficient when it came to anything phone-related.

"She said they still had quite a few callbacks to make, that a lot of people they called weren't home. There was a play at the community theater, a shower for Dot Larson's new baby, parents' night at school, and a bunch of church functions. Some of them ran really late, and Mother didn't think that they should call past ten at night."

Hannah knew about one of those church functions. Clara Hollenbeck hadn't come home until after midnight from her Bible study group.

"Anyway, they're going to tie up the loose ends today. Mother wants us all to meet her out at the Lake Eden Inn for dinner at seven tonight, her treat. That way we can talk about the case."

"Who's *us all*?" Andrea asked, and Hannah bit down on her tongue to keep from correcting the awkward phrasing.

"You, Hannah, me, Mother, Carrie, and Norman."

"Okay. You can count me in. Bill's working late anyway."

"Hannah?" Michelle turned to her.

"It's fine with me as long as I have time to run home and feed Moishe before I drive out to the inn."

"But how about that Kitty Valet Mike gave you?" Andrea asked. "I thought it was for occasions when you couldn't get home at the regular time . . . like tonight."

"It *is* for occasions like this. It's just that Moishe's been eating every scrap of food I put in it, and he's always hungry when I come home at night."

"If he's eating that much, it won't hurt him to miss a meal," Andrea pointed out. "Mother's dinners never run long. You can feed him when you get home."

"You're right. I can." Hannah tried not to think of how disappointed Moishe would be when she didn't come home at the regular time to fill his Kitty Valet.

"So what did you find out at Heavenly Bodies?" Michelle asked.

"Nothing," Andrea answered her.

"Nothing?"

"Nothing yet," Hannah amended it.

"They wouldn't talk in front of me," Andrea explained. "I think it's because I'm the sheriff's wife. Hannah has to go back out there alone this afternoon."

"So you're going to talk to all the fitness club members about Ronni?" Michelle guessed.

"We narrowed it down a little more than that," Hannah told her. "Roger, our old fitness instructor, was back in class this morning. He can't do a lot of the exercises because of his broken arm, but everybody understands."

"We talked to him after class," Andrea went on with the story, "and when we told him we were investigating Ronni's murder and we needed to talk to all the women in the classes she taught, he went to the computer and enrolled Hannah in both of her afternoon classes."

Michelle looked worried. "Are you going to be able to do all that extra exercising?"

"I don't know, but I'll try. If I'm really stiff and sore, I can come in late, or quit early, or whatever. The important thing is to catch Ronni's students after class and find out what they thought of her."

"Make sure you get the names of anyone who dropped her class or transferred to another one," Andrea reminded her. "Roger seemed to think there were a couple of those."

"How about interviewing the security guard?" Michelle asked.

"Tad Newberg. I was planning to talk to him right after I finish the classes, but I could use your help."

"You've got it. What do you want me to do?"

"Meet me out at Heavenly Bodies at five. I checked Tad's schedule, and that's when he comes in today." Hannah glanced over at Andrea. "I could use your help, too."

Andrea nodded. "We'll drive out together. Just tell us what you want us to do."

"I want one of you to help me interview Tad. And I want the other one to take cell phone pictures of the interior of the mall security station, including shots of the monitors. I want to know which rooms at Heavenly Bodies have security cameras."

"Why take photos when you could just ask?" Michelle wanted to know.

"Because I'm not official, and they're not supposed to give out that information to just anyone."

Michelle thought about that for a moment. "I get it. If they told just anyone the exact locations of their security cameras, crooks could avoid them."

"I'll take the pictures," Andrea volunteered. "I just got a new cell phone, and the camera's really sharp."

"Okay, then I'll help with the interview." Michelle turned to Hannah. "What sorts of questions do you want to ask him?"

"I'm sure someone from the sheriff's department has interviewed him already, but he's on duty five nights a week. He may know something about the members who came out on a regular basis for personal coaching from Ronni."

"Background," Andrea said.

"Exactly." Hannah paused to yawn widely. "If we had a cot back here, I'd be tempted to take a nap before I drive back out to the mall to take those last two exercise classes."

Lisa came into the kitchen carrying one of the glass display jars they used to showcase the day's cookie selections. "I need more Don't Ask, Don't Tell Cookies. It's a good thing we made extra, Michelle. They're going like hotcakes."

Hannah sighed, catching a whiff of the heavenly aroma as Lisa began to fill the cookie jar. "Chocolate. It's everything I shouldn't have, and everything I crave."

"Relax," Andrea reached out to pat her hand. "You can have one as long as it's only one. You spent double the required time on the cross-country ski machine this morning."

"I did?"

"Yes. I timed you. If I hadn't said anything, you probably would have gone on for another ten minutes."

"But I hate that machine! I guess I must have been so busy

thinking about the case and how to proceed, I lost track of time."

Lisa brought her a cookie and Hannah had all she could do not to stuff it in her mouth all at once. Instead, she made it last a whole two minutes even though it just about killed her.

"Would you like another?" Lisa asked her.

"No! I mean, yes, of course I'd like another. But no, I know I shouldn't have one."

"That's good willpower, Hannah," Andrea complimented her.

"It's not willpower, it's a precaution. Just get those luscious cookies out of my sight before I grab the jar, run out the door, and lock myself in my cookie truck so I can eat every one."

DON'T ASK, DON'T TELL COOKIES

Preheat oven to 350 degrees F., rack
in the middle position.

Hannah's 1st Note: This is an adaptation of Friar Rudolf's recipe for Chocolate Sauerkraut Cake.

1 cup softened butter *(2 sticks, 8 ounces, ½ pound)*
3 cups white *(granulated)* sugar
4 large eggs, beaten *(just whip them up in a glass with a fork)*
2 teaspoons vanilla extract
1 cup cocoa powder *(plain American cocoa—I used Hershey's)*
1 teaspoon baking soda
1 cup buttermilk
5 cups flour *(pack it down when you measure it)*
2 cups chopped *(and drained and rinsed)* sauerkraut

Prepare the sauerkraut by rinsing it off with cold water under the faucet, and draining it in a sieve or colander. Rinsing is very important. Make sure you rinse it well. **(You will chop it later when it's thoroughly drained.)**

Hannah's 2nd Note: This is easier with an electric mixer, but you can do it by hand.

Beat the softened butter with the sugar until the mixture is light and fluffy. Add the beaten eggs and mix them in thoroughly.

Mix in the vanilla extract, cocoa powder, and baking soda. Stir *(or beat on low speed)* until everything is well incorporated.

Add half of the buttermilk *(½ cup)* and half of the flour *(2½ cups)*. Beat until smooth.

Add the remaining half of the buttermilk and the remaining half of the flour. Beat until smooth.

Hannah's 3ʳᵈ Note: If you used an electric mixer, remove the bowl with the cookie dough. You'll have to add this last ingredient by hand. Even finely chopped sauerkraut tends to wrap itself around the beaters.

Dump the sauerkraut on a cutting board, and chop it finely with a knife. You can also chop it in a food processor, using the steel blade and a pulsing motion. It's very important to chop it up into tiny little pieces.

Measure one cup of sauerkraut, packing it down in the cup. Pat the sauerkraut dry with paper towels, and add it to the cookie dough. Stir it in thoroughly.

Drop dough by heaping teaspoons onto cookie sheets that you've greased or sprayed with Pam *(or other nonstick cooking spray)*, 12 cookies per standard-size sheet.

Bake the cookies at 350 degrees F. for 10 to 12 minutes. Let them sit on the cookie sheet for 1 minute, and then transfer them to a wire rack to cool.

When the cookies are cool, frost them with Mocha Icing.

Yield: 8 dozen delicious cookies

MOCHA ICING

½ cup softened butter *(1 stick, ¼ pound)*
1 cup semi-sweet *(regular)* chocolate chips
4 to 6 teaspoons very strongly brewed coffee
3 to 3½ cups powdered *(confectioner's)* sugar

Melt the chocolate chips with *4 teaspoons* of the coffee in a microwave-safe bowl for 1 minute on HIGH. Stir, and if the mixture is still lumpy, remove the spoon and microwave it again for an additional 20 seconds. If the mixture is still lumpy, repeat again, stirring after each 20-second interval. When you are able to stir the mixture smooth, set the bowl on the counter to cool to room temperature.

Once the mixture has cooled to room temperature, stir in the softened butter until smooth.

Whisk in the powdered sugar, and stir until the mixture is of spreading consistency. If it's too thick, add the remaining 2 teaspoons of coffee. If it's too thin, stir in a little more powdered sugar.

Frost the cookies and sprinkle on shredded coconut before the frosting has fully set, if you desire.

Hannah's 4th Note: Lisa just confessed that if she's too tired to frost these cookies, she just dusts them with powdered sugar, plunks half of a maraschino cherry on top, and serves them that way.

Chapter Seventeen

"So Ronni was really hard on Betty Jackson?" Hannah repeated what Charlotte Roscoe, Jordan High's head secretary and a member of Ronni's Swim to Slim class, had told her. It was another interrogator's trick she'd picked up from Mike. You repeated the last comment and then you were silent, waiting to see if the person you were interviewing would fill that silence by elaborating.

"That's right. Betty's feelings were really hurt. You know how sensitive she is about her weight. When I saw her the next morning she was okay, but she told me she was going to think of some way to get even with Ronni."

"Do you think that . . ."

"No!" Charlotte jumped in before Hannah could finish her question. "Don't even think it, Hannah. There's no way she had anything to do with Ronni's death. Betty's too squeamish to do anything like that. She won't even swat a fly. When she said *get even,* she was probably talking about getting Ronni fired, or something like that. Besides, she isn't even in town."

"You're sure of that?"

"I'm positive. We're in the same night class at Lake Eden Community College, and I'm taking notes for her while she's gone. Betty left early Tuesday morning. She drove up to Duluth for her cousin's wedding, and she won't be back until Sunday night."

"Okay. Thanks, Charlotte."

"You're welcome. Is there anything more I can do to help? I didn't like Ronni personally. She was a real slave driver in class, but I'll miss her. I managed to lose an inch around my waist in the first two weeks of her class, and now I can fit into my skinny pantsuit for work."

"Really!" Hannah was glad to hear that. She'd been dreading the swimming class, but perhaps it would help her get into the Regency-style dress even faster.

"Can you find out when they'll open the pool again?" Charlotte asked her.

"Tomorrow. I asked Roger when I signed up for your class. They're keeping the Jacuzzi off-limits, but we'll be allowed in the pool."

"That's definitely good news. I hate doing the exercises on dry land. It's so much easier in the water. The impact is lower and water provides its own resistance." Charlotte glanced at her watch. "Do you need a ride back to town?"

"Thanks, but no. Michelle and Andrea are meeting me out here, and we're going to talk to the security guard who was on duty the night Ronni was killed."

"That's a good idea. You can probably get more information than those rookies at the sheriff's station." Charlotte leaned a little closer and lowered her voice, even though they were alone at a table in the Snack Shack. "I understand they pulled the seasoned detectives off the investigation because they were personally involved."

Hannah remembered the good spin Andrea had put on the situation and decided to do some spinning of her own. "That's true. Ronni taught physical fitness classes out at the sheriff's station gym, you know. They saw her every day, and she was well liked. You know how cops are. They depend on each other, and there's a real bond between them, just like soldiers or fraternity brothers. They considered Ronni one of their own, and losing one of their own is always hard. I think Bill's afraid that some of his detectives might get a little too zealous if they got their hands on her killer . . . if you know what I mean."

"I certainly do! And then *they'd* be in trouble. That was a wise move on Bill's part."

Hannah silently congratulated herself on a job well done. What she'd said wasn't a mere rotation, or an ordinary revolution of the facts. She'd created an out-and-out whirling Moebius strip that outspun Andrea and then some!

"It's a good thing you're helping them out, Hannah. They'll never catch the killer without the best minds on the force."

"I'm not helping them officially, but I do want to do my part," Hannah continued to spin. "And you don't have to worry about rookie detectives, Charlotte. Bill's brought in a really good detective from the Minneapolis Police Force. Her name is Stella Parks."

"That's good. Well, good luck with the security . . ." Charlotte stopped speaking and looked worried again.

"What is it?"

"That security guard you're going to interview . . . it's not Frank Hurley, is it?"

"No, his name is Tad Newberg. He was the guard on duty when Ronni was killed. Does Frank Hurley work out here at the mall?"

"Yes. He's a really nice guy, Hannah. He used to work for a private security firm up north, and he moved here to be closer to his relatives. I'm glad he wasn't on duty when it happened."

"How do you know him?" Hannah was curious.

"He works for us at the school whenever there's a big basketball or football game, and we wouldn't even think of holding a prom without him."

"The prom I can understand. That tends to get a little wild. But there's that much trouble on big game nights?"

"Oh, it's not *real* trouble. It's just kids acting up and causing an inconvenience. Sometimes they think it's funny to let the air out of the opposing team's bus tires. Frank patrols outside, and he gives them a lecture about how the Jordan High Gulls practice better sportsmanship than that. The kids think he's pretty strict and old-fashioned, but they respect him."

Hannah knew she must have been tired, because it took several seconds for the next question to occur to her. "You said Frank works out here. Does he know Tad Newberg?"

"I'm sure he does. The security staff out here isn't that large, and they must have worked together at one time or another."

Hannah flipped her shorthand notebook open and wrote Frank's name inside. "He could be a valuable resource. Could I have his number?"

"Of course." Charlotte gave it to her, but she looked puzzled. "Why do you need it if Frank wasn't on duty when it happened?"

"Because he works here," Hannah thought fast, "and he knows how the mall security works. I probably won't need him, but I'll keep his name handy in case Tad's not available and I've got questions about scheduling, or procedure, or something like that."

"Oh. Well, he'd probably know all about that. If you need him, call me and I'll introduce you."

"Thanks," Hannah said. And her mind said, *Disaster averted. Good work.*

"So who do you think killed her, Hannah?" Charlotte leaned closer again. "I probably shouldn't say this, but I overheard her on her cell phone one day, and she told someone that she was going to turn her ex-fiancé in for tax evasion. Of course I don't know if she did it or not, but the federal government's nobody to fool around with. If Ronni actually called their tip line and he found out about it, he might have been so mad at her that he killed her."

"Not possible," Hannah said, watching Charlotte's face fall. "Wade Hoffman was in an auto accident, and he was still at Lake Eden Memorial under Doc Knight's care when Ronni was murdered."

"Oh. Well . . . it was just a theory."

"And it was a good one. It's the first thing I checked out."

"Really?" Charlotte looked pleased. "Well, how about Serena Roste? Did you check her out, too?"

"Who's Serena Roste?"

"She's Wade Hoffman's former fiancée. He was engaged to Serena before he got engaged to Ronni."

"I didn't know that."

"That's because it's Elk River gossip, not Lake Eden gossip. We use a substitute teacher from Elk River every once in a while, and she told me that it was a really nasty breakup. Serena and Ronni used to be close friends until Ronni stole Serena's fiancé."

"Serena Roste." Hannah flipped to her suspect page and added the name. "Do you think Serena was upset enough with Ronni to kill her?"

Charlotte gave a little shrug. "I don't know. Maybe. Did you just add her to your suspect list?"

"Yes. Mike says that more murders are committed by spouses or jealous lovers than by any other group of people."

"I didn't know that." Charlotte gave a little grin. "That almost, but not quite, makes me glad I never got married."

"Did you bring the cookies?" Hannah asked, when Andrea met her in the Snack Shack.

"Of course. Michelle's got them. She's getting a guest pass from Roger so she can come in anytime she likes."

"Does the owner know about this?"

"Oh, yes. Roger's handling it for him. He's very worried that Heavenly Bodies will get a reputation for not being safe, and he wants Roger to do all he can to prove that they aren't liable in any way for Ronni's death."

"That figures. And it explains why Roger is being so generous with the guest passes."

"That's only one reason. The other reason is that he wants us to hurry and catch Ronni's killer because Stella interviewed him today."

"Roger didn't like Stella?"

"It's not that. It's just that he told her he was at home with his girlfriend the night that Ronni was killed, and she demanded proof."

"Can Roger prove that he was with his girlfriend all night?"

"He told me he can if it comes to that, but he's really hoping it won't."

"Let me guess . . . Roger's girlfriend wasn't supposed to be staying with him, and she'll get into trouble if she has to swear she was with him, for the whole night?"

"You got it."

"She's underage?" Hannah asked, crossing her fingers and hoping that wasn't the case.

"No, it's just that she's got a scholarship and she lives in the dorms at Lake Eden Community College. Resident students, regardless of age, aren't supposed to be out all night."

"I understand," Hannah said, and she did. "Roger doesn't want to rat on his girlfriend unless it's absolutely necessary to keep him from being arrested for a crime he didn't commit."

"That's exactly right. It won't come to that, will it?" Andrea looked worried.

"Not if I have anything to say about it." Hannah pushed back her chair and got up as Michelle waved to them from the doorway. "Roger must have told you his impression of Stella Parks. What did he say about her?"

Andrea rose and they began to walk toward their younger sister. "Roger said that she was as tough as nails."

"There's that same cliché again." Hannah gave a little laugh. "Stella seems to attract them. I'm actually looking forward to meeting her. It sounds as if she plays hardball. And there goes *another* cliché."

Chapter Eighteen

"*That's* Tad Newberg?" Michelle asked as she spotted the short, heavyset young man in the perfectly pressed uniform standing by the mall security station.

"Yes, that's Tad. Why do you look so surprised?"

"I think I know him from somewhere, but I'm not sure where."

"You probably saw him out here when you were shopping," Andrea told her. "He's been here for about two years."

"Maybe," Michelle said, but she sounded doubtful.

"Tell him you think you met him before," Hannah suggested. "Maybe he'll remember where it was. Even if the two of you can't figure it out, it'll keep him distracted so that Andrea can take pictures of the security monitors."

"Hi, Hannah," Tad greeted her as they stepped up to the station.

"Hello, Tad. I just wanted to drop by and thank you for your help the other night."

"No thanks needed. That's my job."

"Both Andrea and I are grateful that you waited with us until the sheriff's department arrived."

"That's right. We felt a lot safer with you there," Andrea chimed in.

"They brought you some cookies," Michelle held out the box. "They're chocolate with mocha frosting."

Tad looked genuinely pleased as he accepted the box. "Wow, thanks! I'm crazy about chocolate cookies."

"Do you like chocolate sauerkraut cake?" Hannah asked him.

"I like it a lot. My sister-in-law makes one almost every Sunday for dinner. It's my brother's favorite cake."

"These cookies are based on that cake. I call them Don't Ask, Don't Tell Cookies."

"Because of the sauerkraut? Or because of the military?"

"The sauerkraut."

"That's funny. I like the name." Tad turned to Michelle with a contemplative look. "You look familiar. Do I know you from somewhere?"

That was Andrea's cue to take her phone out of her pocket. "Sorry," she said to Tad, after glancing at the display. "It's my babysitter. I've got to take the call."

"I was just thinking the same thing," Michelle said, stepping a bit closer to completely capture Tad's attention. "I mean, I was thinking I know you from somewhere."

"How about high school?" Tad asked her. "I'm a couple of years older than you are, but what school did you go to?"

"Jordan High. How about you?"

As the conversation went on between Michelle and Tad, Hannah glanced in Andrea's direction. She'd managed to walk all the way back to the wall of security monitors and she was pacing back and forth, pretending to hold an imaginary conversation with Grandma McCann. And all the time she was talking, Hannah knew she was using her in-phone camera to take photos of everything inside the security station.

"I don't think I know anybody from Elmdale," Michelle said, "but maybe we met at some kind of statewide school contest. Were you in the band? Or the chorus?"

"Not me, but I was always in line at the Dairy Queen in Little Falls when they opened in the spring. How about you?"

Hannah tuned out for a moment and stepped away slightly so that she could examine the rest of the station. It was fairly large, the size of someone's living room, and other than two small cubicles in the back that were walled off into offices, everything was open to view.

"Maybe I saw you out here when you were on duty," Michelle suggested.

"I don't think that's it. I know I saw you somewhere, but I don't think it was out here."

Hannah tuned out again. She moved back slightly so that she could see what appeared to be bookshelves on the far wall. They were filled with tapes, clearly labeled with the day and date, and there was an obvious gap for the night of Ronni's murder.

Pay dirt! Hannah sidled a bit closer. The span of the tapes covered two weeks, and that was obviously as long as the security team kept them. Perhaps the older tapes were archived. It didn't really matter. What mattered was the gap for the night of Ronni's murder, a bare spot on the shelf.

There was only one conclusion to draw. Hannah assumed that the sheriff's department had taken the tapes. If she carried her theory further, Detective Stella Parks could be viewing them at this very moment.

There were other assumptions to draw as well, although spotting the gap in coverage had nothing to do with it. Hannah had to assume that Ronni's murder had not been caught on tape. If the killer had been identified, an arrest would have been made, and the Lake Eden Gossip Hotline would be buzzing like a whole boxcar of bees. Delores would have wasted no time in calling to tell all three of her daughters, and no such call had come.

Perhaps viewing the tapes would be a waste of time, but Hannah's gut feeling was that they might learn something about the people who had visited Heavenly Bodies that night, gym members who might have seen something that would prove to be important.

Try to get those tapes, Hannah made a mental note. And then she added, *And meet Stella Parks to find out her agenda.*

*   *   *

"What an absolute nerd!" Michelle said as she climbed into the rear seat of Hannah's cookie truck. They'd decided to go out to the inn together in Hannah's truck. On the way back, Andrea would pick up her Volvo in the mall parking lot.

"You're talking about Tad Newberg?" Andrea asked her.

"Who else? The only thing that bothers me is where I met him before. It's one of those questions that'll keep me up for hours tonight."

"Nothing is going to keep me up for hours tonight!" Hannah pulled out of the parking lot and headed for the Lake Eden Inn.

They were just turning onto the access road that led to the inn when Andrea's cell phone rang. "It's Bill," she said, identifying her husband's ring tone. "I'd better take this."

As Hannah guided her truck over the bumpy road that wound through the trees, she heard Andrea's end of the conversation.

"Oh, hi, honey!" Andrea said, and Hannah could almost hear the smile in her voice. "Don't tell me you're coming home early! We're just about to meet Mother at the inn for dinner."

There was a silence, and then Andrea spoke again. "Of course. I entirely understand. You have to make Detective Parks feel welcome. Where are you taking her?"

In her rearview mirror, Hannah saw Michelle lean forward so that she could hear better. Was trouble brewing in paradise?

"You're coming here, too?" Andrea sounded surprised. There was a beat of silence while Bill obviously said something. "But we can't! Of course we'd love to, honey, but Mother planned this out so that we could discuss Ronni's murder case. I don't think you want her to hear about that . . . do you?"

Another beat and Andrea laughed. "That's what I thought.

It's okay, honey. You just tell her all about Lake Eden and how nice it is to live here."

"And if he wants us to join them for coffee afterwards, that would be nice," Hannah jumped in, even though it meant that she had to admit she'd been following what was supposed to be a private conversation.

"Nice touch," Michelle said, patting Hannah on the shoulder.

Hannah smiled. "I thought so. I want to meet her."

"But does she want to meet you?" Michelle countered.

Andrea shushed them both by holding up her hand. "Bill says that'll be fine. She wants to meet us all anyway. They're leaving the sheriff's station now, so they'll be only fifteen minutes or so behind us."

Michelle waited until Andrea had ended the call, and then she tapped her on the shoulder. "Have you met her yet?" she asked.

"No. I just hope she's not . . ."

"Really attractive?" Michelle guessed.

"That, too. But I was thinking more about the department. I hope she's not critical of the way Bill's been running things."

"Right," Hannah said.

"I understand," Michelle added. "Maybe we should point out that Bill has no unsolved murder cases on the books."

Hannah gave a nod. "That's good. We could all sing Bill's praises, but if his cliché is true and her mind really is like a steel trap, she'll see right through it. Maybe we ought to give her some cookies for her office instead. That usually brings people around."

"Good idea." Michelle turned to look at the cookies Hannah always carried in the back. "Do you have anything good to give her?"

"Do I have anything *good*?" Hannah did her best to sound outraged.

"You know what she means," Andrea gave a little laugh. "Do you have anything that a tough-as-nails, brave-as-a-lion, mind-like-a-steel-trap visiting detective would like?"

"I've got Blueberry Crunch Cookies. I packed them up for Mother, but I've got enough for Detective Parks, too."

"Perfect," Andrea pronounced. "They ought to sweeten her up."

"In more ways than one," Hannah said.

BLUEBERRY CRUNCH COOKIES

Preheat oven to 350 degrees F., rack
in the middle position.

1 cup melted butter *(2 sticks, ½ pound)*
2 cups white *(granulated)* sugar
2 teaspoons vanilla
½ teaspoon salt
1½ teaspoons baking soda
2 large eggs, beaten *(just whip them up with a fork)*
2½ cups flour *(no need to sift—pack it down when you measure it)*
1 cup dried sweetened blueberries *(other dried fruit will also work if you cut it in blueberry-sized pieces)*
2 cups **GROUND** dry oatmeal *(measure before grinding)*

Hannah's 1st Note: Mixing this dough is much easier with an electric mixer, but you can also do it by hand.

Melt the butter in a large microwave-safe bowl for 1 minute on HIGH. Add the white sugar and mix it in thoroughly.

Add the vanilla, salt, and the baking soda. Mix it in well.

When the mixture has cooled to room temperature, stir in the beaten eggs. When they are fully incorporated, add the flour in half-cup increments, stirring after each addition.

Mix in the dried blueberries.

Prepare your oatmeal. *(Use Quaker if you have it—the cardboard canister is useful for all sorts of things.)* Measure out two cups and place them in the bowl of a food processor or a blender, chopping with the steel blade until the oatmeal is the consistency of coarse sand. *(Just in case you're wondering, the ground oatmeal is the ingredient that makes the cookies crunchy.)*

Add the ground oatmeal to your bowl, and mix it in thoroughly. The resulting cookie dough will be quite stiff.

Roll walnut-sized dough balls with your hands, and place them on a greased cookie sheet, 12 balls to a standard-size sheet. *(If the dough is too sticky to roll, place the bowl in the refrigerator for thirty minutes and try again.)* Squish the dough balls down a bit with your impeccably clean palm *(or a metal spatula if you'd rather)*.

Bake at 350 degrees F. for 10 to 12 minutes or until golden brown on top. *(Mine took 11 minutes.)* Cool on the cookie sheet for 2 minutes, and then remove the cookies to a wire rack to cool completely.

Yield: 6 to 7 dozen unusual and tasty cookies, depending on cookie size.

Hannah's 2nd Note: These cookies freeze well if you stack them on foil *(like rolling coins)* and roll them, tucking in the ends. Just place the rolls of cookies in a freezer bag, and they'll keep for three months or so as long as no one finds them and eats them without telling you.

Hannah followed the hostess to one of the alcoves Sally and Dick Laughlin, the owners of the Lake Eden Inn, had set aside for private dining. Delores and Carrie hadn't arrived yet, and Andrea had stopped off to talk to Barbara Donnelly, head secretary at the sheriff's station, in the hope that she might let something slip about Stella Parks and the results of the official investigation. Michelle was similarly occupied. She'd stopped to talk to one of her former classmates, who had dropped a class that Ronni had taught.

The alcoves sat against the back wall in the large dining room. They were elevated, and Sally had once explained to Hannah that the fact they were on a two-step podium made people feel more important. Hannah supposed that was true. If you were so inclined, you could peek out from behind the filmy draperies that hid the diners in the alcove from public view, and look down your nose at the patrons below you.

The hostess whisked aside the draperies, and Hannah stopped short as she saw that one chair was taken. So they weren't the first ones here!

"Hi, Hannah," Norman patted the chair next to him. "I saved you a seat."

"Thanks. I can see they're in short supply." Hannah smiled as she surveyed the five empty chairs. Then she moved over to take the one next to Norman.

"I came early so I could go over some notes Mike gave me," Norman explained, slipping a small notebook into his jacket pocket.

"More instructions on how to proceed?"

"Right. He's going stir-crazy, Hannah. He even gave me a stack of books for you."

"Let me guess . . . *Five Easy Steps to Running a Tight Investigation? The Detective's Guide to Solving Crimes? Collecting Clues and Closing Cases?*"

Norman laughed. "Something like that. I had to promise Mike I'd give them to you and tell you how important he thought they were. I didn't have to promise that you'd read them."

"Good, because I'll be so busy trying to figure out who killed Ronni that I won't have *time* to read them. Is there anything else Mike said to tell me?"

"Yes, but I'll wait to tell you when we discuss the case after dinner. The mothers want to be in on the kill this time."

"The *kill*?"

"Metaphorically speaking, they've helped with the hunt before, but they've never been in on it when you've closed in on the murderer."

"Mother was there once. She's the reason I'm still here."

"I pointed that out to her, but she says it doesn't count, that it was just a happy coincidence."

"*Happy*?! That's not exactly the way she felt at the time!" Hannah stopped and thought over what Norman had told her. "Okay. I think I understand what the mothers are trying to say. They're tired of doing phone work, and they'd like to do something more exciting. Does that sound about right to you?"

"I'm almost sure that's what they mean."

"What sort of exciting homicide case assignment can we give to two post–middle-aged women who love antiques and can't run very fast?"

"I'm not sure. All I know is I wouldn't want to get them into any trouble."

"Maybe we could ask them to read the books Mike gave you?"

Norman laughed. "Nice try, but somehow I don't think that's the type of thing they had in mind."

"I suppose not." Hannah sat there for a moment trying to come up with something, and then she shook her head. "I can't think of a thing. Maybe I'm just too tired."

"You need brain food."

"That would be fish, right?"

"That's what they say. I saw Sally when I came in, and she told me about her new appetizer. It's tuna sashimi."

"Isn't sashimi like sushi without the rice?"

"That's one difference between them. When Sally serves her tuna sashimi appetizer, she arranges very thin strips of tuna over a bed of mixed greens. She sauces everything lightly with soy and ginger, and decorates the plate with rosettes of pickled ginger."

"That sounds wonderful. I know I'd like it if I could just get past the raw fish part. Maybe it's because I'm from Minnesota and my father fished."

"Could be. How are you coming along at the gym?"

"I've added a bunch of new suspects to my list." Hannah gave a little laugh. "Ronni insulted quite a few women in her classes. Of course when it came to the men, she was exactly the opposite."

"That figures."

"I was just wondering . . . you joined Heavenly Bodies, didn't you?"

"Yes, but not because of Ronni. I thought you knew me better than that. I'm a one-woman guy, and I've found her. And just because she hasn't said yes yet doesn't mean I'm going out looking."

"That's not really what I . . . well, maybe it was, but I . . ."

"I'm flattered you were jealous." Norman seemed to sense that she was uncomfortable, and he jumped in before she could stutter out any more half-explanations. He reached out for her hand, squeezed it once, and started to say more when footsteps approached and the curtains parted.

"Well hello, you two!" Delores arrived with Carrie, and Andrea and Michelle were right behind her. "Our waitress will be right here with tonight's specials. Let's have a nice meal, and then we can get down to business over dessert and coffee."

Dessert. The word rang in Hannah's mind like a tolling bell. No dessert for her, even though Sally's dessert cart was laden with some of the most scrumptious concoctions she'd ever tasted. Her flourless chocolate cake was fantastic, her mousse of the night was always mouthwatering, and her lemon torte was nothing short of legendary.

"What's the matter, Hannah?" Norman asked.

"Dessert," Hannah said in a mournful tone. "I can't even have fresh fruit."

"Why not?"

"There *is* no fresh fruit in November. This is Minnesota. The only things that grow in Minnesota in the winter are icicles."

Norman laughed, and when Hannah joined in, he slipped his arm around her shoulders and gave her a little hug. "I promise you'll have dessert, Hannah. When the mothers decided to meet out here for dinner, I talked to Sally and we dreamed up a special dessert just for you."

Hannah opened her mouth to say she couldn't possibly eat it, not if it contained over fifty calories. And what dessert *didn't* contain over fifty calories? But then she thought about how hurt Norman would be if she refused to eat his carefully planned dessert.

Life was a balancing act, and this time the scales were really skewed. The dessert was on one side, and Norman was on the other. It was all a matter of priorities. She had to decide which was more important in the giant scheme of things. The fact that she'd have to spend an extra hour at Heavenly Bodies tomorrow, working off the extra calories her special dessert contained, didn't count for much when you weighed it against Norman's disappointment if she didn't eat it.

The scales tipped in Norman's favor. And come to think of it, that was a really bad metaphor under her dietary circumstances. All the same, her decision was clear, and Hannah turned to smile at Norman. "That was really thoughtful of you. I can hardly wait to taste it."

There wasn't a whole lot you could do with a boneless, skinless chicken breast if you couldn't use apricot jam for a glaze. Honey with mustard was also out, and not even barbecue sauce was acceptable. Sally had proven herself a master with salt, pepper, garlic, and tarragon. And although Hannah's entrée was succulent and roasted to perfection, it was still naked chicken. Hannah had eaten enough naked chicken in the past week to populate at least half of Winnie Henderson's prize-winning coop.

The broccoli was good. It would have been even better with cheese sauce, but dieters couldn't be choosers. Kathy Purvis, a member of Ronni's Slim and Trim class, had told Hannah that if she shut her eyes and used her imagination, she could make plain baked chicken taste like filet mignon with burgundy mushroom sauce.

Hannah shut her eyes and tried it. She thought of a succulent filet, so tender she could cut it with a butter knife, so perfectly grilled that the center was still the deep, dark red that she loved. As she chewed the tender beef, the mushrooms would provide a slight resistance to the teeth, and the flavor of good wine paired with the silky, buttery richness of the sauce would form a marriage that would linger long after the morsel was gone.

It was poetic, but it didn't work. It was still plain chicken. No amount of imagery could make it what it was not. It looked like chicken, it tasted like chicken, and it was silly to pretend that it wasn't chicken.

"How is your chicken, dear?" Delores asked, smiling at Hannah across the table.

"It's wonderful, Mother," Hannah said, not untruthfully. Does a chicken by any other imagining taste the same? Of course it does! Even Shakespeare knew that. But a person can take only so much chicken, and Hannah figured that she was chickened out.

It seemed to take forever before the plates were removed and the bread basket, an item she'd been ignoring for close to an hour, had gone off on the busboy's tray. Even the plate of butter had disappeared, and it wasn't a moment too soon. Hannah had spent the past thirty minutes squelching the urge to stab one of the perfectly square pieces of butter and pop it into her mouth.

"Coffee all around?" Delores asked, and everyone nodded. It was a silly question to ask a bunch of Minnesotans who couldn't remember ending a meal with any other beverage.

When everyone had been served coffee, Delores called for the dessert cart, and Hannah noticed that Norman had a word with their waitress. She was almost certain that meant her special dessert was about to arrive. Of course she'd enjoy it. She'd have to be dead not to enjoy dessert. But enjoyment came at a price, and Hannah knew that guilt and regret would set in immediately after she swallowed the last bite.

The dessert cart arrived with little fanfare. It didn't need any bells and whistles. The desserts spoke for themselves on their glass plates and attractive bowls. Three different flavors of crème brûlée, four multilayered cakes, several pies, two choices of puddings, an array of pastries, and various flavors of sorbets and ice creams.

Hannah waited until her mother, her sisters, and Carrie had made their choices. Then Norman nodded at their waitress, and she lifted the cover on six lovely parfait glasses filled with layers of colors that shimmered and caught the light from the candle at the center of the table. The top of each dessert was decorated with three perfect raspberries, and Hannah wondered where Sally had found them this time of year.

"For you." The waitress set one parfait glass in front of Hannah and another in front of Norman. "Sally hopes you'll enjoy this special parfait. She said to tell you to please drop by the kitchen after dessert to tell her how you liked it."

Hannah picked up her spoon to taste the concoction that Norman and Sally had wrought. But she couldn't resist asking, "How many calories? Do you know?"

"Yes," Norman gave her a big smile. "Twenty-five."

"Twenty-five?!" Hannah couldn't believe her ears. Perhaps he'd said something else and she'd heard what she wanted to hear. "Did you say *twenty-five* as in five less than thirty?"

"Yes. Sally calls it Guilt-Free Parfait, and it would be less without the raspberries, but she thought they were a nice touch."

"They *are* a nice touch. I'm going to save them for last."

With that said, Hannah removed the berries and stared down at the brightly colored parfait. There were three layers. The top was red, the middle was green, and the bottom was yellow. But she couldn't think of any ingredients that would add up to only twenty-five calories. What was it? Plastic? She dipped her spoon in cautiously and raised a bite of the ruby-colored top layer to her lips.

"Raspberry," she said, immediately recognizing the flavor of one of her favorite berries. "It's raspberry and . . . something else."

"What does the *something else* taste like?" Norman asked.

"I'm not sure, but it makes my tongue tingle. I like that. It's fun. What is it?"

"Sugar-free raspberry Jell-O and soda water."

"So *that's* the fizzy part." Hannah dug down with her spoon to taste the green second layer. "Lime?"

"Lime with Diet 7 Up. Try the third layer. That's my favorite."

Hannah excavated to the third layer, the sparkling yellow one. "Sugar-free lemon Jell-O," she guessed after she'd tasted it. "But there's something else, something tingly and zingy."

"It's diet ginger ale," Norman told her. "Sally thought the ginger taste would go well with the lemon."

"Sally's right. It does." Hannah spooned up another bite of her dessert. It *was* dessert. She felt she was ending her meal with a parfait loaded with yummy calories, but she wasn't. "Are you sure that this is less than twenty-five calories?"

Norman nodded. "Sally and I figured it out."

"Wonderful!" Hannah said, spooning up another bite. It was amazingly exhilarating to feel indulgent and virtuous at the same time. "Only twenty-five calories," she repeated, giving Norman a big smile. "In that case, I might just have two!"

GUILT-FREE PARFAIT

1 small box sugar-free lemon gelatin***
1 small box sugar-free lime gelatin
1 small box sugar-free raspberry gelatin

*** Sally used Sugar-Free Jell-O brand, .3-ounce boxes, 4 half-cup servings per box.

1 cup boiling water for each package of Jell-O *(3 cups in all)*
1 cup cold diet ginger ale for the bottom layer *(Sally used diet Vernor's)*
1 cup cold diet lemon-lime soda for the middle layer *(Sally used diet 7 Up)*
1 cup cold soda water *(Sally used Canada Dry Seltzer)*

Hannah's Note: You can use any flavors of sugar-free gelatin you wish, but it's prettier if the layers are contrasting colors. You can also use any carbonated diet drinks that you wish in the gelatin layers.

Sally's Note: Use canned diet soda whenever possible. It has more fizz than the large bottles. If you can find it, use a small bottle of soda water or seltzer rather than the 2-liter type.

Norman's Note: Of course you could make this dessert in a dish using just one flavor of sugar-free gelatin. Making it with three layers gives you three flavors and three colors

and makes you feel as if you're eating something very special.

Get out six small parfait glasses. You can also use large balloon wine glasses if you don't have parfait glasses.

Boil one cup of water for the bottom layer. Pour the boiling water in a small bowl, and add the sugar-free lemon gelatin. Stir it until it's dissolved. That should take about one minute.

Let the gelatin cool in the refrigerator for 10 minutes. Set your kitchen timer. You don't want it to harden, just to cool to room temperature.

Open a can of icy cold diet ginger ale. Measure out one cup and add it to your cooled gelatin. Stir it in gently. Avoid stirring too much—that will break down the bubbles. Pour bottom layers in each of the six glasses you've chosen to use.

Rinse out your bowl. You can use it again for the next layer.

Refrigerate the glasses until the bottom layer is set. This will take approximately one hour.

When the bottom layer is set, it's time to make the middle layer. Boil one cup of water. Pour the boiling water into the small bowl you rinsed, and add the sugar-free lime gelatin. Stir it until it's dissolved, about one minute.

Let the gelatin cool in the refrigerator for 10 minutes.

Open a can of icy cold diet lemon-lime soda. Measure out one cup. Add it to your cooled gelatin, and stir it in gently. Stir just enough to blend. You don't want to lose the bubbles.

Take your glasses out of the refrigerator and pour in the middle layer. Return them to the refrigerator, to set for one hour.

Rinse out the bowl you used so that you can use it again for the top layer.

When the middle layer is set, it's time to add the top layer. Boil one cup of water. Pour the boiling water into the small bowl you rinsed, and add the sugar-free raspberry gelatin. Stir it until it's dissolved, about one minute.

Let the gelatin cool in the refrigerator for 10 minutes.

Open a small bottle of icy cold seltzer or soda water. Measure out one cup and add it to your bowl of gelatin. Stir it in gently. Avoid overstirring—you don't want to break down the bubbles.

Take your glasses out of the refrigerator, and pour in the top layer. Return the glasses to the refrigerator. Once the top layers are set, you can cover each glass with a piece of plastic wrap to keep the top fresh.

Add three raspberries to each parfait glass before serving. You can also use a small strawberry, or a thin slice of peach or pear. The calorie count will be approximately the same.

Sally says to tell you she's going to make some with Sugar-Free Strawberry Kiwi Jell-O on the top layer and decorate each glass with a slice of kiwi because that's really exotic here in Lake Eden, Minnesota.

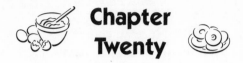

Chapter Twenty

"Norman and I will be right back." Hannah rose to her feet and motioned to Norman. "We're just going to dash to the kitchen and compliment Sally on her Guilt-Free Parfait."

Delores pulled a stack of papers from her briefcase-sized purse. They were stapled together, and Hannah assumed they constituted the list of names her mother and Carrie had called on the phone. "Go ahead, dear. I just want to go over these names with Carrie one more time. If you see our waitress, would you ask her to leave a large carafe of coffee?"

"I'll make sure she does that, Delores," Norman promised.

"Thank you, dear. That's very sweet of you."

Hannah couldn't believe what she had just heard. *Dear?* At some time when she hadn't been looking, Norman had been elevated from *Norman* to *dear.*

"I should call Lonnie," Michelle pushed back her chair. "He may have some information for us. The reception's better in the lobby, so I'll just go out there to call."

Andrea jumped up. "Hold on and I'll go with you. I need to check on the kids."

Hannah gave a glance back at the booth as everyone bailed. Carrie and Delores didn't look at all upset, and she guessed it was okay with them. What on earth could she ask them to do that would be exciting and not injurious to their health?

"You look worried," Norman commented.

"Just trying to think of something the mothers can do."

Norman reached out to take her hand as they walked down the hallway to the kitchen. "That's a tough one. They're going to know if you feed them a placebo."

"Nicely put," Hannah teased him. "Do they teach about placebos in dental college?"

"Dental *school*," Norman corrected her. "It's just like med school, except it's for dentists. We take courses in pharmacology so we can prescribe medications."

They'd reached the plain wooden door near the end of the hallway. It wasn't marked in any way, but both Norman and Hannah knew it led to Sally's kitchen.

"Let's go," Hannah said, pushing it open and stepping into the busy interior of a working restaurant kitchen. "Come on, Norman. Let's find Sally and tell her we love her parfait."

Less than a minute later, Hannah and Norman were standing in the office Sally called her own, a room just off the busy restaurant kitchen. Large picture windows looked out onto the controlled chaos of the kitchen, providing Sally with a view of what her chefs and servers were doing on this busy night.

"Sit down and have one of my special espressos," Sally said, pouring them both an espresso in the doll-sized cups Turkish coffee had made popular.

"The parfait was great," Norman told her, leading off the conversation.

"I know. I tasted it. I'm thinking about adding it to the menu. But enough about desserts. I've got some news for you," Sally leaned across her desk. "You're working to solve Ronni's murder, aren't you, Hannah?"

"Yes, Norman and I are working on it together."

"Well, you might not know it, but Ronni came out here last week looking for a cocktail waitress job. I told her we really didn't have cocktail waitresses, that if there was a big crowd in the bar, our regular wait staff filled in. She said that was fine, and she told me she'd worked as a cocktail waitress at The Moosehead Bar and Grill and that they served food in the bar. She said she quit that job last week because the tips weren't good and it was too far to drive to Anoka and back every other night."

"Did you hire her?" Norman asked.

"I never hire anyone without checking their job history. The last place she'd listed was The Moosehead, so I called the owner to ask about her. He wouldn't tell me exactly what Ronni did, but he told me that she lied when she said she quit."

"She was fired?" Hannah guessed.

"That's right. He said he didn't want to go into details, but they couldn't *afford* to keep her on any longer."

"I wonder what that means," Norman said, looking puzzled.

"I'm not sure, but I thought maybe you might want to drive to Anoka to check it out."

After everyone had a full cup of coffee and their waitress had left a carafe, Hannah pulled out her stenographer's notebook, the one she'd come to think of as her murder book, and started their discussion. "Why don't you go first, Mother? Tell us what you and Carrie found out."

"You may already know this, but Hannah asked us to call around and see if we could find out who Ronni was involved with," Delores prefaced her remarks.

"That's *romantically* involved," Carrie clarified.

"It turned out to be a much bigger job than we thought it would be." Delores tapped her finger on the stapled sheets of paper on the table. "It would have been easier to find out who Ronni *wasn't* involved with!"

"Let's cut to the chase," Carrie suggested. "We made sixty-seven calls, and we wrote down every name that came up."

"We counted the number of times the names were men-

tioned by other people and arranged them according to . . ."
Delores turned to Hannah. "What's the word I want, dear?"

"Frequency?"

"Yes, frequency. If twenty people mentioned a name, we put it ahead of a name that only came up nineteen times." Delores passed the list down to Hannah. "Here's the list, but I don't think it'll do you much good. Every single name except three have alibis. We printed those three names out in red so they'd be easy to spot."

Hannah was almost afraid to look, but she glanced down at the list. Sure enough, Mike's name was in the top ten, and it was printed in red.

"Mike?" Andrea guessed, and Hannah nodded.

"How about Lonnie?" Michelle asked.

Hannah flipped to the second page and found Lonnie's name, also in red. "He's number thirty."

"Bill?" Andrea asked, and her voice quavered slightly.

Hannah turned over more pages until she spotted the third red name. "He's on the last page."

"We're so sorry, dear," Delores said, reaching out to pat Andrea's hand.

"It's okay, Mother. I know all about it, and it's a mistake. People saw them together and misinterpreted it."

"Good for you, dear!" Delores praised her. "Without trust a marriage is worth nothing." Then she turned to Michelle. "How about you, dear? Are you all right?"

"I'm fine. Lonnie told me all about it." Michelle gave a smile that didn't quite reach her eyes. "We were both dating other people at the time."

"Then we're all okay with our findings," Delores continued as she turned to Hannah. "I don't need to worry about you, do I, dear?"

"Not me, Mother," Hannah said, flipping the good-sized booklet over so that she didn't have to focus on Mike's name. "Let me read you the list of suspects I have so far."

Hannah flipped to her page of suspects and went down the

list, one by one. "I have Mike, Lonnie, and Bill. You already know about them."

"You have *Bill*?" Andrea looked shocked. "But you *know* he didn't do it."

"Of course I do. I also know that Mike didn't do it. And I don't think Lonnie did it either, but this is an objective list and nobody gets crossed off until they have an airtight alibi, or until someone else proves to be Ronni's killer."

Neither Andrea nor Michelle looked happy, and an uneasy silence fell over their gathering. Finally it was broken when Norman cleared his throat. "Who's next on your suspect list?" he asked Hannah.

Bless you! Hannah felt like saying, but of course she didn't. Instead she glanced down at her list and found the fifth name. "Bridget Murphy."

"Of course!" Delores exclaimed. "We should have written her down. Several people told us about her confrontation with Ronni at Bertanelli's."

"You know Bridget, don't you, Mother?"

"Of course I do. Why do you ask?"

"Norman said you wanted something exciting to do for the investigation. Would you and Carrie like to interview Bridget to see if she has an alibi?"

"We wanted exciting, not dangerous!" Carrie spoke up. "Bridget Murphy has a temper!"

"I'll do it," Michelle said. "Bridget likes me, and I can figure out some way to ask her that won't sound like I'm accusing her."

"She's all yours," Hannah said, making a note on her page. "How about Betty Jackson? She's next on the suspect list."

"But why?" Delores sounded shocked.

"Ronni insulted her in exercise class, and Betty said she'd get even with her. Charlotte Roscoe told me that Betty went to Duluth to her nephew's wedding, but I haven't checked it out yet."

"I'll do it," Andrea offered. "I have a couple of friends in Duluth."

"Then there's the other suspect Charlotte gave me, Serena Roste."

"Who's that?" Delores asked.

"Wade Hoffman was engaged to Serena before he got engaged to Ronni. Charlotte said it wasn't a pretty breakup, especially since Serena and Ronni were close friends before Ronni stole Serena's fiancé."

"Past tense," Norman noted. "You said they *were* close friends. Did Charlotte think that Serena might have killed Ronni?"

"She thought it was a possibility."

"I'll find out about Serena," Carrie offered. "I have a good friend in Elk River, and I can call her."

"Great. Thanks, Carrie." Hannah jotted it down in her book. "Now how about Loretta Richardson and Trudi Schuman?"

"Why are *they* suspects?" Carrie looked puzzled.

"Ronni insulted them when she substituted for Roger in our class," Andrea explained.

"I'll check their alibis," Michelle offered. "I'll drop in on Carly and find out where her mother was that night. Carly's Mom and Trudi do everything together."

Hannah made another note in her book. "How about Babs Dubinski? Who wants to take her?"

"I will," Andrea said quickly. "I want to check on that rental property of hers, anyway. Somebody told me she was thinking of putting it on the market."

Hannah wrote Andrea's initials in front of Babs's name. There was a reason her sister was the top-selling real estate agent in Lake Eden. "How about Immelda Griese?"

"Wait a minute, dear." Delores looked slightly confused. "What possible reason could Babs and Immelda have for killing Ronni?"

"They're in our class, and Ronni insulted them," Andrea

gave the same explanation. "She also insulted Gail Hansen and Vonnie Blair. Hannah will probably mention them next."

"Was there anyone in your class she *didn't* insult?" Carrie wanted to know.

Andrea nodded. "Me. I think she was about to, but Hannah jumped in and asked her whether she was going to spend the whole hour insulting us, or if we could actually do some exercises."

"Good girl!" Delores beamed at Hannah. It made Hannah feel about six years old, but it was a very nice feeling.

"We'll check on Vonnie Blair," Carrie volunteered. "Delores and I have to go out to the hospital tomorrow to give blood. They're having another drive. And on the way back, we'll stop to see Immelda at the rectory."

"I can take care of Gail Hansen," Norman said. "She's scheduled for a checkup tomorrow afternoon."

"That's it, then," Hannah flipped the page, "except for one thing that only Andrea can do for us."

Andrea looked surprised. "What's that?"

"I need to get the surveillance tapes from the cameras at Heavenly Bodies on the night that Ronni was murdered. I know there won't be any footage of the murder. We would have heard about that right away. But I'm hoping we can spot something that Detective Parks and the rookies didn't notice."

"Done," Andrea said. "I'll ask Bill to bring them home."

"Thanks. That's all I have then." Hannah closed her notebook.

"But I thought you were going to give us something exciting to do," Delores complained. "Talking to Vonnie when we go out to give blood doesn't quite cut it, dear."

"I know. But I really don't have any . . ." Hannah stopped and glanced at Norman. And then she started to smile. "I *do* have something. It's a real clue, and you'll have to be careful how you play it. As a matter of fact, you'll have to go undercover at a bar in Anoka."

"Undercover at a bar!" Carrie turned to look at Delores. "We can do that, can't we?"

Delores laughed. "Of course we can."

"You may have to make a real friend of the bartender to get information," Hannah told them.

"Not a problem." Delores looked supremely confident. "It's the type of assignment that's absolutely made for us. Tell us all about it, dear."

Chapter
Twenty-One

"Andrea!" Delores pulled her daughter away from the curtain that ensured their privacy. "A good wife doesn't spy on her husband."

"If not me, who?" Andrea countered, causing Hannah to cringe at the grammatical infringement.

"If not you, me," Michelle said, putting her eye to the crack where the curtain met the wall. "Where is he sitting?"

"To the left of the fountain. Right now he's alone. She was sitting across from him, but her back was to us and I never really had the chance to see anything but the back of her head."

"What did that look like?" Hannah asked.

"Blond hair, fairly short. It looked like an expensive salon cut, but it's hard to tell from this far away. They just finished their entrées, and I think Bill just ordered coffee."

"Cops drink a lot of coffee," Michelle said. "Lonnie says they go through hundreds of dollars in coffee every week."

"She didn't leave, did she?" Hannah asked.

"I doubt it. She probably just went to the ladies' room."

Michelle watched for several minutes while the rest of them made casual conversation. Suddenly she laughed. "Relax, Andrea! You don't have a thing to worry about!"

"What do you mean?" Delores asked, and Hannah realized that she hadn't told Michelle that it wasn't nice to spy. Evidently spying on a husband was a bad thing to do, but it was okay if you spied on your brother-in-law.

Michelle let the curtain drop and turned around to face them. "The lady cop just came back to Bill's table, and I saw her before she sat down. There's no way Bill would be interested in her."

"She's ugly?" Andrea sounded hopeful.

"No, she's not ugly. But she's a lot older than Bill. You were wrong about her hair. It's gray, not blond. I got a really good look at her and she's really old, at least fifty, maybe more."

"Really . . . *old*?" Delores said, her words clipped and her tone as cold as ice.

Uh-oh! Michelle had put her foot in it this time! Hannah tried to think of something to say to defuse the situation, but before she could come up with a thing, Michelle opened her mouth.

"Did I say old? I didn't mean old. Everybody knows that fifty's not old." Michelle almost stammered in her hurry to extricate herself. "It's just that Bill has got to be at least twenty years younger than . . . well . . . most of the time, younger men don't go for women old enough to be their . . . uh . . ."

Delores held up her hand. "Quiet, Michelle. You're only digging yourself in deeper."

"But I really didn't mean that . . ."

"I said that's enough, Michelle."

Delores hadn't raised her voice, she never did, but Michelle clamped her lips shut tightly. It was childhood all over again, and Mother was angry.

"It's time for us to leave." Delores stood up and motioned to Carrie. "*Old* people need their sleep, you know, and we have a big day coming up tomorrow."

"Thank you for dinner, Mother," Hannah said, hoping to change the subject.

"Yes, thank you, Delores," Norman added quickly.

"Thank you, Mother," Andrea said. "Dinner was delicious."

"Thank you, Mother," Michelle added her thanks. "Would you like me to go out and bring the car around for you? It's pretty cold out tonight."

"Thank you, Michelle, but no. I realize I'm *old*, but I think I can still walk to the parking lot without incident." Delores gave her youngest daughter a withering glance.

"Oh, boy!" Michelle breathed when the curtain had closed behind her mother and Carrie. "Do you think she'll ever forgive me?"

"Of course she'll forgive you," Andrea said. "She has to. She's your mother."

"And because she's your mother, she'll make you eat a caseload of crow *before* she forgives you," Hannah added.

Andrea's cell phone rang. She retrieved it from her purse and flipped it open. "This is Andrea." She listened for a moment and then she smiled. "We can do that, honey. We'd like to meet her, too. We can't stay long, though. I haven't given Hannah your notes yet, so I'm running out there before I come home."

"What notes?" Hannah asked when Andrea had closed her phone and returned it to her purse.

"Bill gave me a list of things he thinks you should do to solve the case. I'll tell you all about it later."

"I've got notes, too," Michelle told her. "One set from Lonnie, and another set from Rick."

"Same here," Norman added. "Mike came in this afternoon and gave me a whole list of things he thought you should do."

"Catching a killer by committee," Hannah said with a sigh. Even though she wasn't looking forward to getting instructions from four different sources, she'd have to listen to all of their suggestions and either accept or reject them. Mike, Lonnie, Rick, and Bill were expecting the impossible if they wanted her to accomplish everything a whole division of detectives would do on a murder case.

"Ready?" Andrea said, pushing back her chair.

"Ready," Hannah answered. It was going to be another long night, just like the previous several nights. As she followed Andrea out of the alcove, she felt a little silly for even hoping that maybe, perhaps, possibly she might get a full night's sleep.

If anyone had asked Hannah to describe Detective Stella Parks in one word, that word would be *formidable*. She was tall, perhaps even an inch or two taller than Hannah. Although her hair was gray and she was clearly a woman in her fifties, she looked to be in excellent physical shape, and Hannah added the phrase *fit as a fiddle* to the list of clichés that Bill had ascribed to her. She wasn't beautiful, and Hannah doubted that most people would call her pretty, but she *was* striking with her silver hair, deep blue eyes, and strong features.

"I'm glad to meet you, Hannah." Stella reached out to shake Hannah's hand. It was a no-nonsense grip, and Hannah added *down to earth* to her list of clichés. "Bill's told me that although you're not officially sanctioned, you've helped the department solve several homicide cases in the past."

"Well . . . yes, that's true," Hannah said, wondering exactly what Bill had told her.

"Are you working on Miss Ward's murder?"

Cuts straight to the chase. Hannah's list of clichés grew longer. She attempted to think of an answer that wasn't an outright lie, and came up with, "You don't have to worry, Detective Parks. I'd never interfere in an official investigation."

"Call me Stella." Her deep blue eyes bored into Hannah's, and Hannah had the fleeting thought that being interrogated by Detective Parks would not be a pleasant experience. "You didn't answer my question. Are you working on Miss Ward's murder?"

"Well . . . yes. Yes, I am. Unofficially, of course."

"Of course. I'm the detective. You're not. I think we're going to get along just fine, Hannah, as long as you keep that distinction clear. Do you think you can do that?"

"I *know* I can do that," Hannah assured her.

"Good. Now let's get down to business." Stella took another sip of her coffee, but her eyes never left Hannah's. "I'm at a disadvantage here. I don't know the people or the area, and I'm shorthanded. My staff consists of two boys who couldn't find their . . ." Stella stopped and cleared her throat. "Who couldn't find their *feet* in a dark room with both hands. I'd like to know that I can count on you, Hannah. How about it?"

"You've got it," Hannah said quickly. "Is there anything in particular you want me to do?"

"Do what you usually do. Talk to people. Listen to people. Bill's told me that information just seems to land in your lap. I want you to share that information with me, even if you don't think it's important. Let me be the judge of that."

"I can do that."

"Good. Just call me every day and tell me what you've learned. I'll be out in the field most of the time, so I'll give you my personal cell phone number. You can always leave voice mail if you can't speak to me personally. Are we clear on that?"

"We're clear."

"Good. Thank you, Hannah. You're a valuable resource and I'm going to enjoy working with you."

Hannah's mind was still spinning when they got back to her condo. She felt as if she'd been co-opted by a master, but she didn't really mind. The important fact was that Detective Parks actually wanted her help.

"The Kitty Valet is empty again," Michelle reported after a quick trip to the kitchen. "How can one cat eat that much?"

"I don't know. And I'm beginning to think it's impossible."

"You think Moishe's carrying off his food and stashing it somewhere?"

"I don't know what else to think. He still jumps up in my arms when I come home, and it doesn't feel as if he's gained any weight. He doesn't look any heavier, either."

"How much food is he going through?"

"Two complete food tubes a day, sometimes three. That's enough to feed a dozen cats. All that food can't just disappear off the face of the earth, so he's got to be hiding it. I just haven't been able to discover where."

"Do you want me to fill up the Kitty Valet again?"

"Might as well. Maybe we can catch him in the act. In the meantime, I'll put on the coffee."

There was a knock on the door, and Michelle went to answer it. Norman and Andrea had arrived together. She ushered them in while Hannah brought out a carafe of coffee and four cups, and they all sat down in Hannah's cozy living room.

"Okay," Hannah said, yawning widely. "I think you'd better give me your notes really fast before I fall asleep in my coffee."

Chapter
Twenty-Two

She was exhausted, but her eyes were wide open and her mind was whirling like a top. She had four sets of investigative instructions to assimilate.

At least Stella Parks hadn't told her how to investigate. The only thing the Minneapolis detective wanted Hannah to do was talk to people and listen to people, something Hannah always did anyway. Too bad Mike, Bill, Lonnie, and Rick didn't have the same faith in her!

There were the books on procedure to read. Mike believed that if she read them and followed the correct investigative procedure, it would lead her to Ronni's killer. But she didn't have time to read all those books, and that wasn't the way she worked anyway.

Bill wanted her to focus on the forensics, and he was providing Andrea with crime scene photos, transcripts of some interviews, and the autopsy report. The report from the Crime Scene Investigator's unit was still to come on fingerprint, hair, and DNA evidence, and they'd have that as soon as it arrived.

Lonnie's take on the proper way to investigate was totally different. He thought that psychology was the most important factor and that Hannah should delve into Ronni's background. Since no one knew quite what that was, he'd suggested that Hannah interview Wade Hoffman at length to see what he knew about Ronni's childhood and her relatives.

Rick had other ideas. He felt that Hannah and her friends should concentrate on the men Ronni had dated, especially if they were married or involved with other women. Rick was candid when he told Michelle that if he'd had the opportunity, he wasn't sure that he wouldn't have killed Ronni for almost wrecking his marriage. But it wasn't just the men Rick wanted them to investigate. He thought they should focus on the women and families who'd been hurt by Ronni's flirtations. He said that if Jessica had been physically capable of doing Ronni in, he wouldn't put it past her. And although he was sure that his mother hadn't taken matters into her own hands, Bridget certainly had a motive, and so did any other mother who'd been embarrassed and hurt by her married son's betrayal.

Four methods to follow to the killer, and Hannah knew there was no way they could accomplish them all. She had to choose which paths to explore and which to set aside. But Mike and Bill were veteran detectives, and they were supposed to know what they were doing. Rick and Lonnie didn't have quite as much experience, but they'd worked on more cases than she had! She had to prioritize. There was no way she could spread herself that thin. But whose advice should she follow? No one had suggested going out to the gym and talking to the members of Ronni's classes. Was that a waste of her time? Or were there clues to be found at Heavenly Bodies that would lead her to Ronni's killer?

Hannah knew she had to stop thinking and get to sleep. It was twelve thirty in the morning, and she had to get up at five. Moishe never seemed to have any trouble getting to sleep. He was stretched out at the foot of the bed, snoring peacefully, making soft little noises. It was a peaceful sound, a familiar sound that usually sent her right off into the Land of Nod, but it wasn't working tonight. She was too busy trying to figure out how she could accomplish everything that people expected of her.

She wasn't really prepared for the phone to ring at twelve thirty-five, but she wasn't terribly surprised either. She reached out to pluck the receiver from the cradle and answered, "Hello, Mike."

"Hannah!" He sounded surprised. "How did you know it was me?"

Because you're the only person who'd call me this time of night when you know I have to get up at five in the morning, she thought, but of course she didn't say it. Mike had troubles of his own. "Just guessing," she said instead. "What is it?"

"Did Norman give you my notes?"

"Yes, he did."

"How about the books? Did you read them?"

Hannah glanced over at the thick book on the table by her bed. "I took *Principles of Investigation* to bed with me."

"But did you *read* it?"

She should have known she couldn't get away with an ambiguous answer. "I flipped through it," she said, not untruthfully.

"Well, make some time and read it tomorrow. It's the best of the bunch I sent."

"Right," Hannah said. Unless they changed the length of a day to thirty hours, she wouldn't have much time for reading.

"Anyway, I'm down in your garage again. I'm in your truck. Come on down and talk to me. And bring some coffee if you've got it."

"Right," Hannah said again, not bothering to argue the time or the fact she'd have to go out in the dead of winter at night in the cold. "I'll be there in less than five minutes."

"Mike's in the garage again?" Michelle called out as Hannah passed the open door to the guest room.

"Who else? I'm going to take him a thermos of coffee. He's waiting in my truck."

"But you lock your truck, don't you?"

"Of course."

"Then how did he get inside?"

"He's a seasoned law enforcement professional. I'm sure they teach them how to break into a truck in cop school."

"You're probably right. Do you want to take him some cookies?"

"No. This isn't a twenty-four hour diner. He's lucky to get fresh coffee."

"Let me guess . . . somebody just moved to the top of your list? And that somebody starts with an *m* and ends with *annoying?*"

Hannah laughed. "That would be Mike, all right. He should know better than to call me this time of night."

"Do you want me to get up and put on a second pot of coffee? I'm awake anyway."

"More coffee's the *last* thing I need. Go to sleep, Michelle. One of us has to be awake and alert tomorrow morning."

"Thanks for coming down, Hannah," Mike said, leaning over to open the passenger door for her. "Is that a thermos of coffee?"

"It is." Hannah slid into the passenger seat. It felt strange to be on this side of her truck. She didn't think she'd ever been in the passenger seat before. "What's so important that you had to get me out of bed?"

Mike stared at her for a moment, taking in her old sweatpants and sweatshirt partially covered by the faded chenille robe she'd picked up at Lake Eden's only thrift store, Helping Hands. "You really wear *that* to bed?"

"Yes. Without the robe and slippers, of course."

"Somehow I never imagined you wearing something that . . . never mind. I just came to ask you if you're making any progress on the case."

"It's too early to say," Hannah said, giving him nothing except a hard stare.

"How's Moishe doing with his Kitty Valet?"

Hannah's mood improved slightly. Mike really did care about Moishe. "He loves it. There's only one thing . . . he's going through two and three full food tubes a day."

"That's way too much! He's going to be as fat as a pig if he keeps that up."

"I don't think he's eating it. It doesn't look as if he's gained any weight, and with that much food, he would have. I think he's taking out the food and hiding it somewhere."

"That makes some kind of sense, especially since he was a stray. He probably hid food as a survival tactic."

"That's what I thought, but I can't figure out where he's hiding it. There's got to be quite a pile by now."

"Well . . . you can't keep an eye on him twenty-four-seven. What you should probably do is install a surveillance camera."

"A surveillance camera for my cat?" Hannah was amused.

"I think it's a good idea. They have nanny-cams. You need a kitty-cam."

Hannah laughed. "You're probably right, but I'm on a limited budget. I really can't afford to buy an expensive surveillance camera to discover where my cat is hiding his food."

"You don't have to buy one. I've got a state-of-the-art model in the car. I test out products for a company that makes security devices. All I have to do is rate them, and then the department gets to keep them. It's a great way to get free equipment."

Hannah thought about that for a moment. "It's also a great way to save the county some money."

"You bet. The security staff at the mall tests them, too. They don't have much of a budget out there."

"Uh-oh. Is this camera going to break down like the one outside the back door at Heavenly Bodies?"

"You don't have to worry about that. For one thing, it's inside. And for another thing, it's a brand-new, improved model. Some of the older models are affected by temperature and moisture, but this new one is supposed to be completely reliable. I can install it in your kitchen right now if you want me to. All I have to do is put in a bracket and two screws, and that won't take more than a minute or two. Then, when we find out which direction Moishe goes with the food, we can move the camera to that room and track him to wherever he's hiding it."

"Okay," Hannah said. "That sounds like a sensible solution to me. I'll drive you to your car to get it. Where did you park?"

"Right next to you." Mike gestured toward the car that was parked in the slot next to Hannah's cookie truck. It was an old, faded green sedan with a fake convertible top that had ripped and was spewing out fiberglass stuffing.

Hannah just stared at the wreck in surprise. "Where did you get *that*?"

"It was Ronni's new car."

"Did you say . . . *new*?"

"Well, it was new to her. She bought it for five hundred dollars from someone at the bar where she used to work."

"And it runs?"

"So far, so good. Ronni could never get it to run right. She was always asking for rides because it was broken down. It's been sitting on the street outside the apartment complex for at least two weeks now, and I figured I'd better move it before it was towed away. But the funny thing is, it runs like a champ for me. I haven't had a single problem with it."

Surprise, surprise, Hannah thought, wondering how such a bright guy could be so naïve when it came to the excuses a sexy woman gave him.

"Anyway," Mike went on, "I decided to use it after I came to see you last night and I had to park way out on the road. My Hummer's too distinctive. There aren't that many around town. But if somebody sees *this* car parked next to you in the garage, they'll never guess it's me."

"True," Hannah said, but she didn't add the rest of the comment that ran through her mind. *One look and they'll think somebody abandoned it here, and they'll have it towed away.*

* * *

"All done," Mike said, stepping back with Hannah's screw-driver in his hand. He glanced down to see Moishe gazing up at him and turned to Hannah. "Do you think he knows we're on to him?"

"Maybe. Moishe's a really bright cat."

"It's for your own good, Big Guy," Mike said, reaching down to pet Moishe's head. Then he straightened up to face Hannah again. "Just flick that red switch on the base of the camera when you leave in the morning, and it'll record six hours of activity."

"Activity?"

"It's state-of-the-art. It won't record if there's no activity at the food bowl. It's motion activated."

"So I won't have to sit through hours of tape showing the food bowl and the doorway, and nothing else."

"Exactly."

"Thanks, Mike," Hannah said, leading him to the door. "You really have to go now. I need to get some sleep. Tomor-row's going to be a rough day."

"You have a lot of baking to do?"

"I don't have to do *any* baking. Lisa and Michelle are taking care of that. I have to meet Andrea out at Heavenly Bodies."

"So you're still doing your early-morning exercises," Mike said, looking pleased.

"Of course. We work out first, and then both of us go to Roger's Classic Body Sculpting class."

Mike eyed her appraisingly. "You look like you lost a little weight, Hannah."

"I do?" It was Hannah's turn to look pleased.

"Definitely. Your face looks thinner."

Her *face*? Hannah had all she could do not to groan. If her face was the only place she'd lost weight, she'd never get thin enough to fit into her Regency dress!

"It takes a while to start losing," Mike said, the man who was all muscle, no fat. "How long is your class?"

"Half an hour. But I've got classes in the afternoon, too."

"Good for you! Which classes are you taking?"

"Every one of the ones that Ronni used to teach."

Mike looked puzzled. "Why are you doing that?"

"To find out if any of the other class members had a grudge against her. I'm exercising, but I'm listening, too. Ronni wasn't exactly complimentary toward some of the ladies she taught, and they're still talking about the things she said."

"Oh, but that was just Ronni. I don't think anybody thought that much about it. Do you really think that some woman she insulted in class got mad enough to kill her?"

"It's a possibility."

"Maybe, but it's a real long shot. Seriously, Hannah . . . it won't do you any good to nose around out at Heavenly Bodies. There's nothing to learn out there, and you're just wasting time. You'd be a lot better off reading those books I gave you and improving your investigative techniques."

They'd reached the front door, and Hannah opened it. She could hardly wait for Mike to leave. She was sick and tired of everyone telling her how she should spend her time.

"Night, Hannah," Mike said, and then he pulled her into his arms for a kiss.

Conflicting emotions assailed Hannah. On the one hand, she was irked at Mike for telling her how to run her investigation, her weight-loss program, and her life in general. On the other hand, he was the best kisser in the whole county, perhaps even the whole state. Hannah felt the tingles spread up from her toes and travel all the way to the top of her head. They made the return trip from head to toes as the kiss went on for second after delicious second.

"I'd better let you get some sleep," Mike said at last, breaking their embrace. "See you soon, Hannah."

Hannah nodded. She was incapable of further speech. As she closed the door behind him, she thought that perhaps she wouldn't mind Mike's high-handedness quite so much if he'd kiss her like that more often!

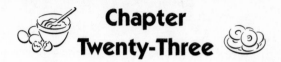

Chapter
Twenty-Three

Hannah refilled the food tube on Moishe's Kitty Valet and secured the lid. Then she put the sack of cat food back in the broom closet and locked the door. Everything was set. All she had to do was remember to turn on the kitty-cam when she left, and her stockpiling cat would be caught red-pawed.

"All set?" Michelle asked, coming into the kitchen in her winter parka and boots.

"I am. But you really don't have to go down to The Cookie Jar this early. If you get there by six, that should be plenty of time to help Lisa with the baking."

"I'm leaving with you. I want to give Moishe plenty of time to hide his food. I bet it's behind the stove."

"You're wrong about that. Moishe can't fit in back of the stove. Besides, the camera wouldn't catch that. It's trained on the living room door. Mike wants to see Moishe leaving the kitchen with the food in his mouth so we can find out which way he goes."

"Do you really think it'll work?" Michelle looked dubious as Hannah reached up to flick the red switch.

"Why not? Unless Moishe's savvy enough to jump up there with a can of spray paint and coat the lens of the camera, we're going to see him heading into the living room with a load of kitty crunchies in his mouth."

* * *

"Here they are," Andrea said, pulling three envelopes out of her briefcase and placing them on the table as if she were dealing giant cards in a game of solitaire. She tapped the envelope on her left with a perfectly manicured fingernail. "The crime lab report," she announced, and then she moved to the middle envelope. "Autopsy. And this . . ." she tapped the envelope on the right, ". . . this envelope contains copies of the crime scene photos."

"Norman and I haven't had our cookies yet," Michelle complained. "Let's start with the crime lab report. Anything else might make us lose our appetites."

"I think that's doubtful," Hannah said. And she watched her youngest sister in amusement as Michelle handed Norman a napkin with two cookies and then took three for herself. If Michelle didn't start watching what she ate, she'd be joining them in their Classic Body Sculpting class before you could say, *Pass the cookies, please.*

It was the eleven o'clock lull at The Cookie Jar, the time of day when most people felt it was too late for a midmorning snack cookie and too early for a lunch cookie. Lisa's husband, Herb, was talking to their sole customer, Earl Flensburg, so that Lisa could join in their crime-solving discussion at the table in the back of the shop.

The crime lab report was short, and everyone listened as Hannah read it aloud. There were no surprises and no clues. Since the gazebo was a public area in a busy spa and gym, there was no useful fingerprint evidence. The hair and fiber evidence was more of the same. The Jacuzzi was used by hundreds of people every day, and there was no telling whether the samples they'd collected were from members, guests, or the killer, who could also be a member or a guest. In short there was nothing found at the scene that provided any clue to the identity of Ronni's killer.

Andrea sighed. "Well, that was a waste. Let's go on to the autopsy report."

"Wait a second," Michelle said, popping the last bite into her mouth and swallowing. "Okay. I'm ready."

Hannah handed the envelope to Norman. "You'd better read it. You know all the medical words, and you can translate it into laymen's terms for us."

"Okay," Norman said, taking a final sip of coffee and clearing his throat.

As Norman read and translated, Hannah found herself holding her breath and hoping that something in the report would exonerate one of her detective "bosses." Since one way of determining the time of death had to do with internal body temperature, Doc had used some scientific formula that allowed for the heat of the water in the Jacuzzi to come up with a time frame. Ronni Ward had breathed her last sometime between the hours of one and two thirty in the morning. And that meant the trio at the sheriff's department were still suspects.

"Doc says the blow to Ronni's head knocked her unconscious and she drowned in the Jacuzzi. He thinks she was in there already, and the killer walked up to the tub and killed her."

Hannah did her best not to imagine Ronni's last moments in living Technicolor. There was something really creepy about leaving an unconscious victim to drown.

"Her blood-alcohol level was three times the legal limit. That means if she hadn't been knocked unconscious, she might have passed out on her own."

"Drunk as a skunk," Andrea said, but she didn't sound censorious. Hannah figured that was probably because Ronni was dead and couldn't cause problems for her any longer.

"There was no evidence of rape, and other than her blood-alcohol level, all of her blood work came back normal. That means no drugs, and no infectious diseases. There was a slight bruising of her lower lip, but it wasn't serious and Doc's not sure what it's from."

Kissing everybody at her birthday party, Hannah thought,

and she looked up to find both of her sisters staring at her. It was clear they were thinking alike.

"The last page is just a listing of physical characteristics."

"What physical characteristics?" Hannah asked.

"Her height, her weight, the size and weight of her organs, and a detailed description of scars and markings on her body." Norman slid the report back into the envelope and leaned back in his chair.

"How much did she weigh?" Andrea asked quickly.

Hannah was puzzled. "What difference does that make?"

"It makes a lot of difference to me." Andrea turned back to Norman. "Look it up for me, will you, Norman?"

Norman nodded and removed the papers from the envelope again. He flipped to the last page and read Doc's description. "Female in her late twenties identified as Veronica Alice Ward."

"Veronica?" Michelle repeated, before Norman could read on. "I thought Ronni was her real name."

"It was a nickname, I guess," Hannah said, turning to Norman again. "Please go on."

"Victim was sixty-three inches in height, one hundred and eleven pounds, fourteen ounces in weight."

"Almost a hundred and twelve!" Andrea exclaimed. "I'm an inch taller and I weigh only a hundred and ten."

Hannah exchanged glances with Michelle. There was no reason to point out that the majority of Ronni's weight had been muscle, and muscle was heavier than fat. That would have been cruel. Instead she decided to change the subject.

"Now that we've got a window for the time of the murder, it'll be a lot easier to check alibis," she said. And then she reached for the third envelope, the one with the crime scene photos, and drew them out to pass around.

To Andrea and Michelle's credit, neither one flinched when it came to studying the photos. Perhaps they were getting used to seeing pictures of crime scenes. Or perhaps it helped that neither of them had liked the victim.

"Look at this last one," Andrea said, passing the photo back to Hannah. "Do you think my flower looks silly?"

At first Hannah thought her sister had flipped round the bend. It was a photo of the back entrance of Heavenly Bodies, and there were two cars parked by the door. Hannah's cookie truck was on the right, and Andrea's Volvo was on the left. She studied the photo for another moment and noticed the flower in question. There was a red rose with the stem wound around the radio antenna on Andrea's Volvo.

"Well, do you? You don't have to be afraid of hurting my feelings. It's not like anybody gave it to me for a present or anything. I just put it there when I took Tracey and her friends to the Minnesota Zoo last summer. Hundreds of people go, you know, and I thought it would make it easier to spot my car in the parking lot."

"I think your rose looks good," Hannah told her. "Winter's so bleak, and it's a bright touch of color."

"I think it's nice, too," Norman said, looking at the photo over Hannah's shoulder.

"I love it," Lisa said, giving a little smile. "Sometimes winter seems so endless. It's like Mom always used to say when I'd complain about how long winter was. *When the sun shines and the tulips go up, we'll all feel a lot better.*"

"Maybe I'll get roses for all of us," Andrea said, lifting her briefcase to the top of the table and flipping it open. "Here are the tapes Bill sent for you, Hannah."

"Videotapes?" Lisa looked puzzled.

"Yes, but they're not just any videotapes," Hannah explained. "They're the Tri-County Mall security tapes of Heavenly Bodies on the night Ronni was killed."

Lisa's eyes grew wide. "They caught the killer on tape?" she asked, and Hannah noticed that her voice was shaking slightly.

"Unfortunately, no." Andrea turned to smile at Lisa. "I know exactly where the security cameras are located. I took pictures of the monitors with my cell phone at the security station. The gazebo that holds the Jacuzzi doesn't have one. And neither does the pool area, the sauna, or the bathrooms and dressing rooms."

Lisa nodded. "I can understand about the bathrooms and dressing rooms. That would be an invasion of privacy. But why didn't they put cameras in the gazebo, and the pools, and the sauna?"

"That's easy," Herb said, and everyone turned to look at him. While they'd been talking, Earl Flensburg had left and Herb was standing there with the carafe of coffee in his hand.

"The invisible waitress trick!" Lisa said with a giggle. "Herb refilled my coffee cup, and I didn't even notice him."

"Right." Hannah gave her the thumbs-up sign, and then she turned to Herb. "Why don't they have surveillance cameras in the sauna, or the pools, or the hot tub?"

"Because the owner's biggest concern is theft. The exercise machines are expensive, so of course they've got cameras in the exercise rooms and the weight rooms. They've got them by the exits, too, so they can see if someone tries to leave with something they shouldn't. But what can you steal from a sauna? Heat? And what can you steal from a pool? Water?"

Hannah had a laugh at her own expense. "It's obvious, now that you explain it, but I didn't even think of it that way."

"Don't feel bad. Most people wouldn't. It's just I've been looking into surveillance systems lately."

"Lisa said you were checking out the red-light camera at the mall for Mayor Bascomb," Hannah said. "Do you really think he's going to put in a stoplight with a camera on Main Street?"

"Not after he gets my recommendation, but it's nice duty for me while it lasts. I'm also looking into smoke and fire detectors. Mrs. Bascomb wants one installed in the new sauna they're building, but it has to be a special type."

"What type is that?" Andrea asked, and Hannah wondered if her sister and brother-in-law were thinking about adding a sauna to the new basement recreation room they'd been planning to build.

"It can't be a heat alarm. If it is, it'll go off every time someone turns on the sauna. It has to be a flame alarm, or a smoke alarm. Smoke's the best bet because the redwood benches in a sauna smoke before they burn."

"I see," Hannah said. "The smoke detector would pick up the problem sooner than the flame detector."

"Exactly right," Herb said. "I'm going to recommend a smoke alarm that's tied directly to the Lake Eden Fire Department. The minute it goes off, they're alerted. That's what they have at Heavenly Bodies. The owner has to pay the fire department a monthly fee to monitor it, but it's worth it. He had to set it up that way to get insurance. There are a lot of ways people can hurt themselves at a gym."

"That's true," Hannah said, thinking about how Ronni had mixed up drinks at her party and then climbed in the Jacuzzi when everyone left. Was the killer someone who'd stayed behind with her? Or was it someone who'd come in after the partygoers had gone?

"You look worried, Hannah," Norman said, reaching out to pat her shoulder.

"I'm not really worried. I'm just wondering how we can possibly watch all sixty hours on these tapes."

"Lisa and I can take six hours," Herb offered. "We'll start watching right after dinner, and if we fast-forward, we'll be through by ten."

"You don't mind?" Hannah turned to Lisa.

"Not at all." Lisa shook her head. "Can we take a tape from the weight room? I just love to see guys straining their muscles and lifting weights."

Herb laughed. "Not a good idea. If there's a cute guy working out, she'll want to watch it three or four times. And then we'll never get any sleep!"

"Herb!" Lisa said sternly, but then she blew it by giggling. "Okay. If my husband doesn't think I should watch handsome men in the weight room, you can give us the hallway. That ought to be perfectly innocuous."

The bell on the door tinkled, and Lisa shot to her feet. "Noon rush," she said, motioning to Michelle.

Lisa said good-bye to Herb while Michelle took her place at the cash register. Then Lisa tied on a serving apron and started to wait tables. The bell was ringing now in a steady cadence.

"My house. Six tonight," Norman said, getting to his feet. "I'll take the tapes with me and set up three or four viewing rooms."

"I can stop somewhere and bring takeout for dinner," Hannah suggested.

"There's no need. I'll make a big bowl of that egg salad you liked. We can have ours on lettuce with sliced tomatoes. Everybody else can have sandwiches."

"I'll bring something for dessert."

"That's fine. Make it something they can eat while we watch the tapes. We'll try to get through as many as we can tonight."

"If we don't finish, I can always take some home to Grandma McCann," Andrea offered. "She can watch some during the day while Bethany's napping and Tracey's in school."

"Good idea. I'll see if I can get Doc Bennett to watch a couple for me tonight. When he came into the clinic this morning, he said there was nothing he wanted to watch on regular television and it was pretty sad to have to judge his bedtime by the number of One Eight-Hundred Dentist commercials he'd seen."

Hannah chuckled at that. "I'd ask Mother and Carrie, but they're going out to The Moosehead tonight. Maybe we can ask them tomorrow if they're in a good mood."

"Maybe," Norman said as he closed the briefcase and snapped it shut. "Bring Moishe with you tonight. Cuddles is home now."

"She got the mouse at your dental clinic?"

"Yes, she did. She's a good hunter."

"You found the carcass?"

"I found *part* of it. She's a good eater, too."

Hannah laughed. She knew exactly what Norman meant. Moishe often left her select mouse parts to let her know that he appreciated living with her.

"See you tonight," Norman said, turning toward the door.

"Norman?" Hannah gave him her most winning smile. "Will you do something just for me?"

"That depends on what it is."

"This time please write down the recipe for your egg salad. It's the best I've ever tasted."

NORMAN'S EGG SALAD

4 cups peeled and chopped hard-boiled eggs.***
*(That's about a dozen extra large eggs—measure
    after chopping)*
½ cup crumbled cooked bacon *(make your own or
    use real crumbled bacon from a can—I used
    Hormel Premium Real Crumbled Bacon)*
1 Tablespoon chopped parsley *(it's better if it's fresh,
    but you can use dried parsley flakes if you don't
    have fresh on hand)*
¼ cup grated carrots *(for color and a bit of sweet-
    ness)*
4 ounces cream cheese
¼ cup sour cream
½ cup mayonnaise *(I used Best Foods, which is
    Hellmann's in some states)*
½ teaspoon garlic powder *(or ½ teaspoon freshly
    minced garlic)*
½ teaspoon onion powder *(or 1 teaspoon freshly
    minced onion)*
salt to taste
freshly ground black pepper to taste

***Norman says not to chop the eggs too finely—some
large pieces are good because they give texture to the egg
salad.

Peel and chop the hard-boiled eggs. Add the crumbled
bacon, the parsley, and the grated carrots. Mix well.

Put the cream cheese in a small bowl and microwave for 30 seconds on HIGH to soften it. If it can be easily stirred with a fork, add the sour cream and mayonnaise, and mix well. If the cream cheese is still too solid, give it another 10 seconds or so before you add the other ingredients.

Stir in the garlic powder and onion powder.

Add the cream cheese mixture to the bowl with the eggs and stir it all up. Add salt and freshly ground pepper to taste, and chill until ready to serve.

Serve by itself on a lettuce leaf, as filling in a sandwich, or stuffed in Hannah's Very Best Cream Puffs for a fancy luncheon.

Yield: Makes approximately a dozen superb egg salad sandwiches.

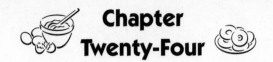

Hannah let the springs on the machine she thought of as the *Push Me, Pull Me* snap back into place with a loud thwack. It was bad for the machine, she knew that, but she simply didn't have enough energy to return the pedals and the handlebars to the starting position any other way. She was weary, worn out, ready to drop, and dead beat. In other words, she'd had it!

Three hours of exercise classes was too much for any normal human being. Hannah was willing to testify to that. Thank goodness she didn't have to go back to The Cookie Jar today! She could go straight home, take a shower, feed Moishe, make some sort of dessert, and drive to Norman's to watch surveillance tapes. Big whoopie.

"Miss Swensen?"

Hannah turned to see an older man with short-cropped gray hair smiling at her. He was wearing a mall security uniform, his bearing was stiffly military, and he looked alert and competent. "Yes?"

"I'm Frank Hurley. Charlotte called and said you might want to talk to me."

"Hello, Frank," Hannah greeted him. She should have known that Charlotte would jump the gun. "I'm glad to meet you, but I don't really have any questions for you. You weren't working the night of Ronni's murder, were you?"

"I was working, but my shift ended at midnight. I heard she was killed a lot later than that. Is that right?"

"Yes." Hannah didn't see any harm in telling the security guard the facts. "Doc Knight says it was sometime between one and two-thirty in the morning."

"It was a terrible thing to happen, but I won't lie and say I'm sorry she's gone. Miss Ward wasn't a nice person. She caused a lot of hurt feelings around here. I'm just sorry that Tad was working that night. I know it was hard on the boy."

"Why do you say that?"

"He's never been at a murder scene before."

"And you have?" Hannah was curious.

"A couple of times when I worked private security for an after-hours club in the Cities. People get liquored up and do crazy things. Most of the time we could break it up before things got too hot, but there were a couple of altercations that got way out of hand."

"You sound pretty calm about it."

"Sure . . . now. That was over thirty years ago, and I don't take that kind of work anymore. It's usually pretty tame duty out here at the mall. That's one of the reasons I wanted Tad to work here." Frank took a step closer and lowered his voice. "Please don't say anything to anybody, but Tad's my nephew and I got him the job. I told the head guy I knew somebody good who was looking for a mall job, and he took my recommendation and hired Tad. He wouldn't have done it if he'd known that we were related. There's some kind of rule against it."

"Don't worry. I won't say anything."

"Thanks. Tad's my sister's youngest, and he's always been like a son to me. As far as I can see, he's only got one weakness."

"What's that?"

Frank looked a bit embarrassed. "It's women," he said. "He picks the wrong ones."

"Quite a few people I know have that problem," Hannah said, giving him a commiserating smile.

"Tad needs a nice girl, one with good moral fiber, if you know what I mean."

"I think I do."

"I've tried to talk some sense into him, but he won't listen. He just keeps trying to get the wrong girls to go out with him."

Hannah nodded, remembering that Charlotte had told her Frank liked to lecture people.

"Well, I'd better get back to work," Frank said, turning to go. "Nice talking to you, Hannah. Just call me if you need me for anything. Charlotte said she gave you my number."

When Frank left, Hannah dragged her tired body to the dressing room, slipped on her coat, and grabbed her clothes. She'd change at home. Right now all she wanted was to be transported to her condo in an instant by the flick of a magic wand, or the click of ruby slippers.

She'd almost made it to her cookie truck when a voice hailed her. Hannah turned to see Tad Newberg heading her way. He was dressed in a parka that said MALL SECURITY over the breast pocket. A fur-lined hat with the same designation embroidered in green was clamped on his head, and he looked a lot warmer than she felt in her perspiration-soaked workout clothes.

"I noticed you were still here," Tad said, giving her a smile in greeting.

"I'm just leaving. What are you doing here so early?"

"I'm pulling a double today. One of the day guys called in sick. How are you girls coming along with the investigation?"

Hannah was surprised. When they'd talked to Tad at the security station, none of them had mentioned that they were attempting to solve Ronni's murder. "Who said we were investigating?" she asked, answering his question with one of her own.

"A couple of the ladies in your classes. They said you and

your sisters always get involved when there's a murder. I was just wondering if you found out anything."

"Nothing yet," Hannah said, deciding it couldn't hurt to share that information. "How about you?"

"Me? It's not my job to investigate murders."

"I know that. I just wondered if you'd noticed anything unusual since the night Ronni was killed."

"Like what?"

"Like somebody who used to come out here every night and hasn't been seen since Ronni died. The regular detectives would miss that, but you'd notice."

"You're right. I would. I don't think . . . no, I haven't noticed anything like that. The only unusual thing that happened since she died was the attempted break-in at Bianco Shoes. They didn't get anything. The alarm scared them off."

A cold wind whipped around the corner of Hannah's truck. She shivered and pulled up the zipper on her parka.

"You're cold. You'd better get going," Tad said, opening the door of her truck for her. "It's supposed to get down to fifteen below tonight, and that's not counting the wind chill."

Hannah shivered again and climbed into her icy cold truck. She reached back for a roll of Molasses Crackles and handed them to him. "Thanks, Tad. Here's a roll of cookies for you. They're frozen, but they should thaw in about twenty minutes after you get back inside."

"That's really nice of you. Thanks, Hannie."

"Hannie?"

"When I like someone, I give them a nickname.You know, like Susan is Suzie. Hannah's a tough one."

She certainly is! Hannah thought, but she didn't say it.

"I hope you don't mind the nickname thing." Tad looked a bit worried. "If you'd rather, I can call you Hannah."

"No, it's okay," Hannah said quickly. She just wanted to cut this conversation short and get on the road. "Good-bye, Tad."

Hannah started her truck to cut off any further dialogue. She was just too cold to chat. Tad took the hint by giving a little wave and heading for the entrance.

As she drove home, Hannah began to smile. It was a good thing Tad hadn't known that Louise was her middle name. He might have decided to call her *Weezie* instead of *Hannie,* and she didn't know which nickname she disliked more.

"Again?" Hannah stared down at the empty Kitty Valet. "Good heavens, Moishe!"

"Rowww." Moishe gave a plaintive meow and brushed up against her ankles.

"Okay. You can have more. Hold on a second and I'll fill it up." Hannah unlocked the door to the broom closet and came back with a scoop of dry cat food. She retraced her footsteps four times until the food tube on the Kitty Valet was full. "There it is," she said, clamping the lid on tightly. "I just wish I knew where you were . . . the camera!"

The minute she thought of it, Hannah reached up to flick off the red switch on the camera. She pushed the button that extracted the tape and retrieved the carrier that Mike had left on the kitchen counter. Her next stop was the living room. Hannah slipped the tape and carrier into her VCR, set it to rewind, and headed toward her bedroom. She'd get out of her soaked exercise outfit, take a lightning fast shower, put on the warmest clothes she owned, grab a fresh cup of coffee from the pot she'd put on when she'd arrived home, and settle down on the couch with the remote control to see where Moishe was hiding his kitty crunchies.

Fifteen minutes later, Hannah was still in the dark. The surveillance camera must have failed somehow, because there were only two shots of Moishe leaving the kitchen. In the first shot, he'd entered the living room and jumped up to the back of the couch to take a nap. At least Hannah assumed he'd been napping. The camera had clicked off. When it reactivated, it caught Moishe in the act of jumping down from the back of the couch and padding into the kitchen again. The third shot showed Moishe leaving the kitchen and heading off toward the laundry room, presumably to use his litter box. And that was all. The rest of the tape was blank.

Hannah removed the tape from her VCR, popped it out of the carrier, and took it back to the kitchen. She'd return it to the camera and run a little test. She'd turn on the camera and leave the kitchen a prescribed number of times. Then she'd turn off the camera and watch the tape to see whether it had activated correctly.

Hannah had just reinserted the tape when her cell phone rang. Since it was in her purse on the counter within easy reach, she answered it.

"Hello? This is Hannah."

"Hi, Hannah. It's Mike. Where are you?"

"I'm home. Why didn't you call me here?"

"Because I didn't know you'd be home this early."

Hannah was puzzled. "You're not calling me from home, are you?"

"Of course not. They might check my phone records. I picked up one of those disposable cell phones with the minutes already loaded."

"Well I'm glad you called. I'm having trouble with this surveillance camera, and I was about to test it out."

"What's wrong with it?"

"I turned it on when Michelle and I left this morning, and I just watched the tape. It only showed Moishe leaving the kitchen twice all day. And when I got home, the Kitty Valet was empty."

There was silence for a minute, and then Mike sighed. "Well, that can't be right. There's no way he could carry that much food in only two trips. He's got to be eating it, Hannah."

"But he's not. I'm almost positive of that."

"Okay. Let's figure this out right now. I want you to put the tape back in the camera and turn it on."

Hannah reached up to flick the red switch. The moment she did, her phone started to make a high-pitched hum. "I think there's something wrong with my phone," she told him. "It sounds like a mosquito."

"I can't hear it on this end. It's probably some sort of interference."

"Then it must be from the surveillance camera. It started the second I flicked it on. I'm going to turn it off and see if it stops."

"Good idea. I'll hold."

Hannah flicked off the camera, and the mosquito sound disappeared. "It's the camera. The sound stopped."

"I'll try it with my cell phone the next time I come over, and if it happens with mine, I'll write it in my report to the company. In the meantime, let's test out that camera. Turn it on again, and crawl into the living room."

"*Crawl?!* Why do I have to crawl?"

"Because you're a lot taller than Moishe. I want to see if the camera's aimed right."

Hannah thought about arguing, but it wasn't worth the effort. She dropped to her knees and crawled through the doorway to the living room. She moved to the side so she wasn't within camera range, and on the count of ten, she dropped to her knees and crawled back into the kitchen.

"Okay. Done," she reported when she'd picked up her cell phone again.

"Great. Now do it three more times to make sure. And then turn off the camera, stick the tape in your VCR, and see if it caught the action."

Crawling through the door and back three more times would kill her. Hannah was quite certain of that. But the surveillance camera picked up movement, and it didn't really matter what was doing the moving, did it? That theory in mind, Hannah opened her pantry and surveyed the contents. What was capable of rolling and wasn't any larger than Moishe? Almost immediately, Hannah had the answer. She grabbed three fifty-ounce cans of chicken broth. They were smaller than Moishe, but that was all right. She bought the cans of chicken broth whenever Florence had a sale at the Red Owl, and stockpiled them in her pantry to use in her Holiday Squash Soup.

Getting back down to the floor with the cans wasn't easy. Hannah resorted to sitting on her haunches since her knees were so sore. Then she picked up one can, positioned it on its side, and rolled it through the doorway.

It was like bowling with soup cans. Hannah laughed out loud as she sent the second can rolling. Once it stopped several feet into the living room, she rolled the third can on its way. A moment later, she'd taken the tape from the camera, slipped it into her VCR, and was watching it on her television screen. In the first shot, she emerged on hands and knees through the doorway, but on the next three shots, the cans of chicken broth took center stage.

"It worked," she reported, picking up her cell phone again.

"That was fast! I thought it would take you much longer. It's difficult for people over thirty to crawl. I think we forget how unless we make it a part of our daily fitness routine."

"I think you're right," Hannah said, her tongue firmly in cheek. "This must be one of the benefits from all that exercise I'm getting."

Most cat owners could tell the difference between an inquiring meow, a grateful meow, and a downright thrilled meow. Moishe's meow was a combination of all three as Hannah pulled up in the circular driveway at Norman's country home.

Before Hannah could even reach in the back of the truck to snap on Moishe's leash, the door opened and Norman came out. He walked straight up to the passenger door and started to open it.

"I don't have his leash on yet," Hannah called out.

"That's okay." Norman opened the door all the way and held out his arms. Moishe jumped into them, purring all the while. "I've got him, Hannah."

"I thought he only did that with me," Hannah said. And although she tried not to react, she felt a tiny little stab of jealousy.

"He doesn't do it for me very often. It happens only when I've got Cuddles waiting inside."

That made her feel better, especially when she reminded herself that Norman had built this house with Cuddles in mind. There was a kitty staircase leading to nowhere in the den, with several marvelous views of the purple grackles that gathered on Norman's lawn. Both Cuddles and Moishe loved it, and they spent hours chasing each other up and down the carpeted steps, stopping every once in a while to look out at the aviary feast they longed to catch.

"Did you find out where the Big Guy is hiding his food?" Norman asked, scratching Moishe under the chin.

"Not yet. I talked to Mike on the phone, and he told me how to re-aim the camera to get the best results. I'll have to wait until I get home to see if it worked."

"I hope it did." Norman juggled Moishe to a new position in his arms. "I'm with you, Hannah. I don't think he's eating more. He seems to be the same weight as always."

Hannah retrieved her brownies from the cat-safe cooler in the back. "Can I use your stovetop? I didn't have time to frost my dessert."

"Of course. It's as much your stovetop as it is my stovetop."

Hannah smiled. She loved Norman's stovetop. She'd chosen it when they'd entered the Dream House contest. It had been fun to design the ideal family home and choose appliances and furniture without even considering price. It had come as a total surprise when their dream house had won the contest. It had also come as a complete surprise when Norman had actually built their dream house and asked her to marry him!

There had been many times since then that she wished she'd said yes. But there had been just as many times she'd been glad she was still single. As Hannah followed Norman into the lovely dream house they'd designed together, she decided this was one of the "yes" times. And she was sure of it when she saw Moishe leap out of Norman's arms and race off to play with Cuddles.

"So what did you bring for dessert?" Norman asked her.

"Bonnie Brownie Cookie Bars. All I have to do is frost them."

"I've never heard of those before. Are they something new?"

Hannah laughed. "Yes. It's a new recipe that owes its existence to the fact that I didn't want to drive to the store."

"So you substituted?"

"Exactly. That's how great recipes are born. I was going to make peanut butter brownies, but I didn't have any salted peanuts. I did have some butterscotch chips, so I made these instead."

"What sort of pan do you need for the frosting?"

"Just a medium-sized saucepan. I brought all the ingredients with me." Hannah gestured toward the small soft-sided cooler she'd carried in with her.

Norman got out the saucepan, and then he stepped behind Hannah and massaged her neck for a moment. "You look so tired. I'm going to be glad when we solve this case and you can get some sleep."

"So am I!" Hannah said, turning to give him a hug. "I don't think I've had more than six hours total since Ronni was killed."

They stood there for a long moment. Hannah no longer felt like making the frosting. She wanted to cuddle up with Norman, and perhaps it wasn't very romantic, but she wanted to go to sleep in the warmth of his arms. Or maybe that *was* romantic, especially in the true sense of the word. She really wasn't sure, but she knew it would be pure heaven.

The doorbell rang, and Norman pulled away reluctantly. "I'd better get that. If you're too tired to make the frosting, I've got powdered sugar in the pantry. We can just sprinkle some on top and serve your bar cookies that way."

"Good idea!" Hannah answered gratefully.

"The only thing that's good about this night is your egg salad," Hannah said, rubbing her eyes. They'd fast-forwarded through six hours of tapes, and her eyelids felt like they were propped up with toothpicks. "You did write down the recipe, didn't you, Norman?"

"Yes, but Cuddles helped me a little. She walked over the ink while it was still wet and made little cat tracks."

Hannah laughed. She'd had similar experiences with Moishe. There was something about the point of a felt-tip pen that was fascinating to those of the feline persuasion. "Can I still read it?"

"Yes. I typed it up on the computer and printed it out for you."

"Thanks, Norman." Hannah snuggled a little deeper into the cushions of the couch in the den. Moishe and Cuddles were sleeping, curled up together, in the round kitty bed in front of the large-screen television set. "What time is it, anyway?"

"Almost ten. We've been at this for over three hours."

"And we've gone through six hours. That means sixty hours of tape, fast-forwarded, roughly translates to thirty hours. Can you watch any more, Norman?"

"I don't think so. I gave Doc Bennett six hours, Lisa and Herb took six hours, and Grandma McCann has six hours. If Michelle and Andrea have watched six hours apiece, that means we have twenty-four hours of tapes to go."

"Is that like twenty-four bottles of beer on the wall?"

Hannah asked, remembering the song they used to sing on the pep squad bus when she was in high school and they went to "away" basketball games.

"Yes, except it might be quicker to drink . . . never mind. It wasn't a rational thought. Delores and Mom have a VCR down at Granny's Attic. Maybe they'll take turns watching tomorrow, and we can subtract another six hours."

"Maybe, if they're having a good night tonight." Hannah stopped talking and frowned.

"What is it?"

"It's crazy. They're grown women, but I'm a little worried about them. I called Sally and asked about The Moosehead. There's a hotel next door, and they've got a shuttle to the airport. I was thinking there might be some out-of-town salesmen and executives that stay there."

"And you're worried about our mothers?"

Hannah thought about that for a minute. "It's not like it's unfounded. Mother was crazy about Winthrop."

"True." Norman reached out and gave her a little hug. "Do you want to take a run to The Moosehead and see what's going on?"

"Hi, guys!" Michelle called out, stepping inside the den. "I'm done with my six hours."

"Me, too." Andrea was right behind her. "We don't have to watch more, do we?"

Norman shook his head. "Not if you're as bored as we are."

"I'd rather watch my fingernails grow. It's a lot more interesting." Michelle walked over to one of the chairs next to the couch and plopped down. "I conferred with Andrea, and we agree that we have nothing, absolutely nothing, to report."

Andrea nodded as she took the other chair. "If we'd gotten the tapes from Mike, I'd think this was a runaround. But we didn't. There's just nothing but empty exercise rooms on the tapes we watched."

"Same thing with our tapes," Hannah said, giving a little

shrug. "The most exciting thing we saw was a spider making a web on the water cooler."

"At least you had a spider," Michelle said. "Maybe the other tapes are more interesting, but we just can't watch any more."

"Hannah was a little concerned about your mother," Norman told them, ignoring the sharp look that Hannah gave him. "What do you think? Will she be okay in a bar with out-of-state salesmen and business executives?"

"I don't know." Andrea gave him a hard look. "Will Carrie be okay with out-of-state salesmen and business executives?"

"I'll drive," Norman said.

There was a moment of silence while the three sisters exchanged glances, and then Hannah spoke. "We'll ride with you," she said.

"Good," Norman said, heading for the closet to get their coats. "I printed out directions this morning, just in case. Let's go see how the mothers are doing."

BONNIE BROWNIE COOKIE BARS

Preheat oven to 350 degrees F., rack
in the middle position.

4 one-ounce squares semi-sweet chocolate *(or ¾ cup
chocolate chips)*
¾ cup butter *(one and a half sticks)*
1½ cups white *(granulated)* sugar
3 beaten eggs *(just whip them up in a glass with a
fork)*
1 teaspoon vanilla extract
1 cup flour *(pack it down in the cup when you measure it)*
½ cup chopped cashews
½ cup chopped butterscotch chips
½ cup semi-sweet chocolate chips *(I used
Ghirardelli)*

Prepare a 9-inch by 13-inch cake pan by lining it with a
piece of foil large enough to flap over the sides. Spray the
foil-lined pan with Pam or another nonstick cooking spray.

Microwave the chocolate squares and butter in a
microwave-safe mixing bowl on HIGH for 1 minute. Stir.
*(Since chocolate frequently maintains its shape even when
melted, you have to stir to make sure.)* If it's not melted,
microwave for an additional 20 seconds and stir again. Repeat if necessary.

Stir the sugar into the chocolate mixture. Feel the bowl.
If it's not so hot it'll cook the eggs, add them now, stirring
thoroughly. Mix in the vanilla extract.

Mix in the flour, and stir just until it's moistened.

Put the cashews, butterscotch chips, and chocolate chips in the bowl of a food processor, and chop them together with the steel blade. *(If you don't have a food processor, you don't have to buy one for this recipe—just chop everything up as well as you can with a sharp knife.)*

Mix in the chopped ingredients, give a final stir by hand, and spread the batter out in your prepared pan. Smooth the top with a rubber spatula.

Bake at 350 degrees F. for 30 minutes.

Cool the Bonnie Brownie Cookie Bars in the pan on a metal rack. When they're thoroughly cool, grasp the edges of the foil and lift the brownies out of the pan. Place them facedown on a cutting board, peel the foil off the back, and cut them into brownie-sized pieces.

Place the squares on a plate and dust lightly with powdered sugar if you wish.

Hannah's Note: If you're a chocoholic, or if you're making these for Mother, frost them with Neverfail Fudge Frosting before you cut them.

Chapter Twenty-Five

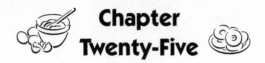

If there had been more time between the opening of the outer door and the breaching of the inner door, Hannah might have reconsidered. The music barreled out to greet them, a rendition of "My Way" by a Frank Sinatra wannabe that was just as loud as it was incompetent.

"It must be karaoke night," Michelle said.

"What?" Hannah moved closer to her youngest sister.

"I said it must be karaoke night," Michelle shouted, very close to Hannah's ear.

There was an empty table near the back, as far from the stage as they could get, and Norman led the way. The lighting was dim, and the stage was the only bright spot in the wood-paneled room. Red plastic banquettes lined two walls, and round wooden tables with wooden chairs were scattered throughout the rest of the space.

There was a candle on every table in a green glass holder, but that provided little light, barely enough to read the menu or the list of special drinks in a Plexiglas sleeve that leaned up against it. Except for the spotlights on the stage and the soft lights behind the bar, the room was deep with shadows.

Hannah glanced around, noting the wooden rafters that loomed above them. And that's when she saw something that made her gasp.

"What's the matter?" Norman asked her.

"It's that moose head hanging over our table. I swear it moved."

The other three looked up at the moose head. It was huge, with a magnificent rack, and Hannah guessed the animal's weight when it was alive would have been close to a half-ton.

"I saw it move," Michelle said, shrinking back slightly. "There! It did it again!"

Norman glanced up at the moose head and down at the table. "I think it's the candle," he said. "Whenever it flickers, it makes the moose head appear to move."

"Let's test out your theory," Hannah suggested, pulling the candle toward her and blowing it out. "There. Now let's see if the moose head moves."

They watched the wall for at least a minute, but absolutely nothing happened. The moose head remained stationary.

"You're right," Hannah told him. "Do you want to light the candle again?"

"I'll do it." The voice came from above, and they looked up to see a waitress standing by the table. She picked up the candle, drew the kind of lighter used to ignite a barbecue from her apron pocket, and lit the candle. "Was the moose head moving for you?"

"Yes," Andrea said. "We thought maybe it was animated or something."

"Oh, it's animated, all right. Some people say it dances to the music if you have enough drinks." The waitress gave a little laugh. "What'll it be, folks?"

The waitress turned to Norman first, and Hannah thought that perhaps it was because she assumed her tip would come from him. "How about you?"

"I'll have a ginger ale. I'm the designated driver." Norman gave his order. "What would you like, Hannah?"

Hannah thought about it for a split second. If she had a glass of wine, she'd probably fall asleep at the table. There was another reason not to imbibe, and that had to do with her diet. A glass of dry white wine had about eighty calories. "I'll have a diet drink. Coke, ginger ale, anything is fine."

"The same for me," Andrea said.

"I'll have an ice-cream drink," Michelle said, glancing down at the list of fancy drinks that had been propped up next to the candle. "You make your Brandy Alexanders with chocolate ice cream, don't you?"

"That's right."

"I'll have one of those, but leave out the brandy, please."

"Okay, but it's going to taste like a chocolate shake."

"I know," Michelle said with a smile.

While they were waiting for their drinks to arrive, Hannah turned to watch the stage. A woman a few years past her prime in an outfit that should have been worn by a teenager was singing a country western ballad about losing her job, and her boyfriend, and her car.

"She ought to just sing it backwards," Andrea said.

Norman looked puzzled. "Why should she do that?"

"Because then she'd get them all back."

There were predictable groans around the table, and Andrea gave a dainty little shrug. "Don't blame me. It's Bill's joke. He says it's going around at the sheriff's station."

Hannah listened to the singer for a few moments and then she asked, "Does anybody know what *karaoke* means?"

"No clue," Michelle said, and Andrea shook her head to show she didn't know, either.

"I know it's Japanese," Norman answered her, "but that's all I know."

"It's a compound word made from two Japanese words. *Kara* means empty, and *oke* is orchestra. When you put them together they mean *empty orchestra*."

"That makes sense," Norman said. "They usually remove the vocals from the sound track electronically, and that leaves only the orchestra."

The singer tried for a high note and missed abysmally.

Hannah gave a little groan and decided to concentrate on something else, anything else except the song and the singer. "Does anybody see the mothers?" she asked, scanning the dimly lighted room.

It took a few moments with all of them looking, and then Michelle leaned across the table. "There's a blonde and a brunette over there in the far corner under the moose head by the Cold Spring beer sign."

"That could be Mother and Carrie. I can't really tell," Andrea offered her opinion.

"I don't think it is," Norman said. "Mother never wears her hair like that."

The country western song ended to loud applause. Hannah wasn't sure if it was because the audience liked it, or whether they were relieved it was over.

"Maybe they left already," Michelle suggested, taking a sip of the milkshake their waitress had delivered while they were scanning the room. "If they got what they needed right away, they could be home in Lake Eden right now."

"I . . . don't . . . think . . . so." Hannah forced out the words from a throat that had gone suddenly dry. She swallowed with difficulty and followed it with, "Tell me that's not Mother climbing the steps to the stage."

Norman turned to look. "It's Delores," he confirmed, "and my mother is right behind her."

"Are they going to sing?" Andrea sounded horrified.

"I don't know what else they'd be doing up there," Hannah told her.

"Good for them!" Michelle looked delighted. "I didn't know Mother could sing."

"She can't," Hannah said and left it at that. There was always the possibility that the floor would open up and swallow them. Or perhaps the karaoke machine would malfunction. Or maybe the microphone would start screeching with feedback and they'd have to shut it off.

Hannah watched in shock as the mothers reached the top

step and turned to walk to the center of the stage. Delores picked up the microphone and held it between them as the first bars of the song they'd chosen began to play.

"What song is it?" Andrea asked.

"I don't know," Hannah answered her, and then she groaned as Carrie and Delores linked arms. "They're not going to dance . . . are they?"

"I think they're going to do some kind of step," Michelle said.

"*Bye Bye Love*," Norman said, and when all three Swensen sisters turned to look at him, he hurried to explain. "That's what they're going to sing. I recognize the intro. It's an old Everly Brothers song."

A few beats later, the mothers opened their mouths and began to sing. They looked as if they were having great fun as they stepped back and forth in perfect unison, and sang the lyrics.

Hannah had all she could do not to cover her ears. One glance around the table and she realized she was not alone. Norman looked pained, Andrea looked highly embarrassed, and Michelle looked as if she wanted to burst out laughing. As for Hannah, every extremely flat and loudly amplified note that reached her ears made her head throb and her teeth hurt. It had to be the worst rendition of an Everly Brothers song that had ever been performed.

The agony went on through verses too painful to enumerate, but it was met by a wave of raucous applause. When it was over, Hannah breathed a huge sigh of relief and wished she'd ordered that glass of wine. "That was really awful," she said. "They weren't in tune at all."

Norman turned to smile at her. "That's true, but both of them were equally flat, and that means that they were harmonizing."

"I thought it was kind of cute," Michelle said. "They weren't nervous at all and the audience liked it."

Hannah had to admit that Michelle had a point. The audience was still applauding, and a guy at the front table was calling for an encore.

"It wasn't as bad as I thought it would be," Andrea said, and Hannah knew she was trying to be charitable. "At least they *looked* good."

Hannah glanced toward the stage again and what she saw made her eyes widen. "Smiles everyone, and remember . . . we thought their performance was fantastic. They must have spotted us while they were singing, because here come the mothers!"

When the mothers reached their table, Michelle was the first to jump to her feet. "That was amazing, Mother," she said, giving Delores a little hug. "I've never heard anything like it."

Hannah stifled a chortle. Michelle had come up with a wonderful way of saying something that sounded like a compliment. And since she'd given Delores a hug, she was obviously trying to get back into their mother's good graces.

"What did you think, dear?" Delores turned to Hannah.

"We all agreed that you and Carrie were in perfect harmony," Hannah said, stealing Norman's line.

"And you were in perfect step, too," Andrea said, smiling at the mothers. "That must have taken some practice."

"Five minutes in the ladies' room," Carrie admitted, turning to Norman. "What did you think, son?"

"It was quite a show," Norman said, giving Carrie a kiss on the cheek. "All these years, and I never knew you could sing like that."

Five minutes later, they were seated at a blue plastic booth in The Yum-Yum coffee shop, sipping mugs of coffee. Since the mothers needed caffeinated fortification for the trip back to Lake Eden and it was far too noisy to talk inside The Moosehead anyway, they'd all met at the small restaurant at the end of the block. Some last-minute arrangements had been made. Michelle would be driving Delores and Carrie home and staying the night with Delores. They'd only had two drinks at The Moosehead, but Michelle had offered and

Delores and Carrie had accepted. Hannah was glad. It was a sign that forgiveness was right around the corner for Michelle's untimely age-related remarks.

"Before I forget," Delores said, turning to Hannah, "we found out why Ronni quit her job."

"Except that she didn't really quit," Carrie added. "She was fired for skimming."

Delores nodded. "She totaled her customers' bar tabs early, took their credit cards, and rang them up. And then, when they wanted another round of drinks, she asked them to pay in cash and she slipped it in her apron with her tips."

"How did she get caught?" Hannah asked.

"The bartender spotted her, the same bartender who was on tonight. The owner was giving him grief about coming up short. He knew he wasn't giving away free drinks, so he kept an eye on the cocktail waitresses and caught Ronni in the act."

"Ronni begged him not to turn her in," Carrie took over the story. "She told him she needed more money so that she could quit her job at Heavenly Bodies. She said she was being stalked by someone when she was at work."

"Stalked?" Hannah asked. "Did she get a look at the person stalking her?"

Delores shook her head. "No, but she told the bartender that she'd stopped using the Jacuzzi at night when she was alone. She said she was sure someone was spying on her in there."

"You don't think she was actually stalked, do you?" Andrea asked Hannah.

"I don't know. Unfortunately, it's a little late to ask her, but I think I'd better add a possible stalker to my suspect list." Hannah pulled out her steno pad and flipped to the suspect page, but before she could start to write, she heard Michelle give a little gasp.

"What is it, dear?" Delores asked her.

Michelle swallowed hard, and Hannah noticed that her

hands were shaking slightly. "It's . . . it's . . . the stalker! I just remembered where I saw Tad Newberg before!"

"Where?" Hannah leaned closer. Whatever Michelle had remembered had upset her.

"He was a night security guard at Macalester when I was a freshman. I used to see him outside the Fine Arts building on Wednesdays when I went to my night class."

"So you knew him?" Hannah asked.

"Not really. He was one of those familiar strangers, like a person you see on the bus every day or a checker at the grocery store. A couple of weeks before midterms, our professor told us there was a stalker, and he warned us to walk in pairs on campus at night. And then, the next time the class met, he said they caught him and it turned out to be one of the security guards."

"And you think the stalker was Tad?" Andrea asked her.

"I don't know. He didn't give us a name. All I know is, I never saw Tad in front of the Fine Arts building again."

"We have to find out who the stalker was," Hannah decided. "I'll call Detective Parks in the morning and see if she can find out. If the stalker was Tad, I'll add him to my suspect list."

"That reminds me," Carrie said to Hannah. "You can cross Vonnie Blair and Immelda Giesse off your list. Vonnie spent the night at her mother's house."

Delores nodded. "And Immelda's sister came for a visit. Father Coultas said they sat up talking until all hours of the morning."

"Great," Hannah said. "Michelle eliminated Bridget. And Carly said her mother and Trudi hosted a sleepover for a dozen of her little sister's friends."

"Serena Roste couldn't have done it, either," Carrie told them. "My friend in Elk River read her wedding notice in the paper. She got married last week and they're on a two-week honeymoon in Jamaica."

"And I found out that Babs Dubinski was at Marvin's babysitting all night," Andrea said. "You know Babs. She's crazy about her grandsons. She'd never leave the boys alone at night."

"Did you get the listing?" Hannah asked, remembering that Andrea had intended to ask Babs about her rental property.

"Of course I did, and I think I already have a buyer. But let's get back to business. I called my friend in Duluth, and she said Betty Jackson couldn't have done it. She was at a bridal shower the night that Ronni was killed."

"Cross off Gail Hansen, too," Norman told Hannah. "She drove to the airport in Minneapolis to meet her husband. His plane was delayed, and they didn't get back here until almost three in the morning."

"That's it, then," Hannah said with a sigh. "The only suspects I've got left are the ones I know didn't do it, the mysterious stalker Ronni told the bartender about, who might or might not turn out to be Tad, and the unknown suspect with the unknown motive that we haven't discovered yet."

The drive back to Norman's was uneventful, and Hannah had all she could do to keep from nodding off. She was profoundly tired, and she wondered how in the world she'd be able to stay awake on the trip home, especially now that Michelle wouldn't be riding with her. All she really wanted to do was crawl into a warm cocoon and pull the covers over her head.

"Hannah? We're here," Norman said, reaching out to touch her shoulder.

For one brief moment Hannah was disoriented, but then she realized that she was sitting in the passenger seat of Norman's car and they were in the driveway in front of his house.

"I'd better get home," Hannah said, fishing in her purse for her car keys.

"You have to get Moishe," Andrea reminded her.

"Right. It completely slipped my mind. Will you help me get his leash on, Norman?"

"Sure," Norman agreed quickly. "Just sit there for a second, and I'll walk Andrea to her car. I'll be right back for you."

Hannah was about to say that she was perfectly capable of getting out of Norman's car by herself, but why argue? She'd just use the few minutes it took Norman to walk Andrea to her car to shut her eyes and take a brief rest before starting on the drive home. She'd have to fight to stay awake, perhaps roll down the window to let the cold air in or turn the radio up so loud it hurt her ears.

It was peaceful here in the country. She heard the soft whistle of the wind in the distance, the low hooting call of an owl, and the rustling of small animals in the brush at the sides of Norman's driveway. She was toasty warm. Her parka was pulled up to her chin, and although the fur tickled her, it felt cozy and comforting.

"Hannah?"

It was Norman again, and Hannah opened her eyes. She must have nodded off. "Yes."

"You're too tired to drive home tonight."

He was right. She was. But propriety must be observed. "Can't," she said, forcing her tired mind to work again. "You're here alone. What would people think?"

"Do you care?" Norman asked her.

"Yes. Maybe"

"How much do you care, Hannah?"

"Not enough," Hannah said and let him escort her into the house and up the stairs. They stopped at the doorway to the master bedroom.

"You take the master," Norman said. "I'll sleep in the guest room."

"But it's your bedroom."

"It's *our* bedroom, but I don't think you're up to discussing that now. Here's a sleep shirt. Go put it on." Norman handed her a folded bundle of clothing and pushed her off toward the master bathroom. "While you're changing, I'll light a fire and turn down the covers for you."

Her limbs felt like lead, but somehow she managed to get out of her clothes and into the red flannel sleep shirt. Red was her favorite color and it was brand-new. Even though her brain felt like overcooked oatmeal and she was too tired to figure anything out, she knew that he'd bought it for her.

She opened the bathroom door, wondering what would await her, and found Norman sitting on the side of the bed. "Climb in and get warm, Hannah," he invited, patting the blankets. "I'll go get the cats."

"Cats," Hannah said, slipping under the eiderdown coverlet and resting her head against the most comfortable feather pillow she'd ever encountered. The fire flickered, its light was golden, and the room was exactly the right temperature.

"Here you are, Big Guy," Norman's voice was soft as he brought the two cats into the room. "Go ahead, Cuddles. You can sleep with Hannah, too."

There was a thump as Moishe landed and padded up to lick her cheek. A second later, there was another thump, a less heavy one, and Hannah heard Cuddles start to purr. As she drifted off to sleep, Hannah knew that life was good and everything was almost perfect.

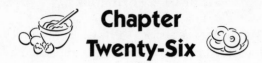

Chapter
Twenty-Six

She was sleeping on a cloud, and it was incredibly soft and fluffy. That meant it was a dream cloud, not a real cloud. Real clouds were cold and damp, a thick mist that glommed together in a semi-amorphous shape to hang in the air above people's heads. She'd learned that in grade school science, but it was so contrary to the image clouds presented from the ground that she'd chosen to ignore the fact and embrace the misconception.

She was awake . . . almost. Hannah rolled over and dislodged the cat who'd been sleeping next to her on the pillow.

Cuddles. And Moishe was right next to Cuddles on the neighboring pillow. But what was Cuddles doing in her bed?

Not her bed. And these were not her pillows. She had two expensive goose down pillows on her bed, and this bed had four. It also had an eiderdown coverlet, something she'd priced but couldn't afford.

Not her room. Hannah realized that the window was in the wrong place. And so was the door to the bathroom. And the fireplace . . . the fireplace!

Hannah sat up with a gasp. She was in Norman's bedroom! She blinked, concentrated, and tried to remember what had happened the previous night. It was just starting to come back to her when she realized that there was a border of sunlight around the heavy curtains at the window.

What time *was* it?! Hannah glanced at the clock on the bedside table and gave a loud groan. Eight o'clock. Too late to meet Andrea at Heavenly Bodies. Too late for Roger's Body Sculpting Class. She'd overslept by almost four hours, and she had to go home right away!

One step inside the luxurious master bathroom and Hannah changed her mind. Perhaps she didn't have to go home immediately. Ever since they'd designed this wonderful room, she'd wanted to try out the surround shower. It had jets on all four walls, and it was reputed to be the closest thing to a massage you could get without a masseuse.

Two fluffy red towels awaited her on the warming rack. The letter H in a flowing script was embroidered on each towel, and Hannah gave another little groan. Towels with her monogram. When Norman had built this house, he really had planned for her to share it with him.

No time for regrets now. She had to take a shower and get on the road. Norman was probably gone already, and she had to take Moishe home and change clothes before she could show up at The Cookie Jar.

The shower was heavenly, and Hannah took longer than she knew she should. She stood in the center of the enclosure on the sunburst made out of multicolored tile to get the full benefit of the massaging jets.

"Incredible," Hannah breathed, letting the water wash her exhaustion away. She started to feel halfway human, and then fully human, and then so good that she smiled and hummed a little tune.

She really didn't want to get out, but she did. She could have stayed in the rejuvenating enclosure all day. But there were places to go, people to interview, tapes to watch, and killers to catch. Hannah toweled off, delighting in the thick richness of the towels, and then she dressed quickly, brushed her teeth with the new toothbrush Norman had left for her on the counter, and brushed her hair with a brush that was a clone of the one she had at home.

Hannah felt so good she almost skipped down the stairs. It was amazing how invigorated she felt after a full eight hours of sleep, and a massage in the surround shower. She burst into the kitchen, hoping that Norman had left some coffee in the pot for her, and stopped short as she saw that he was sitting at the kitchen table.

"Norman!" she said, completely surprised. "I thought you'd left by now."

"And miss the chance to show off my cooking skills by making your breakfast?" Norman laughed and rose from his chair.

"But I can't eat anything good."

"You mean you can't eat anything fattening," Norman corrected her.

"Same thing."

"No, it's not. Hold on for a second and I'll show you. Everything's ready, and it's in the warming oven. While I'm dishing it up, have some coffee. I just made it fresh, and your mug's on the counter next to the coffeepot."

Hannah honed in on the coffeepot and poured some coffee for herself. Then she took a seat at the table and hoped that what Norman had made for her wouldn't irretrievably blow her diet. She was going to eat it, even if it meant she'd gain weight today. Having breakfast served to her in the morning was a real luxury. It made her feel special, and pampered. The clock on the kitchen wall read eight-thirty, and Hannah gave an exasperated sigh.

"What's the matter?" Norman asked her.

"I really ought to call Andrea on her cell phone. I'm sure she's wondering what happened to me."

"No, she's not. I talked to her last night when I walked her to her car, and she urged me to keep you here. Both of us agreed that you were too tired to drive home by yourself."

"So Andrea knows I spent the night with you?" Hannah asked, a bit nervously.

"She knows you *might* have spent the night with me, but I

told her that if you insisted on going home, I'd drive you there."

"Oh."

"So nobody knows, not even Michelle, because she stayed with your mother. You can say anything you like about where you spent the night, Hannah."

Perhaps it was only her imagination, but Hannah thought that Norman looked a bit disappointed. Perhaps it was a guy thing, and it would be a blow to his ego if she lied about spending the night with him. "If anyone asks, I'm going to tell them exactly where I spent the night," Hannah said, "unless you don't want me to, that is."

A smile spread over Norman's face, and Hannah knew she was right. It was definitely a guy thing.

"Whatever you decide is fine with me," Norman said, walking over to set the plate on the place mat in front of her.

Hannah glanced down at the plate. "A popover!" she said, and immediately, her mouth began to water. "It looks delicious."

"That's not all," Norman told her. "Take off the top and see what's inside."

Hannah removed the top, which had been sliced off and then replaced, almost like one of her cream puffs. "Eggs. And bacon. And . . ." Hannah stopped and took another sniff. "Parmesan cheese?"

"That's right. There's a little freshly chopped parsley in there for color, too. You'll see when you start to eat it. Do you want to know the calorie count?"

Hannah was almost afraid to ask, but obviously Norman had totaled it up. "Yes, I want to know. How many calories for the whole thing?"

"I'll break it down for you. Seventy calories for the popover, one-ten for the egg, thirty-seven for one slice of crumbled bacon, and seven for the sprinkling of fresh parmesan. The parsley is negligible. That's a grand total of under two hundred and twenty-five calories. And it's good, isn't it?"

"Mmmmph," Hannah said, even though she could have swallowed and then answered his question.

Norman laughed. "I'll take that as a yes."

Hannah was amazed at how fast she ate the breakfast that Norman had prepared. It really *was* good, and she was hungry. When her plate was empty, she got up to refill their coffee cups and sat back down again. "That was the best breakfast I've had in a long time! You're wonderful, Norman. You thought of everything to make me comfortable; my own sleep shirt, a fire in the bedroom fireplace, warm towels for my shower, a new toothbrush, and on top of it all, a gourmet breakfast. I could get used to being treated like this."

"That's the general idea."

He was smiling at her in a way that let Hannah know he was about to say something about sharing their dream house again. It was time to change the subject unless she wanted to say yes. And she did . . . at least part of her did. But the other part still wasn't sure she wanted to give up her independence. "I still can't believe you went to all the trouble of figuring out the breakfast calories."

"It wasn't any trouble. I just looked up the ingredients online. There are a couple of Web sites with free calorie counters."

"Well . . . thanks. I really appreciate it. The breakfast was great, and the shower was heavenly, and the towels were splendid, and your bed is magnificent. I think I got the best night's sleep I've had in years!"

"Under any other circumstances that last comment might not be a compliment."

Hannah laughed. And then she blushed slightly. It was best to change the subject again. "What are your plans for today?"

"I'm going to see if I can farm out the tapes. Another night of staring at empty hallways and closed doors is going to drive us crazy. What are your plans?"

"I'm going to avoid getting any more instructions from

anybody," Hannah said. "I've been thinking it over, and the advice I've been getting from Mike, and Lonnie, and Rick, and Bill just isn't very helpful. It'd be fine if I had a whole team of detectives to send out for this and that, but I don't. I can't run *their* investigation, so I'm going to concentrate on *my* investigation. I'm just going to trust my instincts about what to do next and hope I end up catching Ronni's killer."

She hadn't been home for more than five minutes when the phone rang. Hannah said a few choice words she'd never utter around her young nieces and plucked it from the cradle. "Yes?"

"Hannah!" It was Mike's voice and he sounded worried. "Where have you been? I've been calling you every hour since midnight!"

He'd called her at midnight. Again. Mike wasn't concerned that she hadn't had a full night's sleep since Ronni was murdered. He'd probably wanted her to meet him in the garage again with a thermos of coffee and cookies so that he could give her more instructions on investigative procedure.

"So where were you?" Mike asked, sounding more than a little irritated.

Here was the acid test, and it wasn't even difficult. "I spent the night at Norman's," she said.

"At Norman's?"

"Yes."

"I should have known somebody would tell you, but I didn't think you'd run to Norman on the rebound."

You should have known somebody would tell me what? Hannah felt like asking, but she didn't. It was better to let Mike hang himself with his own rope.

"It didn't mean anything, Hannah. It was just . . . convenient, you know? She was right there across the hall from me and . . . these things happen. You're an adult. You know that."

So *that's* what an adult was. She had to remember to share that little gem of knowledge with her sisters.

"Well, anyway . . . now we're even, and we can start over. I'll call you tonight, okay? I've got to get off the phone now. Herb's going to call and tell me where to meet him. He said he needs to talk to me about something important. Talk to you later, Hannah."

There was a click and the line went dead, just as dead as Hannah's respect for Mike. He'd lied to her about being involved with Ronni, and then, when he thought she'd found out about it, he'd tried to explain his behavior away by saying it meant nothing. Even worse, he'd jumped to the wrong conclusion about the night she'd spent at Norman's house.

There was a sound from the top of the couch, a low growl. Hannah glanced up to find Moishe standing there with his fur bristling. He gave another low growl, just like he did when he spotted Delores coming up the stairs, and then he jumped down to the cushions and hopped on her lap to lick her cheek.

"It's okay, Moishe," Hannah said, petting her loyal friend. And then she settled down again to watch the tape she'd decided she'd view before she headed off to The Cookie Jar to meet her sisters.

The tape was clearly labeled with the date and camera number. The mall security staff was well organized. She didn't have the list of camera numbers and their locations that Andrea had written up for them, but it took Hannah only a second or two to realize that the outdoor camera had generated this tape. There was a quick pop of the parking lot by the backdoor to Heavenly Bodies. It lasted a minute or two, showing nothing but parked cars and no movement. Hannah recognized several of the cars. There was Mayor Bascomb's new Saab, Roger's black Jeep, and Ronni's old green wreck. Then horizontal lines began to stretch across the screen, and the image deteriorated until it was nothing but what her Grandmother Swensen, who'd had less than adequate television reception on her antenna out at the farm, had called "snow."

Hannah hit the fast-forward button, but the snow remained

snow. This must be the camera that had malfunctioned and failed to record Lonnie and Mike leaving the area, thereby causing them to be considered as suspects. Even though Hannah doubted that the camera would suddenly heal itself, she watched the tape until the end.

Something niggled at the back of her mind, something that wasn't right. Hannah thought back to the beginning of the tape when the image had been clear, and she realized that Ronni's old car was the problem. Mike had told her that the car had been sitting untouched on the street in front of the apartment building for at least two weeks. But that wasn't true. There it was in all its dubious glory, on the security tape from the night Ronni was killed.

Had Mike lied to her? Again? It was certainly possible, but Hannah couldn't think of any reason he'd lie about something like that. And perhaps it wasn't a lie. Perhaps Mike simply didn't know that Ronni had taken her car to work the night of her death. But there was an even more puzzling question. How had Ronni's car gotten back to the same parking spot on the street in front of the apartment complex? Had someone at her birthday party driven it home for her? Or had the sheriff's department gone through it for possible evidence and then towed it back to The Oaks?

It was something she had to check out, but there wasn't time to do it now. One glance at the clock and Hannah knew she had to leave. She was expected at The Cookie Jar at eleven. After a quick scratch under the chin for Moishe and four of his favorite salmon-flavored treats, she flicked on the surveillance camera and went out the door.

She was almost to her cookie truck when she heard someone calling her name. Hannah turned and saw Sue Plotnik putting Kevin into his car seat.

"Hi, Sue." Hannah walked over to greet her. "You're out early."

"Not really. We have to be at Kiddie Korner by noon, and I need to stop to pick up some cookies for story time."

"Cookies? Consider yourself stopped. I've got three dozen Triplet Chiplet Cookies in the back of the truck if you want them."

"You bet I want them!" Sue finished buckling Kevin in and waited for Hannah to come back with the cookies. "Thanks for the job, Hannah. I just adore it. We're having so much fun, it's almost a crime Janice pays us."

"She needs you, Sue. The last time I dropped in on her at Kiddie Korner, she was really stressed out."

"I know. Sometimes it's not the work. It's just that you need another adult to talk to. Being around children as your only companions all day is . . . well . . . it's wearing. But there's two of us now, and we're having a really good time."

"I can believe it." Hannah smiled at her downstairs neighbor.

"There's something new every day, especially at Show and Tell time. You wouldn't believe what some of the kids say!"

"Tell me," Hannah said. If she was a bit late, it wouldn't matter, and it was wonderful seeing Sue so happy and energetic.

"Well . . . the first day I started, Sonny Newberg got up and said, *Mom had a big fight with Uncle Tad because he didn't pay back the money for Nikki's flowers. Mom said he shouldn't buy flowers for a bimbo like that. What's a bimbo, Mrs. Plotnik?*"

Hannah just shook her head. It sounded as if Tad Newberg's sister-in-law didn't approve of the girl he was dating. "What in the world do you say to a question like that?"

"I just said I wasn't sure what his mother had meant, and then I asked him about flowers and what kind he liked best. A couple of the other kids told me which flowers they thought were the prettiest, and then somebody else got up to tell about going to the Minnesota Zoo. Kids are fairly easy to distract at that age."

"Car go, Mommy!"

Hannah and Sue turned to look at Kevin, who was twisting the little steering wheel attached to his car seat.

"I think he's getting impatient," Hannah said.

"Definitely impatient. I'd better go, Hannah. I'm going to be at work early because of your cookies." Sue shut the back door of her car and climbed into the driver's seat. "Thanks again, Hannah . . . for everything."

Hannah got into her cookie truck and followed Sue up the ramp and out of the parking garage. It was good to know that something she'd arranged had gone well. Now all she had to do was solve Ronni's murder, lose enough weight to fit into the dress for her mother's book launch party, and pretend that it didn't matter at all that Mike was a skunk.

TRIPLET CHIPLET COOKIES

Preheat oven to 350 degrees F., rack
in the middle position.

2 cups melted butter (*4 sticks, one pound*)
3 cups white (*granulated*) sugar
1½ cups brown sugar
4 teaspoons vanilla
2 teaspoons baking soda
½ teaspoon salt
4 beaten eggs (*just whip them up in a glass with a
    fork*)
5 cups flour (*not sifted—pack it down in the cup
    when you measure it*)
1 cup white chocolate chips (*6-ounce package*)
1 cup milk chocolate chips (*6-ounce package*)
1 cup semi-sweet (*the regular kind*) chocolate chips
    (*6-ounce package*)
2 cups chopped salted cashews

**Hannah's 1ˢᵗ Note: If you can't find white chocolate
chips, you can substitute butterscotch chips, peanut butter
chips, or any other chips you like.**

Melt the butter by heating it in a microwave-safe bowl
on HIGH for 3 minutes, or in a pan on the stove.

**Hannah's 2ⁿᵈ Note: This dough gets really stiff—you
might be better off using an electric mixer if you have one.**

Mix the white sugar and the brown sugar with the butter. Add the vanilla, baking soda, and salt. Mix well.

Feel the bowl. If it's not so hot it'll cook the eggs, add them now and mix well.

Add 2 cups of the flour and stir well. Then add the chips, and the chopped nuts. Mix it thoroughly.

Add the 3 remaining cups of flour, and stir them in well.

Drop by rounded teaspoons onto greased *(or sprayed with Pam or other nonstick cooking spray)* cookie sheets, 12 cookies to a standard-sized sheet. If the dough is too sticky to handle, chill it for an hour and try again.

Bake the cookies at 350 degrees F. for 10 to 12 minutes or until nicely browned. *(Mine took 11 minutes.)*

Let the cookies cool for two minutes, and then remove them from the baking sheets. Transfer them to a wire rack to finish cooling.

Yield: Approximately 10 to 12 dozen crunchy, nutty, chocolaty cookies that everyone will love.

This recipe can be cut in half if you wish.

Chapter
Twenty-Seven

Her cell phone rang just as she exited the condo complex, and Hannah pulled over on the side of the road to answer it. "This is Hannah."

"Where are you?" It was Andrea's voice, and she sounded anxious.

"I'm just leaving the complex. I should be there in twenty minutes."

"Okay, I'll wait fifteen minutes, and then I'll pour coffee for you. Frank Hurley's here, and he's got something to tell you."

"What?"

"He won't tell us, only you. Do you think he's interested, Hannah?"

"You mean interested in *me*?"

"Well, maybe not. He's got to be almost thirty years older than you are. It's probably because you're leading our investigation and he wants to talk to the head person."

"That's probably right."

"Lisa says to tell you that there was nothing on their Heavenly Bodies tapes. They watched all six hours. Then she went to bed, and Herb stayed up to watch a tape from the red-light camera at the mall. He says I should tell you he found out something very interesting."

"What is it?"

"He won't tell anybody except you and Mike."

"Mike? What's *he* got to do with it?"

"I don't know. Herb knows he's off the case, so it can't have anything to do with Ronni's murder. And then there's Mother and Carrie."

"What about Mother and Carrie?"

"I don't know that, either. They're here, but they want to wait until you come in to tell us some big news. Where are you now?"

"What do you mean, where am I? I'm right where I was when I answered the phone."

"You're not driving?"

"Of course not. Cell phones are distracting. I never drive and talk on the cell phone at the same time."

"Right. I forgot about that. Only one more thing. I was supposed to remind you to call Detective Parks and ask her to check on the Macalester stalker."

"I did that. I left her a voice mail."

"Okay, then. I'm hanging up now. Hurry in because I'm dying of curiosity and nobody'll tell me anything unless you're here."

Hannah pulled out on the road again and tromped on the gas. She was curious, too. The snowplows had been out, the roadway wasn't slippery, and her tires hummed along as she drove just slightly over the speed limit. What did Frank Hurley want to tell her? What did Herb want to tell Mike and her? What was Delores and Carrie's big news?

Her mind was sluicing through the possibilities as she turned in the alley and pulled into her parking spot at the back of The Cookie Jar. She shut off her truck and wasted no time rushing in the kitchen door, tossing her parka on the rack, and pushing through the swinging door to the coffee shop.

Every stool and chair was occupied with customers who all looked up as she came in. It seemed that everyone here wanted something from her. She just hoped she'd be able to provide it.

"Hannah!" Andrea rushed over to greet her. "We're going to put you at the workstation in the kitchen since so many people want to talk to you in private."

"Okay," Hannah said, feeling a bit like Marlon Brando at the wedding in *The Godfather*. "Are there really that many people?"

"Not *that* many. Only six or so, unless somebody new comes in. I'll bring your coffee and usher people in when you're all set up."

Hannah went back through the swinging door and sat down on a stool at the workstation. She had several seconds to think about horse heads and sawed-off shotguns, and then Andrea came in.

"Here's your coffee. Do you want a cookie before we start?"

"Diet," Hannah said, shaking her head.

"Right. Well, if you're sure I can't get you anything else, I'll bring Frank Hurley back."

Hannah had time for three sips of her coffee before Frank came through the swinging door. He took the seat across from her at the workstation and gave a little sigh. "I'm really sorry, Hannah. I forgot to tell you something about the night Miss Ward was killed."

"What's that, Frank?"

"It happened earlier, on my watch. I just didn't connect the dots before. There was somebody hanging around the mall entrance to the spa. You know, where the window is. I wouldn't have thought anything about it, but he just walked back and forth in front of the window, and there wasn't anything to see inside. The receptionist was gone, and there were no lights in the front. I thought maybe he was waiting for someone to come out so he could sneak in, so I went over and asked him if he was a member. He said no, that he was just browsing. *Browsing* is a strange word to use at a spa. You browse in a store, you know? I got the impression he wasn't all there, if you know what I mean."

"I know what you mean. Can you describe him for me?"

"A male Caucasian in his midthirties, light-brown hair, average build, average height. He was wearing jeans and a dark blue parka with fur around the neck."

"Do you think he was homeless?"

Frank shook his head. "I didn't see anything that pointed in that direction. He was clean, his clothes were clean, and he was dressed for the weather. He just sent up red flags for me, you know? I told him to move along, and he went out to the parking lot. I didn't see him again, and I left at midnight."

"Is there any way he could have gotten into Heavenly Bodies?"

"That's what I'm worried about. I should have told Tad about it when he came in at eleven, but I really didn't think it was important. The guy was gone. That was that."

"But now you're giving it a second thought?"

"Yeah. The thing is, people were coming and going for Miss Ward's birthday party, and that back door was opening and closing a lot. He could have slipped in with one of the guests."

After Frank had left, Hannah took out her shorthand notebook and added the man in the blue parka to her suspect list. It wasn't much to go on, but there had to be some reason he'd been hanging around the mall entrance to Heavenly Bodies. Then she closed her notebook and slipped it into her large shoulder bag, the one her mother hated and her fashionable sisters kept trying to replace.

"Ready?" Andrea asked, opening the door partway.

"Ready," Hannah answered, hoping her coffee would hold out.

She'd gone through five people with tidbits of information for her that had proved to be less than useful. Then Delores and Carrie had come in to tell her that they'd won the karaoke contest at The Moosehead and now had a fifty-dollar credit at the bar. When the door opened and Herb walked in with

Mike, Hannah hoped they'd have something interesting to tell her.

"You can go back to baking cookies now, Hannah," Mike said with a grin that couldn't have been any wider.

"What do you mean?" Hannah gazed from Mike to Herb and then back again.

"I reviewed the red-light camera photos from the night that Ronni was killed," Herb explained. "The camera's mounted by the traffic light at the mall exit, and it catches anybody running the red light to get on the freeway. It shows Mike entering the intersection on yellow at twelve thirty-five."

"And Ronni was killed between one and two-thirty in the morning," Hannah said, recalling the time from Doc Knight's autopsy report.

"That's right." Mike gave a little nod. "The only reason the highway patrol didn't write me up is that I was driving a patrol car."

"We're taking the photo out to the sheriff's department to show Bill," Herb said.

"And I'll be back on the case this afternoon." Mike gave her a little kiss on the top of the head. "You've done a good job, Hannah. Write up what you've learned so far, will you? I'll take over now."

"He actually said that?" Michelle looked outraged.

"He actually did."

"You're not going to do it, are you?" Andrea asked, bringing up the rear with Norman as they climbed the steps to Hannah's condo.

"Do what?" Hannah asked her.

"Write up a report for Mike."

Hannah turned around as she reached the landing. "Of course I am. But he told me to go back to baking cookies, and reports take time to write. It'll probably be a week or so before I have the chance to put anything down on paper."

When she got inside, the first place Hannah headed was

the kitchen. She glanced down at the Kitty Valet and let out a whoop of excitement. "Moishe's out of food again. Now we'll get to see if the kitty-cam worked."

Hannah put on the coffee, Norman took the tape out of the kitty-cam, and Michelle and Andrea refilled the food tube on Moishe's Kitty Valet. In less than five minutes, they were all settled in the living room with fresh mugs of coffee and a box of Lois Brown's Lemon Cookies that Hannah had brought home from The Cookie Jar, ready to watch the tape from the surveillance camera.

"These are great lemon cookies!" Michelle said, reaching for her second in less than a minute. "There's a lot of lemon, and that makes them nice and tart."

"Sometimes I sprinkle them with powdered sugar before I serve them," Hannah told her. "Does anybody want me to do that?"

There were headshakes all around. It seemed they all liked the tart, lemony flavor.

"Okay, then . . . let's get started," Hannah said, taking a sip of her coffee. "At least we won't be bored silly. Moishe's kitty-cam is motion activated. If nothing moves, it doesn't record."

"No more hours of closed doors and empty rooms?" Andrea asked her.

"Not unless an ant is crawling across the floor." Hannah turned to Norman who had the remote control. "Okay Norman. Let's see what Moishe's been up to while I've been at The Cookie Jar today."

"It looks like he just took a big mouthful," Michelle said. She was holding Moishe, and he was purring so loudly they could all hear him. Evidently he didn't mind being caught in the act as long as he got star billing on Hannah's television screen.

"But he's eating it," Andrea commented, and Hannah thought she sounded slightly disappointed.

The Moishe on the screen swallowed and then moved to the water bowl to take a drink. A moment later, he was back at the food bowl, head buried up to his ears and chewing.

"Maybe he *does* eat it all!" Andrea said, watching Hannah's cat eat.

Michelle lifted Moishe up from her lap, held him a moment to judge his weight, and put him back down again. "I don't think so," she said. "I'm almost sure he's not gaining weight."

"And he would be if he ate rations for four cats twice a day," Hannah said, frowning slightly. "Just wait and see what he does when he's full. That's probably when he hides the rest of the food."

Several minutes passed as they all watched Moishe eat. Never had a cat's dietary habits been so closely observed. At last Moishe pulled back from the food bowl and began to wash his face. This lasted for almost three minutes, and then he ducked his head in his food bowl again.

"The Big Guy's got a lot of food in his mouth," Norman observed. "His cheeks are puffed out."

At first Hannah thought Norman was anthropomorphizing, but Moishe's cheeks did look fuller. Perhaps that was something a dentist would notice.

"He's going to the refrigerator!" Andrea sounded shocked. "He doesn't know how to open the door, does he, Hannah?"

Hannah laughed. "No. He's a smart cat, but he hasn't figured that one out yet . . . at least I don't *think* he has."

Almost in tandem, they all leaned forward as Moishe passed by the front of the refrigerator and ducked into the narrow area between the side of the kitchen appliance and the broom closet. He had to squeeze to get in, but he wiggled his way out of sight in the narrow space.

"That's where he always loses his duck's foot," Hannah said. "And all the times I've fished it out for him with the yardstick, he could have gotten it himself!"

"He must be hiding his food back there," Michelle guessed.

"I hope he doesn't get stuck!" Andrea exclaimed, and all three of them turned to look at her. "What?" she asked, and a moment later, she gave an embarrassed laugh. "I guess that didn't happen, since he's sitting right here on Michelle's lap."

A moment later Moishe emerged, and it was Hannah's turn to gasp.

"What is it?" Andrea asked her.

"He came out headfirst and there's no room to turn around back there!"

"There must be a hole or something," Norman suggested.

"Let's go look," Hannah said, heading for the kitchen at a trot. She unlocked the door to the broom closet, took out the bag of cat food, and motioned to Norman.

"I see it!" Norman said, leaning in with the flashlight and shining it on the wall near the floor. "There's the loose board I told you about when I fished out his duck's foot. The Big Guy's got a nice little entrance to the broom closet back there. But there's nothing on the floor. What's he doing with his food?"

"Putting it back in the bag?" Hannah guessed, looking inside the bag. "It didn't occur to me before, but I haven't bought any cat food since Mike gave me the Kitty Valet. This bag should be just about gone by now, but it's still three-quarters full."

"You're right! He's putting it back in the bag!" Michelle sounded absolutely astonished.

"That's the only logical conclusion. He eats what he wants and then he puts the rest back where it came from."

Andrea laughed. "He eats and then he puts away the left-overs. That's so cute."

"If you've got a hammer and nails I'll fix that board right now," Norman offered.

Hannah was about to say yes, when she reconsidered.

"Thanks, but I don't think I want it fixed. Moishe's playing a game with his new feeder. It keeps him occupied, it's not hurting anything, and he seems to enjoy it. I'll just let him do it for a while, at least until he finds something else to intrigue him."

"I think you're probably wise," Norman said.

Andrea nodded. "Me, too."

"If you keep him from his game, he's just going to find another one," Michelle said, "and maybe it'll be more destructive."

"One mystery solved," Hannah said, heading for the coffeepot for a second cup. "Let's go watch another tape from the mall and see if it'll shed any light on the second mystery we have to solve."

LOIS BROWN'S LEMON COOKIES

Preheat oven to 350 degrees F., rack
in the middle position.

½ cup softened butter (*1 stick, ¼ pound*)
¾ cup white (*granulated*) sugar
1 egg, beaten (*just whip it up in a glass with a fork*)
1 Tablespoon lemon zest***
2 teaspoons lemon juice
1 teaspoon baking powder
¼ teaspoon baking soda
¼ teaspoon salt
1⅔ cups flour (*pack it down in the cup when you
    measure it*)
½ cup milk (*I used whole milk*)

Topping:
¼ cup lemon juice
¾ cup white (*granulated*) sugar

***Lemon zest is the yellow part of the lemon peel,
finely grated. Be careful not to use the white part, because
that's bitter. If you decide you don't want these cookies
tart, use only 1 teaspoon lemon zest.*

Hannah's 1st Note: These cookies are wonderfully lemony
and quite tart. You may want to sprinkle them with powdered sugar before you serve them to those who like them
sweeter.

Beat the butter and the sugar together until they're light and fluffy.

Add the beaten egg, lemon zest, and lemon juice. Mix it all up together.

Mix in the baking powder, baking soda, and salt. Mix well.

Mix in half of the flour and half of the milk. That's approximately a cup of flour and a quarter cup of milk. *(You don't have to be exact—just eyeball it.)*

Stir everything all up, and then add the remaining flour and the remaining milk. Mix well.

Drop by teaspoons onto an *ungreased* cookie sheet. Make these cookies small, about the size of a cherry. If you make them too large, they'll spread out on the cookie sheet and crumble when you remove them.

Bake at 350 degrees F. for 12 to 14 minutes. *(Mine took 13 minutes.)*

Hannah's 2nd Note: I use parchment paper because then I can just slide it onto a wire rack after the cookies come out of the oven.

While the first pan of cookies is baking, mix up the topping.

Heat the lemon juice just a bit in the microwave. *(The sugar will dissolve more easily if the juice is warm.)* Add the sugar and stir it all up. Place the topping next to your wire cooling rack, along with a pastry brush.

When the cookies come out of the oven, remove them to a wire rack with a piece of foil placed under it or, if you've used parchment paper, just pull the paper with the cookies from the cookie sheet and onto the wire rack.

Brush the topping onto the hot cookies. The faster you do this, the quicker the topping will dry into a glaze.

Yield: Approximately 4 dozen cookies, depending on cookie size.

Hannah's 3rd Note: This recipe can be doubled.

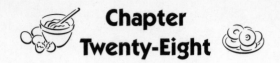

Chapter Twenty-Eight

"No dialogue, no story, no lights, no music," Hannah said with a sigh. "No wonder these tapes are so boring."

"You forgot no action," Norman reminded her, his finger on the fast-forward button. They'd watched the first third of the tape, and so far the Snack Shack was in shadows and absolutely nothing had happened. "There's nobody in there to . . . whoa!" He stopped as the door opened and the lights clicked on. "Here we go! It's show time!"

"It's Ronni," Hannah identified the blonde who walked to the far end of the room and took several small bottles from behind the counter. "And that's diet green tea. This must be when she starts drinking Green-Teanis."

Michelle looked puzzled. "I wonder why she didn't change out of her exercise outfit for the party."

"Maybe she didn't have anything tighter," Hannah offered her opinion.

"That wasn't nice!" Andrea chided her.

"Maybe not, but I bet you were thinking the same thing."

A shade of pink very much resembling the pink of the pillow shams in Hannah's guest room started to appear at Andrea's neckline. It moved slowly up to the top of her cheeks, and Andrea gave a guilty sigh. "You're right," she said. "I was."

"Here comes the rest of the party," Norman said, pointing at the screen. "Mike's got your cream puffs, Hannah."

Hannah watched Mike come in, carrying her tray of cream puffs. She noticed that he'd stuck a candle into each puff, but the platter was covered with plastic wrap. He set it behind the counter, where no one could see it, and gave Ronni a big kiss on the lips that lasted a lot longer than Hannah wanted it to. Then the partygoers began to file in, and Mike took a proprietary place at Ronni's side with his arm around her waist.

"Mike's acting like the host," Andrea said, and then she glanced over at Hannah. "Sorry. I shouldn't have said that."

"Why not? It's true."

"Yes, but . . . oh look! There's Mayor Bascomb!" Andrea sounded grateful that something else had come up on the screen.

Before much more time had passed, the room was filled with people. Someone had contributed a case of beer, and others drank soft drinks or concoctions from the blender that one of the sheriff's deputies was manning behind the counter.

"Lonnie," Michelle breathed, and Hannah turned to glance at her youngest sister. Michelle looked worried, and Hannah wondered if she feared that Lonnie would give the birthday girl the same kind of greeting that Mike had. But instead of heading over to greet Ronni, he gave a little wave in her general direction and got himself a beer from the case at the end of the counter. Then he started talking to a couple of other deputies who were there, and Hannah saw Michelle visibly relax.

"No women," Norman said after another few minutes of watching.

Hannah turned to look at him. "You're right! It's all men."

"Maybe that's because she worked at the sheriff's department, and it's mostly men out there," Michelle suggested.

"Are you kidding?" Hannah just laughed. "There are a

couple of women deputies, not to mention quite a few secretaries."

"Maybe she invited them and they didn't come," Norman suggested. But after a look from the three Swensen sisters, he gave up on that excuse.

"There's Tad," Michelle said, pointing at the man who'd just walked in the door. "Just look at that gorgeous bouquet of flowers! Would a stalker bring his victim flowers?"

"It does seem unusual," Hannah said, thinking of what Tad's nephew had confided to the class at Kiddie Korner and wondering if it was relevant.

"What is she *doing?*" Michelle's mouth fell open as she watched the screen. "Ronni won't even take them! She's pointing to the door, and . . ."

"Tad's leaving with the flowers," Andrea said, just as shocked as Michelle. "And he looks really embarrassed. She must have said something mean to him."

"Look at her now. She's laughing," Norman said, and his brows knit together in a disapproving frown.

"She's laughing at *him,*" Hannah said.

"I can't help but feel sorry for him." Michelle looked sympathetic. "Those flowers must have cost him a bundle."

"He looks like he's ready to break down in tears," Andrea commented as the security guard passed by the camera. "I wonder what Ronni said to him."

Hannah motioned to Norman. "Can you put it on pause?" And then she turned to Michelle. "Find out."

"Find out what Ronni said to him?"

"Right. Lonnie was there. He must have heard it. Call him, and we'll wait."

It took only a few moments to get the answer, and when they did, they could scarcely believe their ears. "She actually called him a little toad?" Hannah asked.

"That's right. Lonnie repeated her words exactly. She said, *Get out of here you little toad! I wouldn't invite you to my birthday party if you were the last man on earth.*"

"That's really harsh," Norman said, shaking his head. "No wonder he looked so dejected."

They watched for another few minutes, but it was more of the same. And then Mike lifted Ronni up on the counter and she said something to the crowd that had them applauding. Everyone began gathering up glasses, bottles, and snacks. Mike went behind the counter to get the platter of cream puffs, and in less than two minutes the room was vacant and the lights were off again.

"They moved the party to the Jacuzzi," Hannah said, knowing she was right. "And that's all we're going to see on this tape."

Norman fast-forwarded to the end just in case someone had left something and come back to get it, but the lights stayed off and the Snack Shack remained vacant. He rewound the tape, returned it to the sleeve, and shrugged. "That was a waste of time."

"Not for me," Michelle said, and Hannah knew she was thinking about how honest Lonnie had been in his account of the party and how completely unromantic he'd been around Ronni.

"Not for me, either," Hannah said for exactly the opposite reason.

"What now?" Andrea said, after Michelle and Norman had left. Michelle was meeting Lonnie at the hospital to visit with Rick's wife, and then they were going out for pizza. Norman had promised Carrie and Delores he'd drop by Granny's Attic to help them move some heavy antiques. They would meet up later at The Corner Tavern for dinner, and they had a reservation at seven.

Hannah glanced at her watch. "It's only three. We've got four hours until dinner."

"I know. I'm thinking about running out to Heavenly Bodies and catching up on my exercises. I didn't go this morning."

"Neither did I, but you know that already. You discussed it with Norman last night."

Andrea looked a little nervous. "I hope you don't mind, but it was for your own good. I was really worried you'd fall asleep on the drive home. I hope you stayed over . . . unless he drove you home, of course."

"Yes."

"Yes, what?"

"I didn't drive home alone last night."

"So Norman took you home? Or you stayed with him?"

"Yes."

Andrea stamped her foot so hard Hannah was almost afraid she'd poke a hole in the ceiling of Phil and Sue's downstairs unit.

"Which! I want to know which!"

Hannah took pity on her sister. Andrea looked ready to fall on the floor and start beating her fists on the rug in frustration. "I stayed with Norman."

"Oh. Well . . . good." There was a moment of silence, and then Andrea spoke again. "I don't suppose you're going to tell me anything about it. I mean, *where* you slept and . . . and things like that?"

"No."

"Oh, well." Andrea sighed deeply. "I didn't figure you would. So do you want to follow me out to the mall and finish our exercise routines for the day?"

"Sure. It beats mopping the floor and watching it dry."

They parked right next to each other at the back door. Andrea got out of her Volvo first, and she was standing at the entrance with her hands on her hips when Hannah joined her.

"Well! If that doesn't beat all!" she exclaimed, clearly frustrated. "My key doesn't work, and the sign says they're closed."

Hannah stepped closer to read the sign. The outer door to Heavenly Bodies was closed, and the sign said they wouldn't reopen until six o'clock tomorrow morning. "Does that mean we get to drive to Bertanelli's for a pizza instead?" she asked, only half-joking.

"Not if you want to fit into your dress for Mother's party. Let's go in the mall and see what happened."

There weren't very many people shopping. The mall was practically deserted. When they approached the security station, they saw Frank sitting behind the desk at the front. "Hi, ladies," he said.

"Hi, Frank." Hannah took the lead. "We were hoping that you or Tad would be working. We've got a question."

"Tad doesn't come on until seven tonight, but I'd be happy to answer your question. Is it about Miss Ward's murder?"

Andrea shook her head. "It's about Heavenly Bodies. Do you know why it's closed?"

"Sure do. They closed at noon because there was a problem with the thermostat. It's fixed now. The industrial heating and air-conditioning guys just left."

"Can we go in and do our exercises?" Andrea asked. "Hannah and I missed class this morning."

Frank shrugged. "I don't see why not. I'll activate the locks for you. It might be pretty cold in some of the rooms, but you can always hop in the Jacuzzi if you get chilled."

"Thanks, but no thanks!" Hannah shivered slightly. "The Jacuzzi is where Ronni was killed. I'm not overly superstitious, but I don't really want to get in there again."

"I can understand that. As a matter of fact, most of the other members feel the same way. That's why the owner replaced the hot tub with a new one. He even took out the old bar and bar stools and replaced them with other furniture. The only thing that hasn't been changed is the wallpaper, and they'll probably get around to that one of these days."

"They redecorated so fast?" It was clear that Andrea was impressed.

"That's right. The owner said it was a shame that nobody was using it, and he wanted to change the whole look. Instead of all that latticework, it's a thatched hut, now, with wooden shutters that fold down to make tables on the inside. Wait until you see it. It's really nice."

After Frank had let them into the gym, Hannah and Andrea stashed their coats in the dressing room and went straight to the exercise room they thought of as their own. Andrea chose to start with the cross-country ski simulator, and Hannah began her routine on the machine she called the *Walk to Nowhere*.

Ten minutes passed, and they switched to other equipment. Hannah was amazed at how much easier it was getting. At first she'd had trouble even using the machines. She'd forget which foot to push and which handle to pull. Now it was like second nature. If this was an example of the muscle memory the fitness gurus talked about, she was in favor of it!

Fifteen minutes into their routines, Hannah noticed that Andrea was shivering. It was cold in the exercise room, and even though they were moving, the chill seemed to seep through their skin and into their muscles and bones.

"Jacuzzi?" Hannah asked.

"Yes! I'm freezing!"

They hopped off the machines and walked at a fast clip to the recently renovated gazebo. Frank was right. The latticework frame was gone, and in its place was a thatched hut with open space for windows.

"Nice," Andrea said, climbing up the stairs and stepping inside. "I think this is an improvement."

Hannah was right behind her, and she was surprised at the amount of work that had been done. The area was completely different, and even the hot tub was a different configuration, octagonal instead of round.

Andrea reached down to feel the water. "It's hot," she said, smiling in anticipation. "I'm getting in. How about you?"

"I'm right behind you."

It didn't take long to slip out of the loose pants they'd worn over their leotards. The leotards could double as bathing suits, and that was one of the reasons they'd bought them. Andrea stepped in first and gave a sigh of pleasure. "It's perfect. Turn on the jets before you get in, will you, Hannah?"

Hannah turned on the jets and joined her sister in the tub. There was nothing quite as nice as sinking into a tub of swirling, bubbling, heated water when you were shivering with cold. "Heaven," she declared, sinking down until only her head was above the surface of the water.

The two sisters sat there smiling for several minutes, thinking their own thoughts and luxuriating in the warmth. Then reality intruded in the form of Andrea's cell phone.

"Uh-oh," Andrea groaned, clambering out of the tub. "I have to get that. Bill said he'd call."

Hannah leaned back against one of the molded backrests built into the tub and half-listened as Andrea talked to her husband. It was obvious that Andrea was pleased about something. She was using words like *wonderful*, and *marvelous*, and *fantastic* as she listened to Bill talk. When she came back to the hot tub, she was smiling from ear to ear. "Bill's got an alibi, and he's back on the case. Isn't that great?"

"It certainly is!" Hannah was just as delighted as Andrea and every bit as relieved that her brother-in-law was in the clear.

"Bill's been doing a little legwork, going back to all the places he went on the night Ronni was murdered," Andrea explained. "Three different people gave him alibis at three different times. That means there's no way Bill could have driven out to the mall, killed Ronni, and still been at those places at those times."

"Good for him for tracking them down," Hannah complimented her brother-in-law.

"Anyway, he's coming home early, and he wants to take me out for dinner to celebrate. I told him I'd be home in thirty minutes, so I'd better go get dressed. I hope you don't mind that I won't be having dinner with you and Norman."

"Of course not." Hannah wasn't at all disappointed. She liked her times alone with Norman.

"Are you going to leave now, too?"

"I'll get dressed and see how I feel. I might do that final ten minutes on the cross-country ski machine."

Hannah got out of the Jacuzzi, wrapped a towel around her shoulders, and followed Andrea to the dressing room.

The first thing Andrea did when they got there was to pull her cell phone from her purse and plug it into one of the wall sockets at the mirrored dressing table. "Don't let me forget it," she said to Hannah.

"You're charging it while you dress?"

"Yes. It's got a built-in high-speed charger so I can do it anywhere. That's one of the features I love about this phone. I don't think it holds a charge very well, though."

"Really?" Hannah opened her locker and took out the sweatpants and hooded sweatshirt she kept there.

"There was a lot of interference when Bill called, and that happens sometimes when the battery's low. I'll let it charge up while I dress and see if it's better when I'm ready to go."

Both sisters toweled off with the large bath towels the spa provided and began to dress. Andrea put on the clothes she'd worn on the drive out, and Hannah pulled on her sweatpants and hooded sweatshirt.

"Don't forget your cell phone," Hannah reminded Andrea.

"Thanks!" Andrea unplugged it and flipped it open. She dialed a number and listened for a minute, and then she nodded. "It's fine now. No interference at all."

"Who did you call? You didn't say anything."

"I called the number for time of day. I didn't want to get involved in a long conversation." Andrea dropped her cell phone in her purse, picked up her winter jacket, and headed for the door. "Are you leaving or staying?"

"I'm staying." Hannah grabbed her purse and her parka and followed her sister out of the dressing room. "I'll still have lots of time to drive home and dress for dinner with Norman."

"I'll touch base with you tonight, then," Andrea said, giving a little wave and heading for the exit. But she took only a couple of steps before she turned and came back again. "Here," she said, drawing a plastic bag from her purse. "I almost forget to give it to you. I got one for Michelle, and Lisa, and Norman too. Now we can all have roses in the winter."

Hannah glanced inside the bag and smiled. Andrea had given her a red plastic rose with a very long stem. "For my antenna?" she asked, remembering their conversation about Andrea's flower on the antenna of her Volvo.

"That's right. There's a wire in the stem so you can just wind it around your antenna and it'll stay there. And because it's plastic, it won't get ruined by the snow and ice."

"This is really sweet of you, Andrea," Hannah said, and she meant it. Andrea had cared enough to shop for the roses and give them to Norman, Lisa, and her sisters. For someone who'd been extremely self-centered a few years ago, Andrea had turned into a thoughtful and caring person.

After Andrea had left, Hannah glanced down at the rose in her hand. Instead of shoving it into her purse where it might not see the light of day for several weeks, she put it, plastic bag and all, in the horizontal patch pocket on the front of her sweatshirt, the one that could be used as a hand warmer. She'd keep it there while she finished her workout routine and put it on her antenna when she got back out to the parking lot.

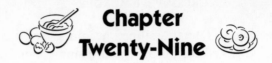

Chapter
Twenty-Nine

The rhythmic swooshing of the cross-country ski simulator was soothing, releasing her mind for other pursuits. Hannah watched the video of a winter scene rolling past on the screen in time with her movements, and she relaxed. Only a small portion of her mind took charge of the repetitive motion and pace, and she began to think of what she'd learned about Ronni's murder.

Swooshing down the hill, push with the left foot, push with the right foot, to the first clue that entered her mind. Sonny Newberg told Sue Plotnik that his uncle Tad gave flowers to Nikki. It was pretty clear that Nikki was a nickname and Tad had nicknames for the women he liked. Ronni's real name was Veronica, but what if Tad gave her his own personal nickname? Could it have been *Nikki*, based on the last part of her name?

According to Frank, Tad didn't have much luck with women. That meant his self-confidence was probably low. When Ronni had refused to take his flowers and insulted him at her birthday party in front of the other guests, it must have been a terrible blow to Tad's ego. Could he have gotten embarrassed enough and angry enough to go back when all the party guests had left and kill Ronni?

Hannah thought about that on a slight downhill slope as

she skied her way past a small stand of pines. Dig in with the right pole, dig in with the left pole, swoosh to the next clue to Ronni's killer. There was the security tape of the parking lot with Ronni's old car in the picture. Mike said Ronni hadn't driven it recently and Hannah believed him. What if the tape she'd watched hadn't been recorded on the night of Ronni's death? What if it was an old tape slipped into a new sleeve, a tape that had been made when Ronni's car was still working?

It would have been easy for Tad to switch the tapes. And if Tad had killed Ronni, he might have wanted to set it up so that everyone who came to Ronni's birthday party was automatically a suspect. It would certainly muddy the waters and hinder the investigation, especially since quite a few attendees were members of the Winnetka County Sheriff's Department.

Hannah's hips swiveled and her legs shot back and forth on the pretend skis. Right leg forward, left leg forward, skiing up a slight rise to the suspect list. Tad wasn't listed as a suspect . . . or was he? The only three suspects left on the page were the stalker, the suspicious man in the blue parka, and the unknown suspect with the unknown motive. Tad saw Ronni every day on the security cameras in the exercise rooms. Ronni knew she was on camera and she certainly wouldn't think of that as spying. But Ronni had specifically mentioned the Jacuzzi to the bartender at The Moosehead and there was no security camera in there.

The Jacuzzi! With a gasp, Hannah remembered the interference on Andrea's cell phone. That had happened in the room with the Jacuzzi. Andrea thought it was a low battery, but Hannah had experienced a similar interference when she'd been standing next to the kitty-cam Mike had installed in her condo kitchen. What if there was a surveillance camera hidden in the room with the Jacuzzi and Ronni had somehow sensed it? Mike had mentioned that the mall security staff tested surveillance cameras for the same company. It was entirely possible they'd been given a camera identical to Mike's and Tad had installed it in the room with the Jacuzzi so that he could spy on Ronni.

There was only one way to find out. Hannah jumped off the ski simulator at the top of a steep incline dotted with bumpy snowdrifts. But instead of tumbling head over heels with arms and legs akimbo as a real skier might have done, she hit the floor running, grabbed her purse, and headed for the Jacuzzi at a trot.

When she arrived at the steps leading up to the thatched-roofed hut, Hannah took her phone out of her purse and switched it on. Then she punched in the number for time of day and listened to the recorded voice. There was no interference. She continued to listen as she climbed the steps and stepped into the hut. There was a high-pitched squeal that grew louder as she approached the spot where Andrea had answered her phone. Another step and the squeal intensified even more. It was loudest right next to the wall.

Since she could no longer hear the recorded voice, and she didn't really care what time it was anyway, Hannah switched off the phone and slipped it back in her purse. And then she began to examine the wall to see if she could spot the lens of the camera.

The thatched-roof hut had been decorated like a tropical paradise with hanging ferns and flowering trees in earthenware pots, and the wallpaper picked up on the lush jungle theme. Glossy leaves, thick green vines, and riotously colored flowers snaked their way up to the ceiling. Exotically shaped tree branches displayed tropical birds in splendiferous plumage, including an impressively large toucan just above Hannah's head.

The best way to proceed was methodically. Hannah started at the top left corner of the wall and let her eyes scan to the right, almost as if she were reading a line of very large print. She told herself to ignore the designs on the wallpaper and concentrate on finding any irregularities in the wall itself. Once she'd reached the right corner, she dropped her focus down six inches or so, and let her eyes move in a horizontal line to the left. She repeated this pattern over and over, lower and lower with each trip from left to right and then back again.

It wasn't until she'd reached an area about a foot over her head and midway between the left and right walls, that she discovered something unusual. It had to do with the toucan. This particular bird had only one eye as the artist had rendered it in profile.

The eye of the toucan bulged out slightly, just like the lens of her kitty-cam. But wallpaper was flat. It didn't bulge unless there was something behind it. Hannah reached up to feel the bird's eye and touched a glass lens. There was a kitty-cam hidden behind the wall by the Jacuzzi. Except it wasn't a kitty-cam. It was a killer-cam! No wonder Ronni had felt that someone was spying on her! Someone was. And that someone was Tad Newberg.

Hannah grabbed her purse and pulled out her phone. She had to call Mike and tell him to arrest Tad Newberg right away. He had killed Ronni. She was sure of it! She punched in the number and waited breathlessly for it to ring. But the interference was so heavy she couldn't hear anything but a high-pitched whine. The best thing to do was to go out to the security station and call from . . .

Uh-oh! Hannah's mind said. *You're out here alone and this is where Tad works. What if Tad comes in early and realizes that you know?* The best thing to do was to get to safety first, and then stop somewhere to call Mike. She raced across the floor, fairly flew down the steps, and crashed straight into the arms of Frank Hurley.

"Frank!" she gasped, shaking with relief. "You have no idea how glad I am to see *you!*"

"And you have no idea how glad I am I caught you before you left," Frank said. "You figured it out, didn't you, Hannah?"

There was a note of menace in Frank's voice that Hannah

had never heard before. It puzzled her and her mind spun through the possibilities until it came to a shuddering halt at a terrible suspicion. She tried to step back, but Frank's arms were like bands of steel around her.

"Figured what out?" she asked, hoping he'd think she was thoroughly mystified by his question.

"You found the camera," he said.

Careful. If you're careful, you may be able to talk your way out of this. You have to give him a kernel of truth so he thinks you're ingenuous and you can't let him guess that you suspect him.

"Yes. Yes, I did find the camera. I'm really sorry, Frank. I know you're just as disappointed as I am."

An expression of doubt crossed Frank's face. "Disappointed?"

"Yes. I really like Tad, but he shouldn't have hooked up that surveillance camera so he could spy on Ronni. That wasn't a nice thing to do. I can't say I blame him though. I know he was crazy about her. I'm right, aren't I?"

"He was crazy about her, all right!"

"Ronni brought this on herself, you know. She was horribly mean to Tad at her birthday party when he gave her those lovely flowers. I can't say I entirely blame him for waiting until everyone else had left and fighting with her in the hot tub. I'm sure he didn't mean to kill her though. Tad's no killer."

"You're right about that! So that's what you figured out, huh?"

"Yes. I just called Mike and he's going to go talk to Tad."

Frank laughed and it wasn't a pleasant sound. "No, you didn't. I was watching you on my laptop monitor. You never got through to him."

"You're right. I was going to call him, but I couldn't get a good signal, not with all that interference. But he'll be here any minute anyway. He's picking me up. I'll tell him to talk to Tad then."

"You won't be telling him anything, not where you're going." Frank pulled his gun, whirled her around, and stuck the barrel against her back. "Walk. It's cold in here, and you're going to spend some time in the sauna. Too bad you're going to overdo it. You'll suffer a heat stroke and die, and everyone will think it's a terrible accident."

"Why are you doing this?" Hannah asked, willing her voice not to shake. "I told you I didn't think Tad killed Ronni on purpose. Once he explains, I'm sure everyone will believe that it was an accident."

"But it *wasn't* an accident." Frank laughed again and prodded her with the barrel of the gun to make her move faster. "And it wasn't Tad either. It was me. I killed Ronni."

"But why?" Hannah gasped, stumbling a bit as she moved forward. She had to keep him talking, distract him, and figure out some way to escape.

"Tad's like a son to me. My sister died when he was born and the poor kid never had anyone. Tad's father always blamed him for my sister's death. Tad's older brother got all the attention. The only one who ever cared about Tad was me. I knew Ronni was a bad influence the first time I saw her flirting with Tad."

Hannah tried to slow her steps, but every time she hesitated, Frank prodded her with the gun again. Her eyes scanned the deserted hallway, hoping for something she could grab, whirl, and use to hit him, but the hallways were perfectly empty. "Did you try to warn Tad off?"

" 'Course I did. What kind of fool do you take me for? I told him she was the kind to play games with men and I proved it by showing him the tapes of her in the Jacuzzi with other men."

There was a broom leaning up against the doorway to the Snack Shack. If she could just get close enough to grab it, she could use it to knock him off balance and . . .

"Don't even think about it," Frank warned her, effectively

reading her mind and pushing her over to hug the far wall. "I'll shoot you here if I have to."

Hannah told herself there'd be another opportunity. There had to be! And then she went on asking questions. "What did Tad say when you showed him the tapes of Ronni in the Jacuzzi with the other men?"

"He was upset, but he wasn't mad at Ronni. He said she hadn't dated the right man yet, but the minute she realized that he was perfect for her, she'd settle right down with him and be happy."

"Are you *serious*?" Hannah asked, stopping in her tracks and turning around to look at him.

"Yes, I am."

"Poor Tad!" Hannah said, and she meant it. But in the meantime, they'd stopped moving forward and were now standing still facing each other. This was good. Hannah knew she had to delay for as long as she could. "He was really that out of touch with reality?"

"Oh, yes. He was delusional when it came to Ronni. Nothing she did was her fault and he wouldn't listen to the truth."

"But you tried to tell him what Ronni was really like?"

"I talked until I was blue in the face. Nothing sunk in. It was like she'd put blinders on him and he couldn't see any of her bad qualities."

"But blinders come off eventually," Hannah said. "It might take a while, but people wise up."

"That's exactly what I was afraid of. I knew the day would come when Tad would see Ronni for what she really was, and . . ." Frank stopped and swallowed with difficulty. "And when that happened, it would destroy my boy. Someone had to put a stop to it and that's what I did."

Hannah was silent. She wasn't sure what to say next.

"Walk!" Frank grabbed her shoulder, whirled her around, and pushed her so hard she almost stumbled. "Get going! I don't want to talk about this anymore."

They rounded the corner and arrived at the door to the sauna. Hannah was still searching for some way to delay him, but she'd run out of all but the final question. "Do you really think you'll get away with it?" she asked.

"Of course I will. You're the only one who even came close to figuring it out, and you can't tell anyone if you're dead." Frank's eyes glittered dangerously. "Too bad you have to pay the price, but my boy comes first. It would kill him if he ever found out what I did to Ronni."

Her purse. If he forgot and left her with her purse, everything would be okay. Her cell phone was in her purse and there would be no interference in the sauna. She could call Mike and . . .

"You won't need this." Frank grabbed her purse and tossed it aside, and then he thrust his hand into the long patch pocket of her sweatshirt and drew out the bag with the rose. "What's this?"

"It's a rose. My sister gave it to me."

"Nice," he said, opening the door, shoving her inside, and tossing the rose in after her. "If it doesn't melt, it'll be a nice start on your funeral flowers."

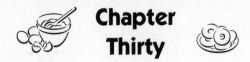

Chapter Thirty

Of course she had tried the door. It was the first thing she'd done. He'd locked it from the outside, and there was no way she could force it open. She prowled around the walls, searching for any weak spots she could use for ventilation. The south wall bordered the parking lot, but she'd leaned up against it yesterday, talking to Andrea after their morning class, and it hadn't been any warmer than the wall on the other side of the backdoor. Even if she did manage to pry off a section of redwood, or cedar, or whatever wood it was, she'd only encounter a thick concrete wall between her and the outside world.

It was getting hotter. The warmth that would have been welcome only minutes ago was now her enemy. Hannah wiped the moisture from her forehead with the sleeve of her sweatshirt. How hot was it? How long would it take her to lose consciousness? Was it true that your life passed before your eyes when you were about to die? She didn't want to know. Not now. Not ever.

It hadn't been long, or at least she didn't think that much time had passed, but she felt dizzy, disoriented, light-headed. Her skin felt hot and it reminded her of sausages on the grill. They split open if you didn't score them with a knife. Would her skin split open before anyone found her?

Heat rose. The moment she thought of it, she dropped to the floor. Could she dig her way down to safety? But the floor was tile and under the tile would be a concrete slab. Out of luck. She was trapped. There was no help to be had below her.

The ceiling. She hadn't checked that out yet. But the ceiling was perfectly smooth . . . except for something that made her draw in her breath sharply. Hope bloomed as she stared up at the round white disk with the holes ringing its circumference.

The conversation with Herb about the alarm systems in the sauna came back to Hannah with startling clarity. It was a smoke alarm, not a heat alarm. If it was set off, it went straight to the Lake Eden Fire Department. Hannah glanced down at the rose she'd placed on the bench of the sauna. Some plastic smoked when it melted. The rose Andrea had given her could be her lifesaver!

It was her only chance. Hannah took a deep breath of the stifling hot air and did her best to pull herself together. Then she forced her body to move. She was so hot, so enervated, but she couldn't give in to the lethargy that threatened to leave her gasping. She'd be a lifeless puddle on the floor if she didn't act now.

Fire. Plastic. Smoke. The words flashed in her fading mind. She had to hold the rose close enough to the heating coils to ignite it. And then she had to climb up on the bench, stand up as tall as she could, and hold the rose up to the smoke alarm.

Hannah crawled. She couldn't stand upright. She was simply too weak. She crawled to the source of the heat, the coils that were so mercilessly draining her life away, and held the rose directly over them. Her vision was wavy, but she saw the rose send up a wisp of smoke and start to melt, the red petals of the flower sinking into the green of the leaves. And a horrible smell began to rise from the smoldering, smoking, melting plastic.

Now, Hannah's mind told her, and she forced herself to climb up on the redwood bench. It took all the strength she had, but somehow she managed to raise her arm and hold the melting, malodorous rose as close to the smoke alarm as she could.

There was no way she could breathe. The stench of the smoking plastic or the smoldering wire, she wasn't sure which, was unbearable. She was probably breathing in carcinogens, but that didn't really matter in the giant scheme of things.

Hannah held her position until her arm muscles spasmed and what was left of the rose dropped to the floor. She was right behind it, collapsing on the bench and giving way to the horrible lassitude that consumed her body and her mind.

Time passed, how much she wasn't sure. Life passed and there was a loud, awful ringing in her ears. Images of family, of friends, of things near and dear to her came, and faded, and changed, until they all melded together in one unfinished life. Hannah crawled her way to the wall, the farthest she could get from the cloying lethal heat. And then she curled up, her ears almost deafened by the ringing, her nose to the floor, praying for a breath of fresh air.

"Hannah?" a voice called her name. "Hang in there, Hannah! I'm here!"

A dream. Mike's voice. It was the last voice she'd hear in this world.

"Hannah!" Mike lifted her in his arms. "I'm getting you out of here now. Don't worry. I'll never let anybody hurt you again."

That's nice. That's good, Hannah thought, as her mind began to revolve in concentric circles.

"We got him. We got Tad Newberg. Stella got the call while I was there. He was the stalker at Macalester."

"Not Tad. Frank," she squeezed the words out of her parched throat. "Frank . . . killed Ronni. And he tried to . . . kill me."

She heard him give orders for someone to go after Frank. And then he was carrying her out, out where she could breathe again.

"I've been such a louse," he said, placing her on a gurney. "I am such a louse. But I love you, Hannah. I love you more than anyone else in the world."

He leaned over her as they pushed the gurney to the ambulance. "Just a quick checkup with Doc Knight," he said.

"I need to go home," she said, and her voice was weak and scratchy. "Don't let Doc keep me. Come with me and take me home."

"I will."

"Promise?" she whispered, just to make sure.

"I promise," Mike said.

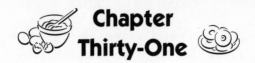

Chapter Thirty-One

Hannah felt like doom was imminent as she opened the door at the Lake Eden Community Center. She was no longer worried about Ronni's killer. Frank Hurley had fled shortly after the smoke alarm activated, but the sheriff's department had caught him and taken him into custody. With one count of murder and a second count of attempted murder, Hannah figured it would be years, perhaps a lifetime, before Frank saw the outside world again.

When Mike's team had searched Frank's house, they'd found the tape from the parking lot camera, which had functioned perfectly, showing everyone leaving the birthday party before Ronni was killed. They'd also discovered the tapes from the hidden camera at the Jacuzzi, including the one that contained footage of Frank knocking Ronni unconscious and deliberately leaving her in the tub to die.

Tad Newberg had been the stalker at Macalester, but he hadn't really done anything illegal. It was just that the romantic attentions he'd paid to one of the young teaching assistants had been both obsessive and unwelcome. She didn't appreciate the flowers he'd left on her doorstep in the middle of the night, or the way he'd called her several times a day to ask for a date. When the head of security at the college had confronted Tad about his actions, Tad had been so embarrassed that he'd resigned.

Hannah opened the inner door and walked across the lobby. Today she faced the real danger, the menace that turned her mouth as dry as dust and caused her legs to tremble as she walked down the hall to the dressing room that brides and bridesmaids used to freshen up before their wedding receptions. It was time to try on the Regency dress that Delores had ordered for her, the same dress that had been much too tight to button only two weeks ago!

"Oh, dear!" Claire Rodgers made a little sound of distress. "It's too large in the waist!"

"Too large in the waist," Hannah breathed, taking immeasurable delight in saying the words. Never, in her wildest imaginings, had she ever thought anyone would use that phrase to describe an article of clothing that belonged to her!

"It'll be fine, don't worry." Claire patted her on the shoulder. "I'll just tie the apron strings tighter. No one will even notice."

"No one will even notice," Hannah breathed, and this time the words took on the character of a dirge. She'd lost so much weight that her dress was too large in the waist. And no one would even notice!

It was the big day, and Claire was there to help them dress. The actual launch party and book signing would be held in the community library with volunteer librarian, Marge Beeseman, handling the sale of their mother's book.

"I'm so proud of you, Hannah," Andrea complimented her. "I knew you could do it, but I had no idea that diet and exercise would work this well. Your dress really *is* too big."

Michelle nodded. "She's right. You must have lost almost twenty pounds!"

"I think it was the sauna," Hannah said, making light of her harrowing experience. "I was in there so long, I must have sweated off ten pounds."

"Are you girls ready?" Claire came back with a digital camera. "Your mother asked me to take a picture. She's going to put it up on her Web site."

"The Web site for Granny's Attic?" Michelle asked, and Hannah could tell she was wondering how a picture of the three of them in Regency dresses would go with photos of collectibles for sale at the mothers' antique shop.

"Mother has a new site," Hannah told her. "Norman's creating it for her. It's just for her books."

"Books, as in more than one book?" Andrea asked.

"That's right. She says she likes writing so much she's already working on the next one. And even more people from Lake Eden are in it!"

Andrea gave a little groan. "I just hope that Mother was complimentary when she wrote about her friends and neighbors."

"Somehow I doubt that," Hannah said, shaking her head. "Remember the night that Mother told us about the book?" When both sisters nodded, she continued, "*I write the people the way they truly are,* Mother said, *the way someone who didn't know and like them the way I do would describe their flaws and their strengths.*"

"Uh-oh," Andrea breathed.

"Uh-oh is right!" Michelle gave a little groan. "But maybe we'll get lucky and people won't recognize themselves."

Hannah looked doubtful. "Maybe, but I still wish Mother had set her romance in medieval England."

"Why's that?" Andrea asked.

"Because then she could have worn a suit of armor, just in case."

"You look great, Hannah!" Mike said, snagging a chocolate mini cream puff from her platter, popping it into his mouth, and swallowing it practically whole. "I just love these things. Do you have a minute? I need to tell you something."

Hannah put her tray down on top of a low bookcase and let him lead her to the back of the library, as far away from the crowd as they could get.

"You have to hear this," Mike said with a grin, pulling his

copy of *A Match for Melissa* from his pocket. "Here's what your mother wrote about me. *The Duke of Oakwood was a fine figure of a man, dressed in exquisitely tailored clothing and boots that glistened from the attentions of his valet.* That's me, Hannah. I always polish my boots so they shine like that. And then she said, *His deep eyes sparkled with humor and gleamed with a keen intelligence, and as he ran his fingers through his hair, a lock eluded him and dropped low to his forehead.* I run my fingers through my hair a lot, and she must have noticed. What do you think of that, Hannah?"

Hannah's mind flipped through the possibilities and came up with a winner. "It's amazing," she said, borrowing the phrase Michelle had used to describe their mother's signing.

"That's what I thought! Your mother must like me even more than I realized. She described me perfectly, and she made me the hero of her book!"

A few minutes later, Hannah was back at work. She'd just served Stella Parks, who'd come to the launch party to congratulate them all on a job well done, when Carrie came rushing up. "Would you care for a cream puff?" Hannah asked her.

"I'd love one, but I've already had three." Carrie stepped a little closer. "Do you have a minute, Hannah?"

Off they went to the rear of the library, and Hannah had a feeling she was about to experience *déjà vu*. She knew she was right when Carrie pulled a copy of *A Match for Melissa* from her purse.

"Just listen to this, Hannah," she said, flipping it open and starting to read. "*Her soft, well-modulated voice was as music to the ear, and her lovely features were a delight to the eye.* Isn't that just wonderful?"

"It's amazing," Hannah said, resorting to the phrase she'd used with Mike.

"I never dreamed your mother would make me the heroine of her book. I'm just too flattered for words! And she even describes the hairstyle I wore when I first moved to Lake Eden. Just listen . . . *Her shining tresses were neatly confined in the twist she had fashioned at the nape of her long and shapely neck.* I'm just so thrilled, Hannah!"

"Of course you are," Hannah said, grateful that the two descriptions, either correctly or erroneously attributed to Lake Edenites had been complimentary. "I'd better get back to work, Carrie. We don't want the author to get mad at us."

The next request for a private conference came only a few minutes later. Before Hannah could find a convenient place to set down her tray, Mayor Bascomb had pulled her to the back of the library.

"You know, I always thought your mother didn't like me," he said. "But I was wrong, Hannah. Just listen to this . . ."

Hannah had all she could do not to groan as the mayor pulled a copy of her mother's book from his pocket. He flipped to a page he'd marked with a square pink sticky from Marge Beeseman's desk, and began to read.

"*His deep eyes sparkled with humor and gleamed with a keen intelligence.* Now tell me that isn't me!"

"I wouldn't dream of it," Hannah said quite truthfully.

"And how about this? *As he ran his fingers through his hair, a lock eluded him and dropped low to his forehead, giving him a boyish attitude and reminding her of a joyful childhood spent with boisterous friends.* Your mother nailed it, Hannah. That's exactly what my childhood was like, and she knows it because she used to be my summer babysitter."

"That's just amazing," Hannah said, and it was. It seemed three people thought Delores had written about them!

"Well, I'd better let you get back to work. I just wanted to tell you how pleased I am that Delores acknowledged me by making me the hero of her book. Do you think I should thank her?"

"No! I mean . . ." Hannah thought fast. If Mayor Bascomb mentioned it to Delores, she might deny it, and then there'd be trouble. "I think Mother would be embarrassed that you unraveled her little secret. And she'd probably say it wasn't you, just to throw you off the track."

Mayor Bascomb thought about that for a moment and then he nodded. "You're absolutely right. I won't say anything about it."

During the next hour, no less than five people came up to Hannah to tell her they were the heroine or hero of *A Match for Melissa*. They all had their own reasons. Claire Rodgers told Hannah, a trifle hesitantly, that she thought she might be the heroine because of the way Delores had described the color of her gown.

"Listen to this, Hannah," she'd said. "*The sea-green color set off her sparkling eyes perfectly, and the vivid hue accentuated her flawless skin.* I wore a dress just like that to church, and your mother asked me to describe the color. And then she said it went perfectly with my eyes and my skin."

"Amazing," Hannah had said, for the fourth time.

The next to corner Hannah had been Bonnie Surma. "Oh, Hannah!" Bonnie had said, smiling so widely Hannah wondered if the corners of her mouth might crack. "I think your mother modeled the heroine of her book after me!"

"Really?" Hannah had asked, wondering which phrase Bonnie would use to substantiate her claim.

"This is why I think so." Bonnie had flipped to a page in the book. "*Her comportment was so charming, all who encountered her smiled with delight.* Your mother once told me that my manners were charming and some other members of our Regency Romance Club could take a lesson from me."

Earl Flensburg had been the next one to approach Hannah. Once they were alone at the back of the library, he'd said, "Your mother made me the Duke of Oakwood, Hannah."

"Really?" Hannah had asked, waiting for him to read the salient phrase to her.

"Just listen to this . . . *It was at this moment that a gentleman on horseback appeared, riding neck-or-nothing toward the disastrous event that was about to occur. He leaned dangerously low in the saddle and snatched the young boy from the jaws of certain disaster.*" Earl stopped reading and turned to her. "You see what I mean, Hannah?"

"You think Mother's describing you," Hannah had said, knowing that she was right.

"Of course. She must have remembered our senior class picnic. We held it out at Ehrenberg's farm, and a couple of us brought our horses. I did a little trick riding for the girls."

"Amazing," Hannah had commented, wondering how many times she could listen to the same assumptions without laughing.

The last two candidates for starring roles in her mother's romance were Al Percy and Cyril Murphy. Al thought *The Duke of Oakwood was a fine figure of a man, dressed in exquisitely tailored clothing* referred to him, since Delores had complimented him on the new suit he'd worn at the last church supper. Cyril had a different take on the end of the same paragraph Al had used. He thought that *He leaned against the garden wall in a relaxed pose, presenting a handsome profile* must refer to him since Delores had once said he had a very distinctive profile.

"Hannah?" her mother hailed her from across the room and Hannah hurried to the table Marge had set up for the book signing. There was a nice-looking, rail-thin, well-dressed woman standing at her mother's side and Hannah was almost certain she'd never seen her before.

"Yes, Mother?" Hannah arrived a bit breathless.

"I'd like you to meet the woman who's been such a great help to me." Delores smiled up at the stranger, the stranger smiled back, and then Delores motioned Hannah closer. "This is Doctor Love," she said in a whisper.

"Call me Nancy," Doctor Love said, giving Hannah a friendly smile. "I'm here incognito."

"Hi, Nancy," Hannah said, smiling back.

"I came to get a copy of your mother's book. I've only had

time to page through it, but it looks marvelous and I do love a good romance. I plan to mention it on the air tomorrow if you'd like to listen."

"That's very kind of you!" Delores looked completely delighted.

"The world needs more romance and I'm eager to run home and delve into yours. Tell me, Delores. Are your characters based on real people?"

"Somewhat," Delores said, "but not entirely."

"Good answer!" Nancy reached out to pat Delores's shoulder. "I'm willing to bet that most of the men in this room think they're the hero, and most of the women think they're the heroine."

"You're right," Hannah said. "At least a half-dozen people have already pulled me aside to read me passages from Mother's book and tell me they *know* they're the main character."

Nancy laughed. "Just as I thought! Keep your eyes open, Hannah. If you find a man who doesn't think he's the hero, grab him and give him a hug because he's the only realist in the bunch!"

Another fifteen minutes passed and four more people pulled Hannah aside to tell her that they knew they were Melissa or the Duke of Oakwood and read her the appropriate passage to prove it. She was just about convinced that there wasn't a realist in the room when Norman walked up.

"Hi, Norman." Hannah held out her tray. "Would you care for a cream puff?"

"Not right now, thanks. I just wanted to catch you alone and tell you how good you look."

"Thank you!"

"You're welcome." Norman held up his copy of *A Match for Melissa*. "You know, this is a pretty good book."

"Mother will be glad to hear that you think so," Hannah said politely. And then she couldn't resist asking, "Do you think she modeled the Duke of Oakwood after you?"

"After *me?*" Norman looked absolutely astounded. "What are you talking about, Hannah? I'm not tall, dark, and handsome, I don't ride well, and I've never had a whole line of women praying that I'll ask them to dance. The Duke of Oakwood is about as far from my character as you can get."

Hannah smiled in delight. If Doctor Love was right, Norman was the only realist in the room. But he was selling himself short and there was something she could do about that.

"Maybe that's true," she said, "but I'm almost sure that Mother modeled every single one of the duke's good qualities after you." And then she set down her tray and hugged him.